THE FOURTH DESCENDANT

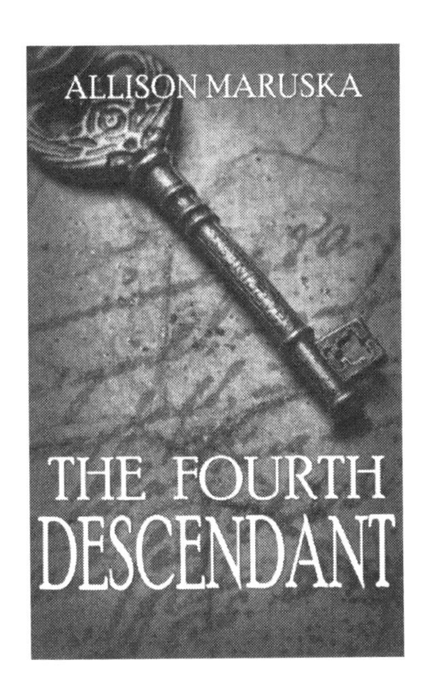

Allison Maruska

This book is a work of fiction. Names, characters, places and incidents are products of the author's imagination or are used fictitiously. Any resemblance to actual events or locales or persons, living or dead, is entirely coincidental.

Cover design by Perry Elisabeth Kirkpatrick
http://perryelisabethdesign.blogspot.com
Image (c) nejron | 123rf.com

Advance Praise for The Fourth Descendant

"I rarely read a story that I can't wait to get back to, and The Fourth Descendant was one. It's full of drama and suspense. It's fresh and new, something very much needed, and it's totally unpredictable."
– John Darryl Winston, author of IA: Initiate

"Allison Maruska hits a homerun with The Fourth Descendant - an intriguing mystery novel that brings into question your ethical beliefs! Four strangers, four keys, and a secret buried underground for generations. While the descendants set about on a life-changing journey to unfold their past, others believe keeping their secret buried is worth paying the ultimate price."
– Lisa Tortorello, author of My Hero, My Ding

"In the Fourth Descendant, author Allison Maruska introduces us to four main characters. She has skillfully developed each one into someone we want to know and care about. They become our friends, who then take us along with them to solve a great mystery. The mystery escalates into a thriller as we contemplate what will happen next. How far will they go to protect their secret? As this book comes to a close, you will be left wanting more. You'll be looking for the sequel."
– Virginia Finnie, author of the Hey Warrior Kids! Children's Book Series

"From the wildly creative mind of Allison Maruska, The Fourth Descendant shines with bright characters, intriguing plot twists and gorgeous sentences. The story of strangers swallowed up by a century-old mystery and linked forever by the events that follow makes for great reading. I couldn't put the book down from the opening paragraph to the epilogue. Michelle, Damien, Jonah and Sharon and their unexpected adventure will stay with me for a long, long time. I highly recommend this book!"
– Carol Bellhouse, author of the Fire Drifter series.

DEDICATION

This book is dedicated to my husband, Joe, and our sons, Nathan and Silas. I only get to spend so much time creating fictional people and worlds because of your support.

The last of the four locks snapped into place.

He ran his fingers along the brass key and placed it in the envelope, bidding a silent farewell to his family.

His secret was in their hands now.

Part One: The Keys

Chapter One

The call came from an unfamiliar number. Michelle almost ignored it, but the prospect of talking to another adult was too promising to pass up. Her children kept their eyes glued to her as they walked home from the playground. Apparently, the event was rare enough to warrant their full attention.

"Is this Michelle Jenson?" the caller asked.

"Yes. Who's this?" *Great. A sales call.*

"My name is Alex Pratt, and I'm calling as a representative for the Richmond Historical Society."

The caller now had Michelle's full attention as well. "Richmond? In Virginia?"

"Yes ma'am. We believe your family is connected to something we found in our courthouse. Can you tell me if your great-great-grandfather was named Gao Zhang?"

"I don't know the first name, but Zhang is my mother's maiden name."

The sound of rustling papers came through the phone. "I'm sure we have the right family. This might sound strange, but try to bear with me. Last month, the city began restoration projects on some of our historic buildings, including our courthouse. The workers found a wooden box hidden under the floorboards, and we thought it was a time capsule, but it contained only a letter signed by four men. One of those men was your great-great-grandfather." He cleared his throat. "The letter gave directions to a safe we found built into a basement wall. The safe is unusual, because it's locked with four large deadbolts. The letter indicated the descendants of each man who signed it would possess a key, and that we need all four keys to open the safe."

"And you think I have one of these keys?" Her son pulled on her arm; she tried to ignore him, wishing she could complete the call without interruption.

"That's why I'm calling. The men who signed the letter have many descendants, and we can't know who might have the keys or if they were thrown away long ago. You're the first person in your family I've been able to reach, and–"

"Can't you just pick the locks?" Her keys jangled as she unlocked the front door, and the kids ran inside to watch cartoons. After hanging her jacket on the hall tree, she walked into the kitchen and retrieved three plates from the cabinet.

"Perhaps, but we want to know what these men had in common. The Historical Society is funding this exploration project, with the possibility of preserving the safe and whatever's inside, depending on what we find. We want to know what it was about these men that brought them together to form such a strange pact."

"Strange? Why was it strange?" She stopped gathering lunch supplies and leaned on the counter.

"Historically speaking, these men shouldn't have been in the same social circles or worked together in the courthouse at all. Your great-great-grandfather was the son of Chinese immigrants; the other three were an Irish immigrant, the grandson of a freed African slave, and a descendant of an original English colonist."

"Well, it sounds interesting, but I don't know anything about a key." Maybe he would try to call someone else in her family. Her husband wasn't likely to let her participate in a treasure hunt anyway.

"I understand. I do want you to know what we're planning, however. We're in contact with film producers to make a documentary about this story. This is why we want to include the families of the men: if whatever is in the safe warrants the attention, you, your family, and the other descendants will be featured. The Historical Society is covering all travel expenses." He cleared his throat again. "Obviously, this will only work if all four families find their keys."

"But what if there's nothing valuable in the safe?"

"I would be surprised if that's the case. We're waiting for the family members to open the safe so we can document the reveal. It will be so much more meaningful if the descendants use the original keys a century later."

Her mind registered one of his earlier comments. "So if I find this key, you'll pay for me to go to Richmond to open a door?" *I'll get to travel? For free?*

"Assuming the other three descendants also find theirs, yes."

Grant yelled at Sophie; Michelle needed to wrap this up before the argument became physical. "Okay, look, my kids are getting impatient. Your number's in my phone. I'll call you if I learn anything about a key."

"I appreciate that."

She disconnected, and after checking on the kids, she started assembling the sandwiches.

Finding a key after a hundred years would be next to impossible. This was important enough to make a documentary about it, though, and a little time in the spotlight would be a refreshing change of pace.

And she would get to travel across the country.

She couldn't help but get excited at the prospect of getting away. If she didn't have to pay for the trip, Mark might even let her go.

In the middle of spreading peanut butter on a slice of bread, she froze as her hopes faded.

She hadn't been away from her kids for more than half a day since they were born. Mark was determined to have the household run as he saw fit, meaning her job was to raise the kids and keep the house while he worked to support them. Working extra hours so she wouldn't need an income was his sacrifice, he would say, though she doubted his avoidance of any child-rearing-related dirty work was a real sacrifice. He liked to make her feel guilty if she wanted some time to herself; neglecting her needs and devoting all her time and energy to the kids was her expected sacrifice.

This time would be different. The historian had called her because her family was part of something important. She wouldn't let Mark make her feel guilty for wanting to find out what it was, no matter how big of a fit he threw.

As she set the children's lunch plates on the table, she brainstormed who in her family might keep an old key and imagined what it would be like to take a flight by herself.

She tried to suppress a smile.

****

"Nah, man, it goes up to the four." Jonah had stopped the band from playing so he could show the chord progression to the potential new guitarist. He was starting to doubt the wisdom of searching for another one via Craigslist. "Give it a try."

Jonah stepped back and leaned against the basement wall, resting one hand on his guitar and placing the other on the back of his neck, under his thick dreadlocks. His dreads were the topic of an earlier argument; maybe he should cut them off, like Olivia wanted. The ornery part of him wanted to keep them just because they irritated his girlfriend.

He wished his band had a gig coming up, so they'd have a reason to practice. He and the drummer, Chris, who also happened to be his roommate, jammed frequently without the hassle of formal practices, but they couldn't have a real band with just the two of them. Tonight they practiced a song Jonah wrote. He smiled when he heard the band play it for the first time, though they'd only made it through one verse before he stopped them.

The newbie played through the progression a few more times before the rest of the band joined him. Drum beats and amplified guitar progressions reverberated off the cement walls. Jonah stopped playing when his phone vibrated in his pocket; he retrieved it and glanced at the unfamiliar number. Area code 804? Where was that? He let it go to voicemail.

After practice, Jonah went upstairs and returned the message. He was still squinting at his phone when Chris appeared next to him in the kitchen. Chris set his drumsticks on the table. "Hey man, why so serious?" He went to the fridge and grabbed a beer, his usual post-jam ritual.

The beer reminded Jonah that he wanted to talk to his roommate about their unequal consumption of the beverage; he'd grown tired of supporting Chris's beer needs. That conversation would have to wait, however.

"This weird guy called me when we were downstairs. I just called him back."

Chris sat at the table and stared at Jonah. He swigged his beer.

"All right." He told Chris everything the historian said about the courthouse, the box, the missing keys, and the potential documentary.

"Whoa, *mysterioso*." Chris chuckled. "Are you gonna look for it?"

Jonah pocketed his phone and walked to the fridge. "I don't know. Maybe I'll call my dad. The guy seemed to think our ancestor was the Irish immigrant guy who signed the letter." He used the magnetic bottle opener to remove the cap to his beer and flicked the cap into the sink, where it bounced off the stainless steel and dirty dishes. After he took a drink, he added, "It kinda feels like a bad joke, ya know? 'An Irish guy, a Chinese guy, a black guy, and a colonist dude walk into a courthouse…'"

Chris laughed. "I'd love to see a stuffy historian put you in front of a camera."

"Yeah, if he'd Skyped me, he probably wouldn't have mentioned the movie." He took another swig and considered the idea. If this key thing was important enough to film, maybe it was worth the time. He retrieved his phone as an alert sounded from Chris's pocket.

Chris glanced at the screen. "Damn, another winter storm warning. Would be nice if it was technically winter. Should I get us some more beer?"

Jonah grinned. "Yeah, go do that." He found the contact he needed and exhaled as he prepared himself for a conversation with his father.

****

Damien sat alone in the bright cafeteria, having successfully avoided his chatty coworkers. His upcoming deadline required nothing else: the less time he spent eating and visiting, the more time he had to develop the intricacies of his new water sanitation idea. He'd formed a habit of bringing a notebook with him on his lunch break, and even if he didn't have anything project-related to do in it, pretending to be busy helped to keep the other employees away from his table.

He cleaned up his dining spot and walked towards the elevator while sipping from his water bottle. He swished and checked his teeth in the door's reflection to make sure there wasn't any food stuck in them.

"Damien! Hey!"

Sydney was waving at him from the end of the hall. She held a messy stack of papers with her other hand, and she used her waving hand to adjust her glasses, which rested on top of her wavy, brown hair. She walked towards him.

Politeness required that he smile, but he hoped the elevator would arrive before she reached him. It didn't.

She looked up to meet his eyes. "Did you hear about Steve's project? It's going on the space station!" Her eyes seemed to bug out of her head when she spoke.

"Really? That's great."

"Yeah, it is. He's been working really hard on it. How's your project coming along?"

"Still working on it." He gestured with the notebook.

The elevator opened, and he entered it. For some reason, she followed.

"Aren't you eating?" He pushed the button for the fourth floor.

"I will. I feel like I never get to talk to you anymore, since they moved me across the building."

Damien knew Sydney wanted more from him than a conversation partner, but he'd kept a professional distance. The dating scene wasn't something he was looking to join. "I'm just trying to stay focused, you know?"

She grinned. "Yeah, I know." The doors opened again, and she put her hand on his arm. "It's good seeing you."

"You too." He stepped out of Sydney's reach and turned left down the hall. A moment later, the voicemail alert on his phone chimed. Someone must have called while he was on the dead-zone elevator.

He listened to the message: an historian named Alex from Richmond wanted to talk to him. When he returned the call, Alex asked him about a key his family might have.

"You think four families have managed to keep four keys for a century?" Damien asked, hoping the guy would hear how ridiculous the whole thing sounded and let him off the hook.

"We realize it's terribly unlikely. But our job is to seek the truth about our history and preserve historical elements. We would be remiss to ignore the families of the men involved." Alex told him they wanted to make a documentary about it.

Damien paced around his lab; just the idea of being in front of a camera made him nervous. "I'm in the middle of a project for work." *Get a clue, please.*

"I understand you have a busy schedule, Mr. Thomas, but we would greatly appreciate any assistance you could provide. Perhaps you can direct us to another family member who may be able to help?"

"You haven't talked to anyone else?"

"No. I've called others, but you were the first to return the message."

Damn. Sometimes, being punctual had its drawbacks.

He felt pressed to say something useful; he tried to not present himself as a complete jerk. "I'll see what I can find, but I might not get back to you right away."

"That's fine. If you find you can't help us, feel free to pass this along to someone else in your family. You have my number."

Damien ended the call and tried to fix his attention on the project on his table. He shifted his focus between that and his computer, but he had trouble keeping his concentration.

That guy knew about his ancestor, the slave who won his freedom when Lincoln issued the Emancipation Proclamation. Well, about the slave's grandson, at least. And if only four men were connected to this mystery in Virginia, a mystery worth documenting in a movie, maybe his ancestor was a part of something important.

He made another call after having to redirect his attention for the third time. Ten minutes later, he had plans to visit his mother's house in Las Vegas. He hoped it would be worth the effort.

****

Sharon looked through the window at the falling rain, enjoying the first Monday morning of her retirement. She listened to the silence that dominated her small house, a silence she'd grown to understand in the three years since Cliff died.

She walked to the bathroom counter and pulled her graying, blonde hair back with a headband before changing into sweats and a grubby T-shirt. The painting project she'd started in the family room over the weekend wasn't going to finish itself, and she planned to resume it after breakfast.

Upon entering the kitchen, she turned on the single-cup coffee brewer. While it warmed, she put two slices of bread in the toaster and turned on her radio.

The talk radio hosts discussed the latest oil spill. She shook her head, wondering if her grandchildren would be able to experience a clean ocean when she took them to her condo on the beach during spring break. She made a mental note to call her cousin, who recently won a seat in the US Senate. Maybe she would have some pull in regulating the oil company.

Her ringing landline added to the noise of the brewer and the jabbering radio hosts.

The caller identified himself as Alex something and told her about a buried box in a Virginia courthouse, but only after she verified that her ancestor was an original Jamestown colonist – a source of pride for her family. Her cousin even mentioned it in her campaign. Alex asked about a key her great-grandfather might have had.

"What kind of key?" she asked.

"One large enough to open a dead bolt and likely made of brass. Do you know of anything like that?"

"Not exactly, but I'll look into it." Her toast had popped, and she wanted to butter it before it cooled.

"Thank you. There's one more thing." He told her he wanted to make a documentary of her and the other descendants opening the safe.

Whatever was behind the door was valuable enough to pay for four airfares and a film crew. Maybe she should look for the key.

"Can I leave you my number?" he asked.

"Sure." She wrote his name and number on a notepad, hung up the phone, and set her toaster on the lightest setting to re-warm her breakfast.

The following afternoon, Sharon stood and stretched her back after applying the last stroke of forest green paint near the baseboard. She admired her handiwork and smiled when she realized Cliff would have never allowed her to paint such a bold color on a wall in their house. She laughed when she imagined what his reaction would be if he saw it.

After she cleaned and stored her painting supplies, she walked upstairs to take a shower. She had dinner plans with her friend in just over an hour, and she didn't want to be late. As she chose a new pair of tan slacks and a purple cardigan set to wear for the evening, she thought about her conversation with Alex.

How could he know so much about her family? There weren't many people who could say they descended from the Jamestown colony, and if she got to be in a movie, she would likely get to talk about it. She tried to remember if she'd seen a key anywhere that might have been the one Alex meant.

She finished putting on her jewelry and made her way downstairs. As usual, when she reached the small landing on the stairs, she glanced at the collage her grandmother – the daughter of Sharon's box-burying great-grandfather – had given her many years prior. Her grandmother had created an image of a colonial house using a variety of items: a coin, some buttons, a bullet casing, a bottle cap.

A key.

She removed her reading glasses from the top of her head and put them in front of her eyes. She squinted and leaned towards the picture, trying to analyze the key. It was partially covered by a match book. She weighed her options for a moment before deciding what to do.

She took the collage from the wall and carried it to her dining room table, where she removed the backing from the frame and freed her grandmother's project from it. She ran her fingers across the part of the key she could touch.

Her grandmother had insisted Sharon keep the collage, made her promise not to lose or sell it. Perhaps it contained something important, and if this was the key that covered a secret in Virginia, it would certainly qualify as such.

"Sorry, Grandma," she spoke towards the ceiling before she started picking apart the collage. After she destroyed a small portion of it, she held the dark, brass-colored key in her hand. It appeared old, but she had no way of knowing if this was the key Alex hoped she would find. She carried it into the kitchen and referenced the phone number on the note pad. Three rings passed before he answered by identifying himself. "Alex Pratt."

"Hello, Mr. Pratt, this is Sharon Ellis. You called me this morning about a key."

"Oh yes, of course."

"I think I found it."

Chapter Two

Michelle mentally replayed her husband's words from the previous night.

You need to be here. Mail that weirdo your key, if you manage to find it.

Mark's refusal to allow her to travel strengthened her resolve to find the key. He'd be more likely to change his mind if she actually had the thing.

She'd called her mother as soon as she could after Mark once again dashed her hopes of doing something interesting. Her mother didn't know anything about a key, but she thought Michelle's uncle might know something.

If you manage to find it.

"Michelle?"

She snapped back to reality. "Oh. Sorry, I was just zoning out."

Anna laughed. "I figured. I was asking what made you decide to visit on short notice."

Michelle sipped her coffee as she sat on the couch with her cousin, enjoying the quiet that resulted from their kids running upstairs to play. Anna's seven-year-old daughter, Britney, loved to show her room off to her cousins.

"It's kind of a long story." Michelle told Anna about Alex's call, then added, "I spoke with Uncle Li yesterday. He thinks you might have the key."

"Really? Why would he say that?"

"Something about boxes that came from his house?"

Anna glanced towards the ceiling, like she was thinking. "I think I know what he's talking about. Most of them came from my old room, but there was a leather case with some things in it that my dad made me promise not to throw away. He didn't tell me why. David went through a few of the boxes when he was looking for things for Britney's dollhouse, but I don't know what he found. Do you want to go through them?"

Michelle nodded. "That leather case sounds promising." She placed her coffee cup on the end table.

"The boxes are in the basement, tucked under the stairs. I'll stay here and listen for the kids."

The steps creaked under Michelle's feet as she descended into the dark, unfinished basement. She pulled a chain, and a light bulb flickered to life.

The leather case was in the second box. She ran her fingers across the dust before she opened it. It contained a hodgepodge of items: a tarnished silver spoon, a thimble, and old stamps, among other things. She sifted through the items until she was satisfied the key wasn't there.

She spent the next half hour going through the boxes, and her confidence deflated with each unsuccessful minute. As she lifted a picture, her finger caught on the corner of the frame, cutting her. She swore, dropped the frame, and cradled her bleeding finger. Scowling, she replaced the items she'd removed from the boxes before she rejoined her cousin in the family room. "If it's down there, I didn't find it." She took a tissue from the box on the end table and wrapped it around her finger.

Anna lowered her novel to her lap. "Sorry. I'll go through the boxes more thoroughly this weekend. Is your finger okay?"

"I'll live."

Michelle tried to hide her disappointment. Her new adventure could be over before it had a chance to start. At least Mark would be happy.

She walked upstairs to check on the kids before returning to the couch. She and Anna caught up on each other's lives until Sophie started crying.

Michelle glanced towards the ceiling. "I'll be right back."

She followed her daughter's cries and entered Britney's room to find Grant holding a plastic baseball bat. She wondered why he wasn't smart enough to at least put the evidence on the floor or hide it in the closet. Britney kneeled next to Sophie, stroking her back.

Michelle approached Grant. "All right, young man, what happened?"

He looked up at her with his big, brown eyes.

"He hit her on the back. I saw him." Britney seemed pleased to give the report.

Michelle held out her hand. Grant didn't want to give up the bat at first.

"Do you want to go home? You know it's not okay to hit."

He shook his head and handed the bat to her. She put him on Britney's bed for a time-out. He tucked his chin into his chest and folded his arms, and Michelle almost chuckled at his dramatic display.

She sat on the floor, leaning against the bed. Sophie crawled into Michelle's lap and snuggled against her. Michelle wiped her daughter's tears with her thumb.

After Sophie calmed down, Britney plopped herself next to Michelle. "Did you see my new dollhouse?" Her smile covered her small face.

"No, I didn't, but your mom told me about it. Why don't you show it to me?"

Britney walked to the side of her room and scooted a house half her height to the middle of the floor. She spun it around so Michelle could see into all the miniature rooms.

Britney grasped a doll small enough to occupy the house and held it in one of the rooms. "This is the kitchen." She wiggled the doll a few times to demonstrate how a doll would make pancakes, then the doll showed Michelle the rest of the rooms. At the end of the tour, Britney changed her voice to a silly doll voice and said, "And before I leave for the store, I have to lock up!" Britney pulled a key that was almost as large as the doll from a small hook in the tiny living room.

"Britney, where did you get that key?" Michelle asked. The key couldn't have been part of the dollhouse set. Aside from its size, it was dirty and old, like antique brass.

"My daddy gave it to me. He said all homeowners have keys." She went back to playing with her doll, trying to make the doll hold the key.

Could finding it be this easy? Michelle's pulse quickened. "Do you mind if I borrow it for a little while?"

Britney scrunched her eyebrows. "Why?"

"I'm just curious about it. I'll give it back to you when I'm done, I promise."

The girl shrugged. "Okay. I guess." Britney handed the key to Michelle, who felt the cool metal between her fingers.

****

"Damn, boy, do something with your hair."

"Nice to you see you too, Dad." Jonah gave his father a quick hug, wondering if the man would ever stop giving him grief about his dreads. "Can we go inside? The drive was horrible."

"Yeah, sure, but let me warn your mother first. She'll want to know you still look like you do drugs." He led Jonah into the house.

"I don't do drugs."

"I know, but ya' look like it."

Jonah shook his head. He hadn't seen his parents in person since last summer; the seven-hour drive from Cincinnati to Memphis prohibited more frequent visits, a fact that had inspired Jonah to move so far away in the first place. Jonah looked forward to seeing his mother and brother, but he could only handle his father in small doses.

They entered the house and found his mother waiting for them at the kitchen table. Jonah's twenty-four-year-old brother, Samuel, sat with her. He examined a small, metal bus by holding it just inches from his eyes, as his nearly complete visual impairment required. His father claimed the empty seat next to Samuel.

His mother rose from the table and squeezed Jonah in her arms. "It's so good to see you!" She pulled away enough to frame his face in her hands and kissed him on the forehead. "You need a haircut."

He chuckled. "So I've been told." He walked to his brother's chair and kneeled. "Hey, Sammy, it's Jonah."

"Jonah!" His brother turned towards his voice and smiled with delight. His free hand found Jonah's head. Jonah took

Samuel's hand from the top of his head and held it between them. Jonah loved how Samuel expressed joy with his whole face. Having "special needs" had its benefits; his brother seemed to be happy about everything most of the time.

"Where'd you get that bus?" Jonah asked.

Samuel pulled the bus close to his eyes again and laughed his deep, throaty laugh. "Brina!"

Jonah looked to his mother for an explanation.

"Sabrina. She's a new aide at the respite home."

Jonah nodded and turned back to Samuel. "Got a girlfriend, huh?"

Samuel laughed again.

Jonah released Samuel's hand and walked to the fridge to grab a soda.

"How was the drive?" his mother asked.

"Long. Winter got us early this year. It took an hour to get out of the weather." He took a drink. "How's it been here?"

He felt a little guilty for staying away so long. His parents were completely consumed in caring for Samuel, and Jonah enjoyed spending time with his brother so they could have a break. Samuel was nearly two years old on the day of Jonah's birth, an event that wasn't supposed to happen because of the risk of the same genetic problem Samuel had being passed to any future children. His mother liked to call Jonah their "surprise blessing."

"Oh, you know, same old same old." His mother looked at her older son, who rolled the wheels of his bus along his palm.

"Do you and Dad want to go out tonight?"

"No, we took Samuel to the respite home last weekend, so we're fine. I'd rather stay here with you." She took a sip from her water glass. "So, why the surprise visit?"

"Dad didn't tell you?"

She shook her head.

He glared at his father for a moment and took the last remaining seat around the table. He told his mother about Alex's call before asking, "Do you have any idea what he's talking about? Is there an old key around that you know of?"

His parents looked at each other.

"Samuel, show Jonah your key," his mother said.

"Key!" Samuel exclaimed as he pulled a chain from inside his shirt. An old, brass key rested on his chest a moment later.

Jonah scowled at his father. "That was too easy. Do you really think that's it?"

His dad shrugged. "Well, I can't know for sure without trying it in whatever lock it's supposed to match. Sammy found that in a dresser drawer at your grandparents' house over Labor Day weekend and wanted to keep it. He's worn it around his neck ever since."

Jonah's father's insistence on a personal visit made sense now. Samuel had claimed the key as a special token, and he didn't relinquish those easily. When they were teenagers, Samuel had taken a liking to the electric tuner Jonah used when he was still taking guitar lessons. Jonah quietly snatched it back once he figured out why he kept losing it, but after the fifth time, when Samuel came running into Jonah's room while yelling and scratching at Jonah to get the tuner back, Jonah decided it would be easier to buy another one.

His dad glanced at Samuel before facing Jonah. "Your grandparents might know more about it. I didn't ask because I didn't think it was important, though your grandpa asked me to make sure Sammy doesn't lose it. I thought he was just being protective of his things."

Jonah nodded. "I'll go see them tomorrow."

****

Damien almost turned the car around and returned to Tempe three times before he was halfway to Las Vegas. The longer he drove, the more he resented the historian for putting this task on him. He had more important things to do than engage in a stranger's treasure hunt. Maybe he should have passed the key-finding mission to his sister, like he had considered before planning this trip. Maybe he still could.

He parked in the driveway of his mother's house. She came outside to meet him at the car, smiling and running to him with open arms.

"It's about time you remembered where we live." She hugged him. He stood in the space between his car and the open driver's door, as far as his mother had let him proceed. He had to bend over to cover the several inches that separated them to hug her properly.

"I know. Sorry I haven't been around." His last visit had occurred during the previous Christmas season almost a year ago. He didn't tell her he'd nearly decided to prolong his absence.

She released him from her hug, took his hand, and pulled him towards the house with such force that he had to use his foot to close the car door because his arm was quickly out of range. She pulled him through the front door and announced to the empty front room, "Marie! He's here!"

His sister emerged from behind a wall that separated the front room from the kitchen. Her brown, curly hair was pulled back in a tight pony tail, as always. She shrieked and ran to him, wrapping her arms around him the same way his mother had done. He could always count on a warm reception when visiting home, in spite of his own grumpy demeanor.

She released him and smacked him on the chest with the back of her hand. "It's about time! Jackson probably doesn't even remember who you are!"

He brought his hand to his chest, where Marie had hit him. "Where is he, anyway?" He wondered if his three-year-old nephew would recognize him, now that Marie mentioned it.

"Upstairs, napping. Come get a drink." She took his hand and pulled him towards the kitchen. This was a universal truth for the women in his family: they loved to lead people around by their hands.

"Hold on, let me get my stuff from the car. Mom pulled me away so quickly I left the keys in the ignition."

She laughed. "All right. I'll pour you a glass of tea."

Marie and his mother retreated to the kitchen, and he walked to his car, thankful that he followed through on this visit; he hadn't realized how lonely he was before his arrival. His mind went to Sydney, the wiry woman from work. Her random appearance in his thoughts at this moment surprised him.

He reminded himself there was a reason he didn't let women occupy any part of his life, including his head. He didn't need to get hurt again.

After taking his bag to the guest room, he made his way to the kitchen. His mother and sister sat at the table, flipping through magazines and drinking tea, which they'd apparently been doing since before he arrived. He claimed his glass and leaned against the counter, trying not to be bothered by the cluttered table.

"Oh no. Sit." His mother pointed to the empty seat next to her.

"No, thanks. I'm tired of sitting."

"All right, suit yourself." She took a stack of magazines from the table and plopped them into the chair. He laughed.

"So what brings you here? It's not even a holiday! Big news to share? A girl, maybe?" His sister crossed her arms on the table and leaned towards him.

He grinned. "No, I'm afraid not."

She huffed, shook her head, and looked at her mother. "I'm gonna lose the bet."

His mother snickered.

"What bet?" he asked.

"Our bet that you'd be married before you're thirty. I bet you would, but seeing as I have less than a year…" She pursed her lips.

He faced his mother. "I'm glad you're making money off me. I wondered why you stopped being so pushy. How long ago did you make this bet?"

She smiled. "When you turned twenty-five."

"How much?"

"Fifty."

He nodded and took a sip. "Not bad. Use it to take me out for dinner."

"Sure, dinner with a girl, since I can start being pushy again!"

He sighed. At least they were bugging him to date any girl instead of pressuring him to track down his ex-girlfriend. Maybe six elapsed years made them realize it wouldn't happen. He hadn't told them the truth about the breakup, how she'd betrayed him with such voracity that he swore he'd never get so close to a woman again. His family had loved her and wanted him to marry her, and they'd assumed he was at fault when the relationship fell apart. He didn't have the energy or desire to correct them. "Not that this conversation isn't fun, but can I tell you why I'm here?"

"Go for it," his mother said. She continued to flip through her magazine and dog-eared a page.

Damien told them about Alex's call, then asked, "Do either of you know anything about a missing key?"

Marie looked to her mother, who raised her eyebrows. "Not that I can remember. Seems like this guy's hoping for a lot. I doubt four different families have managed not to lose four separate keys in a hundred years." His mother squinted at him. "This doesn't seem like something you'd care about."

He shrugged. "I've been back and forth. The guy knows about our freed-slave ancestor. He's done his homework. I guess I want to know how our family is involved."

He waited to see if Marie would show even a slight interest in the subject. If she did, he'd ask her to take over the mission.

She focused on her magazine.

"Well, how about the three of us go through those boxes in the crawlspace after Jackson goes to bed tonight? That's probably our best chance," his mother said.

That evening, Damien worked with his mother and sister as they rummaged through old dishes, albums, clothes, and other items his family had stored over the years, which required Damien to pull box after box from the dusty crawlspace and into the family room. The women kept conversation going as they worked, which exhausted him more than the digging did. At one point, they insisted he share the intricacies of the water sanitation device he was designing, which in itself was wearying because he had to simplify almost every aspect of it for them to understand how it was supposed to work.

They eventually gave up trying to comprehend what Damien did for a living and moved on to another topic. His family's ability to be social for countless hours amazed him. He imagined he was the only introvert in their entire gene pool.

When they reached the bottom of the last box, his mother announced, "Well, that's about it! No key!"

Damien slumped and returned a few items to the boxes before deciding to take a break. "I need a drink. You two need anything?"

They shook their heads, and he walked up the stairs towards the kitchen. He washed the dust from his hands and froze when he saw what hung on the side of the cabinet nearest the sink.

He dried his hands and removed the large, iron key ring from the nail. He walked down the stairs. "Mom, what's this?"

She smiled. "Oh! Isn't that neat? My grandma gave me that. Told me to hang on to it because it's important."

He examined the ring, which held at least twenty large, old keys. "Did she say why it was important?"

She shook her head. "Nope, just that it was important. I love how it looks all rustic, so I hung it up where I'd see it all the time."

"You didn't think of this before we spent hours going through boxes looking for a key?"

She raised her hands. "Hey, sorry. I forgot, okay?"

He examined the keys, hoping one of them was the one he needed.

****

"Hi, Sharon. It's good to hear from you."

Sharon smiled. She sat in her recliner, thankful she was able to connect with her cousin, Liz. Or Senator Griesson, as others called her. "How's your new job treating you, Senator?"

"Senator-elect, until January. It's busy, but it's wonderful. I received an envelope full of cards from a second grade class yesterday. One asked if I could make it okay for her to bring her dog to school."

Sharon laughed. "Seems reasonable to me." She remembered Liz's affection for dogs and imagined Liz was inclined to work on the girl's request. She'd called to feel out her cousin on the oil spill, but once Liz was on the phone, all Sharon wanted to do was chat about the inconsequential.

They talked for ten minutes before Liz said she had to go, citing a need to get back to work. "Thanks for calling, Sharon. Love you."

"Love you too. Don't have too much fun up there on The Hill."

Liz laughed. "Don't worry about that." The call ended.

Sharon sighed, full of pride for her cousin. Part of her wished she had done something so important.

She moved on to her next task. On the night she called him, Alex told her she was the first one to find the key, and he wouldn't make any plans for anyone to meet in Richmond until the other three found theirs, if that happened at all. She knew next to nothing about her box-burying great-grandfather, so she decided to do a little research.

The internet didn't yield as much information as she'd hoped. She found a site that said he'd worked for a pharmaceutical company in New York, but there weren't many more details, so she drove to the public library to examine the microfiche slides of national newspapers. She didn't know if her library in Dallas would have information about events as far away as Richmond and New York, but she didn't have anything better to do. Maybe there would be a story or two about the company for which he worked.

She quit searching after four hours. The most relevant article described the addition to the Richmond courthouse. If she wanted more specific information about her great-grandfather, she would have to travel.

A week later, her brother, Larry, met her in the passenger pickup area of the Fort Wayne airport. He stood outside his old, blue Ford truck, which he had somehow kept running for forty years. He wore slacks and what looked like a new golf shirt that contrasted with his permanently greasy knuckles, and he appeared to have used some kind of gel to comb back his thinning, blond hair. She laughed when she realized he probably dressed up for her.

She hugged him. "Hey there, stranger."

"Hey Shar." He released her and held the passenger door open for her.

She tilted her head. "Who turned you into a gentleman?"

He grinned. "Blame Josie."

She climbed into the truck as she made a mental note to thank Larry's third wife when they arrived at the house. This marriage was the one that seemed most likely to stick, even though it took until Larry was sixty-seven to meet Josephine.

During the twenty-mile drive to the house, Sharon told Larry about Alex's call and about the key. She removed the key from her purse and showed it to him.

"So you had this the whole time?" he asked.

"Yep, right under my nose."

He laughed. “I think Grandma knew what she was doing when she put it there.”

“Do you think she knew what our great-grandfather hid?”

Larry shrugged. “Who knows? She never said anythin’ to me about it.” He glanced in her direction. “What now, since you found it?”

“The historian wants the descendants to meet in Richmond.”

“That seems silly. Can’t you all just mail him the keys?”

She stared out the window. “He said they want us there for the documentary, and besides, I want to see what it opens. Aren’t you curious about how our family is connected to this? I have the time now, so why not go?”

He shrugged, and Sharon was thankful that Alex called her instead of Larry.

They arrived at Larry’s small, colonial-style house set on a few acres, just enough to feel removed from the city while still technically being in it. She loved that her brother kept their parents’ house; it followed her family’s deep appreciation of their history. When she was a kid, she rode horses and shot at targets in what they now called the front yard. That was before the city absorbed their property. She hadn’t ridden a horse or touched a gun since she was a teenager.

After she greeted Josie, Sharon walked to the bright, unfinished basement and found a state of what she would call organized chaos: cardboard boxes were stacked on the far side of the room, and rows of open shelving cluttered with various items – figurines, decorative plates, and dolls, among other things - filled the rest of the space. This must be where Josephine stored the inventory she sold on eBay.

Sharon made her way to the boxes. What she was looking for was likely old, so she removed the top layers of boxes and started with those on the bottom.

Chapter Three

"I take it you found the key." Michelle's uncle removed two sodas from the fridge and offered one to her.

"If it was in a leather case with a bunch of other junk, then yes." She walked with him to the backyard, where they sat across from each other at the patio set, and she told him about Anna's husband finding the key and giving it to Britney for her dollhouse.

He cracked open his soda and sipped it. "That's the one. My father said to keep it until one of us knew why we needed it."

Michelle grinned, realizing she was the one who knew why they needed it. "Why didn't you tell Anna what she had?"

"When my great-grandfather left the key to our family, he asked that few members of the family know about it. I had planned to tell Anna when she asked about it. My father didn't tell me until I asked. I knew she would discover it before long."

Michelle blinked a few times as she absorbed his response. Her uncle had meant for the key to be easily found. If Anna's husband hadn't taken it from the case, Michelle would have found it minutes after she started looking. "Why did he want only a few to know about it?"

"I'm not sure. Perhaps he didn't want to cause fighting."

What could be hidden that would cause family strife? Something valuable, perhaps? Or dangerous? "Did Grandpa say what was in the safe?"

"No. I don't think my great-grandfather told anyone. What are you supposed to do with it?"

"If the others find their keys, the historian wants to get us all together to open the safe. He said they want to make a documentary about it." She took a sip to hide her smile, feeling a little guilty for wanting to get away so badly.

Her uncle squinted at her. "Are you sure that's a good idea? You don't even know this man. What did Mark say?"

She hadn't yet told her husband she'd found the key. If the other descendants found theirs, she'd tell him she was leaving after Alex sent her the plane ticket. Mark wouldn't make her stay home when other people were counting on her to be there. "I looked Alex up online and talked to someone else at the society. His story about the box and safe checks out. I think our family kept the key for this reason."

"I don't think our ancestor meant for this to be in a movie. He said to keep it in the family." He sipped his drink while staring towards the fence.

"What do you know about your great-grandfather?" She had to get him to stop trying to talk her out of participating in this new adventure.

"Only a little. I can show you some things about our family, if you'd like. Maybe that will answer some questions for you."

"I'd like that. I don't know when I'll be able to come here without the kids again."

"Okay." He rose from his chair and walked into the house, and she followed. He left his drink on the kitchen counter. "Wait here."

She sat at the table. A few minutes later, her uncle returned, carrying an old photo album.

He sat in the chair next to her. "My grandmother made this album." The cover made a cracking sound as he opened it. "She wanted to maintain our history – at least, that's what my father told me." He flipped through a few pages. "Ah, here it is." He slid the album towards her.

She looked at the page.

"This is my great-grandfather, Gao. I believe this is the only existing picture of him." He pointed to a small, grainy, black-and-white photograph of a young, skinny, Chinese man. "He was born in, let's see…" He pulled the album to himself. "1883." He slid the album back to Michelle. "So, six years after my great-great-grandparents immigrated to America."

"Why did they come here?" Michelle turned a few pages in the album.

"The same reason many immigrants did: to find new opportunities. They settled in New York and opened a shop in Chinatown. Gao married in 1903, and my grandmother was born two years later." He took back the album and flipped the pages until he found an old photograph of a Chinese woman. "She was their only child."

"That seems strange. I thought families tended to be larger back then," Michelle said.

"Yes. I don't know why they didn't have more children."

"Hmm." Michelle turned more pages of the album. "If he lived in New York, what was his connection to Richmond?"

"I don't know. Perhaps he had business there." He stared at Michelle for a few moments. "There is one more thing I know about him."

"What's that?"

He closed the album. "He disappeared, in 1912 or 1913."

"That was around the same time he buried the box. What happened to him?"

"No one knows, or at least they didn't talk to me about it. Everyone has their theories."

Michelle put her hand on the album. She'd come here hoping for answers, but instead, she had more questions. She hoped the others could find their keys. Maybe her answers were in Richmond.

****

Jonah's grandmother released him from their hug that started immediately after he entered her kitchen. "It's so good to see you again. Hasn't that girlfriend of yours told you to cut your hair?" Fortunately, he'd grown used to his hairstyle being the first topic of all conversations with his family.

He grinned. "Yes, she has. A few times."

His grandmother handed him a glass of water. She started to say something when a gruff voice from the adjacent room interrupted her. "Maybe you should listen to your woman!"

Jonah glanced in the direction of the voice, then back to his grandmother. "I'll be right back."

He entered the family room and found his grandfather sitting at a card table, on which he had sprawled the 1000 pieces of a jigsaw puzzle displaying Monticello, according to the box sitting on the opposite side of the table. He wore skinny, black-rimmed reading glasses that Jonah wasn't accustomed to seeing. "Hey Grandpa."

His grandpa looked up. "Seriously, though. Listen to her. You look like hell."

"Thank you."

"What brings you this way? Here to see your brother?" His grandpa scanned the puzzle pieces.

Jonah sipped his water. "No, I'm here because of something he found." He was about to share Alex's call when his grandpa interrupted.

"The key?"

Jonah nodded. "Yeah. What do you know about it?"

"Only bits and pieces. My dad gave it to me, said my granddad made him promise not to lose it and to pass it on through the family. He said one of us would know what to do with it one day."

Jonah blinked with disbelief at the idea that he was the one who knew what to do with it.

His grandpa continued, "I forget about things if I don't see them, so I kept it in the real skinny top drawer in the guest room bureau, where I keep extra note pads and such. I look in there often enough to know I wouldn't forget about it." He picked up a puzzle piece and twisted it as he held it up to the light, and he placed it into the picture that slowly grew from the outside in. "Anyway, Samuel was exploring, as he does, and he found it. Must have liked the feel of it. He held onto it all during that day, until I put it on a chain for him. I figured if it was one of his tokens, he wouldn't lose it."

Jonah walked across the room, stood next to the card table, and examined the puzzle pieces. He placed a piece in less than a minute. "Are you sure that's the key your granddad meant?"

His grandpa scowled at him. "Course I'm sure. I would've thrown it away if it wasn't." He examined the piece Jonah had added to the puzzle. "You know you have to find out what it's for now, right?"

Jonah furrowed his eyebrows. "Do I?" He was fairly certain he would make the trip to Richmond, but he wanted to hear his grandpa's argument for going.

"Well, yeah!" He chuckled and coughed. "The family's been saving this key for a hundred years! If we have to store it for another hundred years because you don't want to deal with it, I'll kick your ass."

Jonah grinned and placed another piece.

"You planning to finish this for me?"

"No. I'll stop." He studied his grandpa's scowl and turned to head back to the kitchen. "I'll help Grandma make lunch."

"How are you planning to get it from Samuel?" his grandpa asked before Jonah left the room.

"I'm working on that."

The next day was full of preparations, and the following evening, Jonah sat on the couch across from the recliner where his brother sat. He held an acoustic guitar that he borrowed from an old high school buddy. It wasn't as nice as his guitar back home, but for tonight's purposes, it would do.

"Sammy, are you ready?" he asked.

Samuel nodded emphatically. He squinted towards the light above Jonah's head, the only bright spot in the room he could likely see.

"Okay." Jonah strummed the chords that were ingrained in his memory – the chords of his original song. He sang the lyrics of the first verse, closing his eyes as he did so.

I know we can't live forever,

Would it bother you if we tried?

He finished the verse and opened his eyes when he reached the chorus. Samuel had closed his eyes and rocked gently in his chair. By the time Jonah sang the second verse and reached the chorus again, his brother was humming the melody line.

Moments like these made Jonah truly appreciate Samuel. Despite his brother's limitations, he could connect with people in ways that others couldn't or didn't want to. While anyone else would listen to Jonah's song with a mild interest and maybe a hope that Jonah's career would soar, Jonah believed Samuel felt every note, taking every line into his being, not caring if Jonah was an amateur or a platinum-album artist. As he sang, his emotions caught in his throat, and he had to close his eyes to power through the rest of the song.

Samuel clapped after Jonah played the final chords.

Jonah smiled. "Did you like that?"

Samuel nodded. "Again!"

Jonah set the guitar on the couch and kneeled next to the chair. "I thought you might say that, so I made you something."

Jonah reached for Samuel's hand and put a small mp3 player with headphones and a lanyard into it. "Actually, let me show you." He put one ear bud into Samuel's ear and the other bud into his own ear.

Jonah made sure the volume wasn't too loud before he hit "play". The first chords of Jonah's song played through the ear buds.

Samuel smiled. Jonah took the bud from his own ear and moved it to Samuel's other ear before he guided his brother's fingers over the controls of the player, showing him how to play the song and how to stop it. "And I put it on a lanyard, so you can wear it around your neck. See?" Jonah placed the lanyard over Samuel's head, and the player rested on his chest with the key. "Now you can listen any time you want."

"Thank you!"

Jonah swallowed, not wanting to broach the topic that was the point of borrowing the guitar and having his friend record the song for him. "Sammy, can I see your key again?"

"Key!" Samuel felt around his chest until he found it and held it.

"Can I take it off? I want to look at it more closely." Jonah grasped the chain and pulled it over Samuel's head, pausing to remove the ear buds and to see if his brother would protest. Samuel was busy working the mp3 player. He put the ear buds back in his ears and rocked in his chair.

Jonah held the key in one hand and paused the song with his other hand. "Sammy, I need to ask you a question, okay?"

"Okay!"

"Can I keep your key for a little while, since you have the song around your neck now?" Jonah didn't like manipulating his brother, but he couldn't think of another somewhat-decent way to get the key. A trade seemed the least distasteful of all the options he'd considered.

Samuel felt the player in his hand and pressed "play".

****

The morning after Damien found the key ring, he sat across the kitchen table from his mother. Jackson sat in a booster seat next to her, throwing Cheerios onto the floor and occasionally getting one into his mouth.

"So now what, since you have the key?" his mother asked.

He finished sipping his coffee. "I called Alex earlier. He said the others have their keys and to expect a gathering sometime after the New Year." He held his cup with both hands. "I guess I have to decide if I'm going."

"Why wouldn't you go?"

He glanced at his squealing nephew before looking back at her. "Partly because I don't want to miss work, but partly because…" He paused to gather his thoughts. "This stranger just calls one day, tells me about a key, and I'm supposed to rush out there to find out if it opens something? Seems kinda off to me."

"I'm sure you researched the guy."

"Of course I did. He checks out at the historical society."

"So what are you worried about? It would be neat to see you in a documentary."

He shrugged. "I don't know. Do we have family connections to Richmond?"

She grinned, probably because Damien invited her to tell a story. "I don't think so. After the war, our family settled in New York." She leaned forward, assuming her full story-telling posture. "My great-grandpa met and married my great-grandmother in the early 1900s, and my grandpa was born soon after. He was their only child, which makes sense because my great-grandpa disappeared."

That caught Damien's full attention. "Disappeared?"

"Yeah, just one day, poof. He probably just got scared and ran off. My grandpa was seven or so at the time. Told me he swore he'd never do that to his own family." She sipped her coffee.

"Wait, so the relative who buried the box just disappeared?"

"Sure did. Poof." She laughed. "There's an empty grave plot next to my great-grandmother's grave. She never gave up hope that her husband would return one day, so my grandpa kept the plot available. More for her, I think. No one else thought he'd come back."

"Huh." Now the idea of meeting Alex made him more uncomfortable. Why would he consider going to Richmond? To satisfy an historian's curiosity? That seemed pretty stupid.

"Maybe if you go out there and find out what the key is for, you'll learn what happened to him."

And just like that, Damien knew why he needed to go to Richmond.

He let his mother ramble on for the next fifteen minutes about the later generations of his family, pausing to clean Jackson's face and remove him from his booster seat. By the time she finished talking, Damien was more than ready to drive home with his newly acquired key ring in his bag and an old family mystery in his brain.

****

After two hours in Larry's basement, Sharon had a collection of things she thought were connected to her great-grandfather.

She had sifted through items her family had gathered over centuries, items that should have probably been in a museum. Not only had her family originated in Jamestown, a distant cousin fought in the Revolutionary War, another founded a small city in Ohio, and other ancestors battled against the Confederates in the Civil War. Now, her cousin was a senator. She ran her fingers across the stock of a musket, proud of her family's impact on American history.

She replaced the things she didn't need into the boxes and found an empty box to keep the evidence of her great-grandfather. She walked upstairs and found Josephine working in the kitchen. Sharon placed the box on the table.

"I take it you found something interesting." Josephine was rinsing a head of lettuce.

"I think so." Sharon removed the items she had collected: a large Mason jar, a rusty pan balance, a price list from a store, and a yellowed photograph of a man who could have been her great-grandfather. Larry joined them from outside and waited for Josephine to finish with the lettuce before he washed his hands.

"Whadya find?" He walked towards the table while drying his hands with a paper towel.

Sharon gestured to the table, and Larry picked up the jar. "Why is this important?" He turned the jar, causing the gram or two of white powder inside to roll.

"I'm not sure that it is. I learned our great-grandpa was a pharmacist. I thought these items supported that story. Grandma didn't talk about him, so we're kind of on our own here." She took the jar from Larry, opened it, and sniffed the inside of it, but it didn't have an odor.

"Yeah, she didn't want us to ask about him either."

She pressed and released one side of the balance and watched the pans rock back and forth. "Why do you think our great-grandpa would take off like he did?"

"I'd guess the same reason lots of guys take off. Probably got himself a younger model."

"Watch it, buddy, that's not funny," Josephine scolded from the counter.

Sharon laughed. Josephine was definitely good for her brother.

She put the items back into the box. "I'll take this upstairs to my room."

After leaving the box in the closet, she checked her voicemail. One message came from Alex, saying the other descendants had found their keys, and he was arranging for all of them to meet in Richmond in January.

She smiled.

Chapter Four

Michelle drummed her fingers on the armrest of the plane's window seat, waiting for the second leg of her flight to start. Her kids had been worried about her leaving and kept her up most of the previous night, so she'd slept during the flight from Sacramento to Charlotte. She hoped the ninety minutes of flight time to Richmond were enough for her to mentally prepare herself for the coming days.

Her husband had refused to help her with the kids so she could sleep; he was still mad that she waited until three days ago to tell him she was leaving. By then, the other descendants, Alex, and a film crew were already invested in the trip, and she told Mark the key was too valuable to place in the mail. She'd arranged for her mother to watch the kids during the days, so Mark would only have to put them to bed at night. He finally agreed to let her go, though he didn't talk to her again before she left.

She tried to bury the stress of three days' worth of silent treatment as she looked at the other passengers boarding the plane. A stocky, young guy with thick, brown dreadlocks stood out from the crowd. He looked at the seat numbers posted near the overhead bins and slowly moved towards her row. She silently willed him to sit in one of the few empty seats in the rows in front of her, but he didn't take any of those.

No, please don't sit here, she thought. *I bet he smells weird.*

"Twenty-three B," he muttered when he was two rows ahead of her row, and she slumped: she sat in twenty-three A. She scanned the plane for empty seats in the hopes she could move, but by then, every seat was occupied. She stared out the window. Maybe he would ignore her.

The stranger started talking almost immediately after takeoff. "Flying solo?"

She sighed, faced him, and nodded. "Yeah. First time away from the kids." *That's right, buddy. I have kids. Still want to chat?*

He nodded. "Oh, okay. How old are your kids?"

"Three and five." Avoiding conversation seemed unlikely, and while she would have preferred a quiet trip, she didn't want to be rude. "Do you live in Richmond? Or Charlotte?"

He shook his head. "No, I had a layover in Charlotte. I'm from Cincinnati. How about you?"

"I'm heading to Richmond for business."

He nodded and held out his hand. "I'm Jonah."

She smiled and shook his hand, trying to ignore his calloused fingers. "Michelle."

"Nice to meet you."

"Do you always talk to people on planes?" she asked from pure curiosity. Contrary to her expectations when she first saw him, he was friendly and spoke coherently.

"Well, I don't fly much, but I do like to talk. Gotta be outgoing in my business."

She glanced at his dreads and grinned. "Politician?"

He laughed. "God, no. I'm a musician. I work in IT to pay the bills. What do you do?"

"I'm a professional mommy for now."

"Oh, okay. So the business in Richmond is…"

"Personal business."

He nodded.

The flight attendant stopped at their row to take their drink orders. The black man across the aisle from Jonah seemed especially fidgety. Michelle predicted he would order something containing alcohol and laughed to herself when he proved her correct.

Jonah made small talk with Michelle until halfway through the flight, when he pulled a tablet from his backpack and turned it on. The screen displayed pages of a book.

"What are you reading?" she asked before he became too absorbed by his novel.

"*The Girl with the Dragon Tattoo*. Ever read it?"

She shook her head.

"It's great. My girlfriend recommended it. I love a good mystery."

She smiled. *So do I.*

****

Jonah tucked his tablet into his backpack as the plane started its descent. Michelle, the Asian lady who sat next to him during the flight, kept her focus out the window until the wheels touched the ground.

"Were you looking for something?" he asked.

"No. I like watching the landscape get bigger during landings."

Michelle seemed standoffish at first, but she ended up being an interesting conversation partner. She appeared so proper and clean-cut that Jonah guessed she didn't have many friends like him back home.

The crowd thinned enough for him to disembark, and he walked towards the terminal. As he neared baggage claim, he looked for the carousel he needed and for the sign-holding man who was supposed to give him a ride to his hotel. *Keys*, the sign would say, like it was someone's name. Jonah laughed when he thought of it.

Michelle closely followed him, naturally. Her bag would be on the same carousel. He grabbed his suitcase and turned around, scanning the area for his driver. A slightly overweight, nerdy-looking guy with brown hair and glasses stood near the exit door. He held a sign, but the thick crowd didn't allow Jonah to read it. He walked towards the man.

Michelle followed.

He paused and faced her. "Is your ride outside?"

"No, I'm looking for a guy with a sign."

He resumed his walk towards the man. "No kidding! So am I. Maybe we can help each other. What name are you looking for?"

"Keys."

He stopped walking and stared at her. "Keys? Seriously?"

She furrowed her eyebrows. "Yeah. Why?"

"As in, Alex Pratt?"

She squinted at him. "Yeah." She paused. "You have a key?"

He nodded and smiled. "Awesome. Come on."

****

Damien almost never had a drink, but the heightened anxiety caused by his presence on a plane required it. It was bad enough to be on one airplane, but the layover in Charlotte meant he had to board two flights. He wished he'd taken his sister's advice and obtained a tranquilizer prescription.

Fortunately, the older lady who sat next to him didn't want to talk, so he tried to drink enough to relax. The guy with dreadlocks sitting across the aisle kept talking to the woman next to him. Damien had trouble drowning out their voices and couldn't sleep. *I bet that guy does drugs*, he thought.

He felt comfortably mellow by the time the plane landed, and all he wanted to do was get to the hotel and sleep, knowing Alex didn't expect anything from him until the next day. He rushed to the baggage carousel, hoping to find his bag and his ride in short order.

"Dammit." The older lady who'd sat next to him had tried to grab her bag from the carousel, but she didn't have a good enough hold on it to pull it from the belt. Damien stood down the line from her, so he grabbed her bag and made eye contact with her.

She approached him. "Thank you. The thing just slipped out of my hands." She moved the glasses she wore to the top of her head, pulling back her frizzy, blonde hair, which didn't match the number of years her face showed.

"It's no problem."

"Are you feeling better? I got the impression you were rather nervous during the flight."

He grinned. "Yeah. I've never been a good flyer."

She laughed. "Oh, I've been flying all over the place for years. Never even had a close call." She paused while he grabbed his own bag from the belt. "Well, thank you again for getting my bag."

"You're welcome."

She walked away.

Damien stood in place and squinted, looking for the man holding the sign. The only possibility was a guy with brown hair and glasses standing near the door. He walked in that direction, behind the older lady, but he froze when she put down her bag to shake the sign-holding guy's hand.

No way.

He walked closer and waited for the woman to finish talking to the man before approaching him directly. "I believe you're my ride."

The man nodded and held out his hand. "Alex Pratt."

"Damien Thomas." He looked at the woman and smiled at her.

She held out her hand. "Sharon Ellis. It seems we'll be working together."

He shook her hand. "I guess so."

Alex broke the following silent moments. "Looks like the other two are on their way."

Damien turned back towards the carousel. An Asian woman walked with the druggie guy from the plane. *Excellent*, he sarcastically thought.

"Keys, I presume?" the guy with all the hair said.

Alex chuckled and introduced himself, and the new guy held his hand out to Damien, who took it after a bit of reservation. "Jonah Ward," the guy said.

Damien introduced himself to Jonah and then to Michelle.

This should be interesting.

****

"Well, Mr. Pratt, it appears you arranged for us all to sit in the same row on the airplane," Sharon said as soon as everyone settled in Alex's minivan. They all had insisted she take the front passenger seat.

Alex glanced at her before he began driving. "Didn't you get an email about it?"

Sharon shook her head.

Alex looked in the rear-view mirror. "Did any of you?"

The van was silent until Jonah said, "I didn't."

Damien and the woman, whose name Sharon couldn't remember, responded similarly.

"Huh. I wondered why you didn't already know each other." Alex drove towards the airport exit. "Dave was supposed to send you something. He arranged for everyone to be on the same connecting flight so I could pick you all up at the same time. We rented the van so everyone would be comfortable. I'm sorry, I thought you all knew." He paused for a few moments. "Did any of you figure out your connection before you found me?"

"Just before," the woman said. Sharon tried to remember her name. Melissa? Megan?

"Yeah, like seconds. And Michelle and I talked all during the flight," Jonah said.

Michelle! That was it.

"Funny. Well, we're going to the hotel now, and I'll pick you up to go to the courthouse tomorrow morning. I trust you all have your keys," Alex said.

Jonah gasped. "Oh, crap."

Sharon snapped around. Was this guy serious? He was patting the pockets of his jeans.

"Ok, well that's a problem." Alex huffed. "Everything's been arranged for tomorrow!"

Jonah's eyes widened. "Wow. Chill. I'm kidding. Of course we have them. They're kind of the whole point of this." He pulled his key from his pocket.

Sharon chuckled and relaxed, though Alex didn't do the same. He glared out the window. He must have been stressed about their arrival.

"Can I see that, Jonah?" Damien asked as he reached into his bag and pulled out a large key ring that held at least twenty keys.

Michelle laughed from the seat behind him. "How many locks are you expecting to open?"

"I just hope one of these works, or you'll all be very disappointed." Damien looked at the ring in his lap, moving the keys around it. His polished appearance – short hair, clean shave, and pressed clothes – made Sharon assume he wasn't the type to be unprepared for anything. Maybe his uncertainty about having the right key increased his unease on the plane.

Damien and Jonah spent the following minutes comparing Jonah's key to those on the ring. After several comparisons, Damien said, "This one looks the same." He removed the key from the ring and put it in his pocket before returning the ring to his bag.

Sharon laughed to herself as she watched them. Jonah's shabby appearance was a stark contrast to Damien's, and she wondered if the two would talk to each other if they randomly met in public. Michelle seemed reserved or apathetic, but she might have just been tired. She was the right age to have young kids, and Sharon remembered the days when her kids wanted to keep her up all night.

She thought about her companions, amazed at the circumstances that brought them together. Her great-grandfather had worked with their ancestors to bury the safe. She could only guess those men were as different as the people she traveled with now. Sharon was accustomed to knowing even the smallest details of the lives of her ancestors, and until Alex called her, she'd assumed her great-grandfather's story ended with his disappearance. The idea that her family knew nothing about him for countless years was unsettling, though the fact that he interacted with the ancestors of her current companions intrigued her.

"Where did you all find your keys?" Alex asked after several minutes. He seemed to have recovered from Jonah's attempted joke.

"My mom had that ring hanging on the cabinet above her sink, in plain sight. I wish I'd noticed before we cleaned out her crawlspace," Damien said.

Michelle laughed. "My cousin's husband found mine in a case in their basement. Their daughter used it as a toy in her playhouse."

"So, in plain sight?" Sharon asked.

Michelle nodded. "Pretty much."

Sharon squinted. "Mine was in a collage that's hung on my wall for," she paused to think, "at least forty years. I looked at it every day without knowing what it was."

"That's crazy!" Michelle turned to Jonah. "Where was yours?"

"Around my brother's neck."

Michelle leaned towards the seats in front of her. "He was wearing it? Why?"

Jonah turned sideways in his seat. "He has a genetic disorder. The doctors say his mental capacity is like a four-year-old. He likes to keep things. He found the key at my grandparents' house and wanted to keep it."

"Oh, wow. How did you get it from him?" Sharon asked. Surely Jonah wasn't the type to steal from the disabled.

Jonah faced the front again. "I traded him for it." He looked out the side window.

Sharon wanted to ask for details but decided to wait until she knew Jonah more. "It's strange that we all found one-hundred-year-old keys in the open," she said.

"That's what I thought," Alex said.

"Did anyone else's family say the key was important?" Michelle asked.

"Yeah," the rest said in unison.

Sharon turned to face the windshield and blinked a few times. She couldn't imagine that anything else they discovered would surprise her more than this group and where they had all found their keys.

And tomorrow, they would find out what brought their relatives together.

She couldn't wait.

Chapter Five

Michelle ran her finger around the rim of her wine glass as she sat at a table near the hotel's indoor pool. Jonah and Sharon sat with her. Damien had told them he was tired and retreated to his room shortly after they arrived. Aside from the brief conversation in the van, he seemed uninterested in interacting with anyone.

As Jonah and Sharon discussed the first legs of their flights, Michelle mentally replayed the phone conversations she'd had with Mark and the kids. She laughed when she remembered Grant's questions.

Did you fly high in the sky?

Was the plane blue?

"What's so funny?" Jonah asked.

She sipped her Merlot. "My son asked some funny questions when I talked to him on the phone."

"How old is he?" Sharon asked.

"He'll be four next month."

Sharon smiled. "My granddaughter just turned five last November. She's got quite a little personality on her."

"Yeah, Grant keeps me on my toes. He has a way of making me wish I had wine on hand at home." Michelle took another sip and appreciated the opportunity to enjoy a drink with other adults. She didn't like to drink around the kids, since she was usually the only adult around. If something happened that required a trip to the ER, she wanted to be able to drive without worrying about her blood alcohol level. The worry must have been woven into her subconscious, because her first few sips were laced with guilt in spite of her knowing the kids were safe with her mother on the other side of the country.

"Is your husband taking care of your kids, since you're here?" Sharon asked.

Kind of. "In the evenings. My mother is watching them during the day. Mark wasn't too crazy about me coming out here, less so when he found out he'd be in charge of bedtime. Our daughter insists on saying goodnight to every stuffed toy she owns."

"Why didn't he want you to come out here?" Jonah rolled his empty beer bottle back and forth on the glass table top, making a gritty noise.

Michelle resisted the urge to grab the bottle from him to stop the noise. "I think because of how strange the whole situation is. He couldn't imagine an historian paying for us to come here just to open a safe."

The group was quiet for a few moments. Maybe Jonah and Sharon hadn't had the same thought.

Jonah broke the silence. "It's a good point." His eyes moved from Michelle to Sharon and then back to Michelle. "Do you guys think he's legit? He's awfully uptight."

"I think so," Michelle said. "I mean, we all have keys that look the same. Why would he randomly pull four strangers together? And I checked out the story with the historical society when he called."

"Oh, good idea." Sharon grinned and nodded. "Wish I'd thought of it. I was so caught up in the mystery that I didn't question it."

"Well it's important enough to film. What do you guys think is in the safe?" Jonah asked.

"Who knows? Do either of you know anything about your families that could provide a clue?" Sharon asked.

"I don't think so." Michelle glanced at three kids splashing in the pool. "I found out my great-great-grandfather, who signed the letter and buried the box, went missing about the same time."

Sharon leaned into the table. "You're kidding. My great-grandfather disappeared around then too."

Michelle turned slightly away from Sharon. "Do you think this safe has something to do with it?"

Sharon turned her attention to Jonah. "What do you know about your relative?"

He picked at the label on his beer. "Not a whole lot. He was a construction worker – imagine the poor Irish immigrant. My dad thinks he might have worked on the courthouse."

"Did he disappear?" Michelle asked.

"I don't think so. I didn't hear anything like that." He stood. "I'm gonna get another beer."

****

Jonah waited at the bar for his beer, trying to find a way to feel less out of place than he currently did. Michelle and Sharon had commonalities in that they both had kids, Damien wasn't interested in talking to anyone for more than a minute or two, and Alex seemed the academic type who could win at *Jeopardy* but get mugged on the way out the door after bragging about it. Jonah had given him the benefit of the doubt and chalked up Alex's nervousness to meeting all of them after months of planning, but he hoped he wouldn't have to talk to Alex much. The guy was annoying.

Live music played from the neighboring restaurant, and with a full beer in hand, Jonah wandered towards it. A guy about his age sat alone on a stool set on a small stage; he played an acoustic guitar and sang covers of popular songs on request. Jonah had performed a similar act a few times and sympathized with the guy.

If one more person requests John Mayer, I'm done.

Jonah laughed at the memory. He approached the front of the dimly lit restaurant and found an empty seat near the stage. His phone rang after two songs. He placed a couple dollars into the guy's tip jar and left the restaurant. He entered the lobby and answered his phone just before it went to voicemail.

"Hey, baby."

"Hey." Olivia's voice brought a smile to his face. "How's Richmond?"

"It's all right. Been getting to know the others." He swallowed his anxiety. Talking about his trip wasn't the only reason his girlfriend had to call him. He'd been nervous about her call all day. "Did you find out?"

After a few quiet moments, she said, "Yeah." She sighed. "It was positive."

Adrenaline raced through his body, and he sat on the nearest bench. "Are you sure?"

"Of course I'm sure. I took two tests."

He stared at the bar for a few moments, listening to the next song, before his heart slowed enough for him to form words. "Wow." He couldn't figure out what to say for himself, so he tried to imagine what Olivia might hope he'd say. "Look, I don't want you to worry about anything, okay? I'll do whatever I need to do to take care of you," he paused before he could say the rest of the sentence, "and the baby."

She sniffed into the phone. "I wish you were here."

He closed his eyes. "I can come home. I'll give my key to Alex and leave."

"No, you don't have to do that." She inhaled a shaking breath. "This is your only chance to find out what this is about. It's important to your family. I'll see you in a few days. I love you."

"I love you, too. I'll call you tomorrow."

The call ended. Jonah looked at his phone in one hand and his beer in the other, trying to comprehend how his life became so upended in the last three minutes. When Olivia told him about this possibility the previous night, he hadn't said much because he didn't think she could be pregnant. Apparently, one round of antibiotics was enough to disrupt birth control pills.

His mind filled with a dozen thoughts firing in a dozen different directions, the loudest one saying *I'm going to be a father.*

He sighed, rose from the bench, and walked towards the pool.

****

Damien was the first to arrive in the restaurant for breakfast the following morning. He had no idea when the others would join him, though Alex had said he wanted to leave for the courthouse by nine o'clock. His companions still had an hour and a half to come downstairs.

The hotel had set up a buffet-style offering, and the food looked edible enough, but he'd never been a regular breakfast eater. He fixed a cup of coffee and claimed a seat near a television that was tuned to a cable news network. Ten minutes later, Jonah appeared. He took a pastry from a large tray, fixed a cup of coffee, and sat at a table near the window without looking at Damien.

Maybe Jonah didn't notice him. Damien decided to be cordial and approached Jonah's table. "Mind if I join you?"

Jonah looked at him. "Oh. No. Sorry, I didn't see you there."

Damien took the seat opposite Jonah and assessed Jonah's disheveled appearance: his puffy eyes, wrinkled clothes, and dreads sharply contrasted with Damien's polished look. Jonah would stick out like a sore thumb in a documentary.

"Were you guys out late last night?" Damien asked, assuming Jonah had somehow found other musicians and partied into the wee hours.

Jonah shook his head as he took a bite. "I went upstairs fairly early. I couldn't sleep."

"Why not?"

"I got some unexpected news."

"Bad news?"

"No. My girlfriend's pregnant."

"Oh. Wow." They had waded into unfamiliar territory, and Damien didn't know how to respond.

"Yeah, I said something like that too. It's good, really. I love Olivia. We've been together for more than a year. It's just not how I thought things would go." He took another bite. "Do you have a girlfriend?"

Damien shook his head. "My mother would say I'm married to my work."

"What do you do?"

"I'm an environmental engineer." He wasn't in the mood to try explaining his work project again, so he changed the subject. "What do you think about all this key stuff?"

"Well, before last night, I thought it was interesting. It's weird that all of our keys were basically out in the open." He popped the last bite of pastry into his mouth. "Now, it all seems kinda stupid. I'd just like to get back home."

"If you want to get back to your girlfriend, you can leave your key with me. I'll call you after we find out what's in the safe."

Jonah grinned. "Thanks, but I need to see this through. My grandpa threatened to kick my ass if I didn't. And he's a retired marine, so he could do it."

Damien laughed at the mental image of an old man beating up this grungy guy. "I bet your grandpa loves your hairstyle."

Jonah sipped his coffee. "You have no idea."

****

After Sharon found the others at the restaurant and ate breakfast, she claimed her spot in the passenger seat of Alex's van. With the exception of Jonah, they all appeared to have dressed for the camera. Jonah looked like he didn't know why a shower — or a bed, for that matter —was in his room. He appeared to have not slept a wink.

"Do you mind if we turn on the radio?" she asked Alex.

"Not at all. What do you want to listen to?"

"News. My cousin's being sworn into the senate today. I want to find out if anyone's covering it." She beamed with pride. "You might have called her, actually. Liz Griesson?"

Alex shook his head. "Doesn't sound familiar, but I reached you before I got too far down the list." He tuned the radio to a news broadcast.

"Can you imagine if a senator was here? We'd probably be on camera already," Michelle said from the back seat.

Sharon laughed and listened long enough to be sure the station wasn't covering the inaugurations. She then asked Alex the question that had been bugging her since the night before. "Do you know anything about our relatives disappearing?"

"Disappearing? No, can't say that I do. Whose relatives disappeared?"

"Mine and Michelle's, both around the same time the box was buried."

"Mine disappeared too," Damien said from behind Sharon.

She turned to face him. "Really? Around 1912?"

"I don't know when. My mom didn't tell me, and I didn't think to ask. That's the whole reason I'm here. We want to know what happened to him."

"So everyone's relatives disappeared except for mine?" Jonah asked.

"Looks that way." Sharon winked at him. "Maybe your guy was the bad guy."

Jonah smirked. "Yeah, I'm sure that's what happened."

"Alex, how could you not know about our relatives disappearing? Isn't that something you would have discovered before you called us?" Michelle asked.

"I wish I had. It makes the prospect of finding something historically significant in the safe much stronger. We tracked the generations of your families through birth records and census data. We didn't look into anything that would give information about a disappearance."

Fifteen minutes later, Alex parked on the street near an old, stone building. He led them to the courthouse entrance, through a small security check, and into an empty room that might have been an office. The paint on the walls and the fixtures looked new, but several boards were missing from the wood floor. Alex had them stand near a rectangular hole in the middle of the room.

Sharon's nerves collected in her stomach. They were all about to learn why their families kept their keys for the last century, and she got to be a part of it. She removed her key from her purse and ran her fingers along it in anticipation. There was just one thing missing.

"Mr. Pratt, didn't you say there would be a film crew here?" she asked.

Alex pursed his lips. "Yes, I did. The production company said they wanted to know that it would be worth their time. I have two colleagues downstairs to document the opening of the safe. The crew will do a re-enactment if the findings warrant it."

"Did you know this before? Because we were under the impression that we'd be in a documentary," Michelle said.

Alex sighed. "I knew before I called, yes. But I didn't think you would all come out here without that motivation."

Damien turned and stormed out of the room.

Sharon glanced at the others before following. If he left with his key, they wouldn't be able to open the safe.

She caught up to him and put a hand on his arm. He stopped and faced her.

"Where are you going?" she asked.

"I don't trust this guy. I'm leaving." He reached into his pocket, removed his key, and put it into her hand.

Echoing footsteps sounded from behind her, and Alex appeared next to her a moment later. Damien spun around and made long strides towards the courthouse entrance.

He covered a significant distance in short order. Sharon jogged behind him and called out, "Didn't you say you wanted to find out what happened to your relative? Don't you want to know what's in the safe?"

He stopped but didn't say anything.

Alex was behind her, and they both approached Damien again. He stayed in place and turned to face them.

Sharon sighed with relief. Even though she had his key, it wouldn't have felt right for one of the descendants to miss the reveal.

"Damien, I don't think you came here for the documentary," Alex said.

"Yeah. So?"

"So, I'm not sure why it matters to you now."

Damien leaned towards Alex and whispered, "If you lied about that, what else did you lie about? How do we know you're not a scammer or murderer or something, just waiting to get us into the basement to show who you really are?"

Alex chuckled, which surprised Sharon. "I only lied about the movie, and that will likely happen later. I apologize for misleading you. It's so important to have you all out here. I figured it was worth the risk." He held his arm towards the office. "Please." Alex walked back to meet Jonah and Michelle, who were standing in the office doorway.

Damien glared over Sharon's head, towards Alex.

Sharon stretched up to get his attention. "I think you'll regret it if you don't do this. It's why you're here. Even if we tell you what's there, you'll always wonder what it would have been like to open the safe yourself and make the discovery." She put the key back into his hand.

He scowled at it.

"Come on." She walked towards the office but glanced behind her. Damien followed.

With everyone back in the room, Alex returned to the hole in the floor. He reached into his pocket and removed a pair of latex gloves. "This is where the workers found the letter in the box –

under this floor." He put on the gloves, crouched down, reached into the hole, and removed a small, wooden box, similar to the one in which Sharon kept her jewelry and trinkets.

Sharon laughed to herself. The workers had left the box there just so Alex could remove it in front of them, likely for added dramatic effect. "Has the restoration been on hold just for this?"

He nodded. "Like I said when I first called all of you, depending on what we find in the safe, we may want to preserve things the way we found them, including this box and its location."

Alex stood, opened the box, and removed a small piece of paper. "This letter directed us to the safe in the basement." He held the paper out to the group. He approached Michelle and pointed to a name. "This is your great-great-grandfather's signature."

Michelle looked at it, and Alex showed the others the signatures of their ancestors. Sharon instinctively reached out to touch the place her great-grandfather once touched, but Alex pulled the paper away before she could. He put it back into the box.

She sighed.

"Now, I'll take you to where we found the safe."

Chapter Six

Michelle walked with the rest of the group as they followed Alex down a flight of dusty, concrete stairs. She was disappointed to learn there might not be a documentary, and she felt a little silly for spending extra time that morning making sure she looked "camera ready." She even wore a flowery skirt, and wearing skirts was something she usually reserved for weddings and funerals.

Upon reaching the basement, Alex led them through a long corridor and stopped in an empty room with gray brick walls and a cement floor. In addition to the small fluorescent lights that struggled to illuminate the space, a thin beam of sunlight shone through a skinny window near the ceiling. Two other people waited for them: an overweight, brunette woman who held a large SLR camera and a tall, blond, middle-aged man who held a clipboard. The clipboard guy looked around the room, not focusing on any one thing for more than a second or two, even after the group arrived. He touched his nose and neck often enough to notice.

Alex spoke to Michelle's group. "These are members of the Richmond Historical Society." He gestured to each person as he recited their names. "Bonnie, Dave."

Alex introduced Michelle and her group to the historians before discussing their imminent task, almost ceremoniously. "The day has finally arrived." He looked at his peers. Bonnie smiled; Dave shifted on his feet.

Alex clasped his hands in front of him. "We can't thank the four of you enough for traveling here for this. It's so much more meaningful to have descendants of the original men open the safe. Dave and Bonnie will document the findings."

"May we see the keys?" Bonnie asked.

Michelle made eye contact with Sharon, and they held their keys in their open palms. Jonah and Damien followed their example.

Bonnie held up the camera and took about twenty shots of the moment, nearly blinding Michelle with the bright flashes. Bonnie and Alex beamed like children on Christmas morning.

"Now, without further ado, let's get to the safe." Alex turned and moved a large section of plywood leaning against the stone wall, revealing a small safe set into it like one of the bricks. Its color matched the deep gray of the stone. Someone had chiseled away the front part of the wall to expose the safe. "Whoever installed the safe here covered it with a brick façade. The note told us where to remove the fake front."

Michelle stepped towards the safe with the others and examined it. The incessant clicking of Bonnie's camera and the soft scratching of Dave writing on the clipboard provided their soundtrack.

Alex held a cardboard box full of latex gloves over Michelle's shoulder. "Please, put these on before you touch anything. The oils in our skin could cause damage." He shook the box.

Michelle furrowed her eyebrows. "All right." She removed a pair and wiggled her hands into them while she scrunched her nose. Her hands would always sweat like crazy in gloves like these, though she hadn't had to wear them for six years.

After the other three donned their gloves, they crowded around the safe again.

"This is so odd." Sharon touched a round lock on the edge of the right side of the door. "There's a lock on every side. Does the door pull out and away from the wall?"

"It can't possibly be on a hinge." Damien ran his fingers around the edges of the door. "I've never seen a door like this."

"So, what are we waiting for?" Jonah asked.

Michelle placed her key into the lock on the right side of the door, but she couldn't turn it. "Huh." She removed the key and tried the lock on the bottom edge, but it didn't turn either. "Each of our keys must work a specific lock."

Sharon placed her key into the first lock that Michelle had tried, and she twisted it ninety degrees in a clockwise direction. She removed the key, and the lock snapped back to its original position.

"We have to hold the keys in place for the locks to stay open," Damien said.

Michelle moved around the perimeter and tried the lock on the left. The key turned ninety degrees, and she held it in place with her sweaty, gloved hand.

Damien and Jonah tried the remaining locks. Jonah's key turned the lock on the bottom edge of the door, while Damien's turned the lock on the top.

"This thing might be heavy. Pull on three?" Michelle asked.

"Yep. Let's do it," Jonah said.

Michelle counted. "One, two, three."

****

Jonah almost dropped the three-inch-thick safe door when the group pulled it away from the wall. His lock's position on the bottom meant he caught the majority of the weight, which was substantial. "Okay, set it down." His wrist twisted as he kept hold of his key.

Jonah shook out his hand as they looked into the shallow space. A large, clear Mason jar, half-full of white powder, sat on its side atop two papers.

The flashes of Bonnie's camera caused spots to form in front of Jonah's eyes. Alex stood directly behind him, close enough for Jonah to hear him breathing. A slight whistle came from Alex's nose. Even the way the man breathed was annoying.

Sharon removed the jar. "This is just like a jar I found at my brother's house!" She rotated the sideways jar, making the contents roll. "That jar had a little powder in it too."

"Can you hold that up, please?" Bonnie asked. Alex backed away, and Bonnie took his place.

Sharon faced her. "Okay. Sure." She lifted the jar about three inches, and Bonnie inundated them with camera flashes.

Jonah chuckled to himself. The jar didn't look interesting to him, but these historians seemed to think this was bigger than finding Hoffa.

Jonah reached for the papers and examined the one on top. "This looks like a map." He passed it to Damien. "This is a note." Jonah squinted at it, wishing the floating spots in his vision would go away.

"What's it say?" Sharon asked.

More flashes.

Jonah faced Bonnie. "Can you give that a rest?"

She scowled at him. "For a little bit. It's important that we document this."

"Well, you're documenting the hell out of it. I just want to read this, and your camera is blinding me."

She glared at him.

Jonah rapidly blinked, looked at the note, and cleared his throat. "'The consequences of the creation are too severe for our time, and humanity cannot ethically carry its burden. We hope that elapsed centuries will have changed the present mindset.' That's all it says."

"Elapsed centuries? They must have thought—"

"Dave, what the hell are you doing?" Alex's voice interrupted Michelle's.

Jonah and the other three turned around. Dave had placed the clipboard on the ground and pointed a pistol at the other historians. He moved it towards the group upon seeing everyone's attention was on him. "Call it protecting interests." He pointed the gun from one end of the group to the other. "I knew it was here. They should have believed me." He shook his head.

Jonah clenched his jaw and estimated the distance between himself and Dave. Five feet? He could rush that and tackle him.

"You have another jar?" Dave pointed the gun at Damien but looked at Sharon. Alex took a step towards Dave. Dave turned the gun on Alex. "Don't even think about it. I've got enough ammo to make sure no one leaves this basement." He shifted his weight and licked his lips, like he was thirsty.

Alex held out a shaking hand. "Dave, I don't know what you're doing, but I'm sure–"

Jonah made his move. He almost reached Dave before a loud bang followed by a fire in his left shoulder stopped him. Michelle screamed. Jonah gritted his teeth and covered the wound with his right hand as he stumbled backwards, but he stayed on his feet. His ears rang in response to the gunshot.

Dave furrowed his eyebrows and shook his head. "Anyone else?" He waved the gun towards the others.

Nobody moved or said anything. Jonah willed himself to remain standing in spite of the agony in his arm. Blood dripped out of his sleeve and onto the cement floor. Dave took shallow breaths through his open mouth.

"What do you want?" Alex asked.

Dave glared at Alex before he focused on Sharon, who still held the jar. "You're coming with me." He kept the gun on the group but walked to Sharon and grabbed her arm with his free hand, pulling her out the door. Dave looked back into the room. "You all stay here for thirty minutes. If any of you follows me or calls anyone, she's dead."

Dave and Sharon disappeared down the corridor.

****

It took a few moments for Damien's mind to process what happened. His ears were still ringing from the gunshot, and Jonah had fallen to his knees. Michelle and Bonnie were rushing to Jonah's side. Sharon was gone, and Dave could kill her before they'd left the building.

Damien considered leaving. He didn't know these people, and this wasn't what he signed up for. He regretted not forcing Sharon to keep his key and leaving before they came to the basement.

But now he was a part of this. Leaving would make him the biggest jerk in history, so he swallowed the urge to flee, put the map in his wallet, and stepped towards Jonah until Alex bolted out the door.

Damien followed, catching up to Alex down the corridor. "Wait! What are you doing? He said he'd kill her."

Alex stopped walking and faced him. "I don't think he meant to shoot Jonah. Did you see how edgy he was? He was as surprised as us when the gun went off." He looked towards the stairs. "I don't think he'll do that to Sharon."

Damien leaned towards Alex. "You don't know that." He scowled, frustrated with his own inability to act. "Let's give it a few minutes, at least, okay?"

"She said she knew about another jar." Alex dialed three numbers into his phone and held it to his ear as he walked away from the room.

Damien almost followed but decided to see if the women needed help with Jonah until the paramedics arrived. He left the gloves on, in case he needed to handle something bloody. "Alex called 9-1-1," he said when he re-entered the room.

Bonnie looked at him. "He isn't worried Dave will do something to her?"

Damien glanced towards the door, wishing there was a way to be sure that Alex's call wouldn't spell disaster for Sharon. "Apparently not. Dave probably wants whatever jar her brother has. Do you know who he was talking about?"

"What do you mean?"

"He said 'they should have listened.' Who was he talking about?"

Bonnie shrugged. "I wish I knew. I've never seen Dave like this before. He's usually laid back." She turned her attention back to Jonah.

Jonah had moved his hand away from the wound, and Michelle pulled up the sleeve of his T-shirt. He never opened his eyes, but he occasionally squeezed them tighter.

Michelle studied his arm for a moment before shaking her head. "It looks like a graze, but it's deep." She leaned down to face Jonah. "Jonah, open your eyes."

He did, but it must have made him dizzy because he fell to the side and had to catch himself with his good arm. He left a bloody handprint on the floor.

Michelle put her thumb and finger on his chin. "I need to put something on that gash, and your shirt's already ruined. Can you take it off?"

He nodded, and Bonnie helped him pull his right arm out of his sleeve and the shirt over his head. Michelle pulled it off the rest of the way over his injured arm.

A tattoo of unfamiliar symbols was scrawled across Jonah's chest. Damien wondered what they meant.

Michelle used the shirt to wipe the blood from the wound. "Amazing it didn't hit anyone else." She folded the shirt into a narrow rectangle and tied it around his arm.

Footsteps approached the room and Alex entered a moment later, still fumbling with his phone. "They're on their way. The police are looking for Dave's car. Hopefully, they'll find him before he gets too far away."

****

Sharon wiggled in the passenger seat of Dave's Explorer, trying to ease the cramping in her back caused by thirty minutes of nonstop anxiety. She swallowed repeatedly, as if that would relieve her dry mouth, and wished he had let her hold the jar instead of putting it behind her seat.

"Where's the other jar?" he asked once they were on the highway. He squeezed the steering wheel so tightly his knuckles were white.

"In Indiana."

"Dammit!" He pulled the gun from a pocket inside his jacket and shoved it into her side. "Don't screw with me, woman." His eyes were wide, desperate.

She closed her eyes in an effort to calm her heart. "I'm serious. I found it in my brother's basement. There was barely anything in it."

"A little bit is enough."

"Enough for what?"

"Shut up." He put the gun away and touched his nose before putting his hand back on the wheel.

He needed her to find the other jar, and he was apparently willing to shoot or maim people to get it. She could ask some questions without the imminent threat of him shooting her, as long as she was the only one who knew where it was. "What's in the jar?"

He glanced at her and then back to the road.

"Look, I don't know why you're doing any of this. That powder could be flour for all I know. Just let me go."

"Huh!" He glared at her for a moment. "Your family English or Irish?"

She pursed her lips. "English."

"Thought so."

"What does that have to do with anything?"

He drummed his fingers on the wheel. "Know what your relative did for a living?"

She sighed, relieved to have him engaged in conversation instead of threatening her. His nervous energy seemed to be falling. “I think he was a pharmacist.”

“More like a pharmaceutical researcher. It wasn’t illegal for medical companies to make false claims about their products in the early 1900s. Did you know that?”

Sharon shook her head. He seemed to enjoy talking. Maybe she could figure a way out of this if she could just keep him doing that. “What are you talking about?”

He didn’t answer.

“Where are you taking me?”

“To Indiana.”

Chapter Seven

Michelle darted through the drugstore, hoping to quickly find the things she needed to dress Jonah's wound. She hadn't treated a serious injury since clinicals; part of her wished Jonah had allowed the paramedics to take him to the hospital for treatment. The other part agreed that they needed to hurry if they were going to find Sharon alive. It had already been nearly three hours since Dave left the basement with her. The police interviews had slowed everything to a frustrating crawl.

Michelle purchased a bottle of sterile saline, anti-bacterial ointment, acetaminophen, and several packages of gauze and medical tape, not knowing how long they would be searching or how many times she would have to change the wrapping. She remembered to buy a new shirt for Jonah, though the only ones on hand were souvenir shirts that proudly displayed "Richmond" or "Virginia".

She returned to the van. Damien sat in the passenger seat while Alex sat in the driver's seat and spoke on his phone, probably to Bonnie. He'd dropped off Bonnie at the Society headquarters to dig into Dave's personnel file and to find out where Sharon's brother lived. The police were searching for Dave's car, but that was all the information anyone had that might help them find Sharon. Stopping at the drug store for supplies had been Michelle's idea, but no one seemed to have a plan for what to do next.

Michelle found Jonah asleep in the back row of seats. The bullet had created a deep, three-inch long gash near his shoulder, and it had bled profusely. The paramedics had dressed the wound, but he'd bled through the bandage. She hoped fatigue was the only reason he had to sleep.

She climbed into the car and shook his uninjured shoulder. "Jonah. Wake up."

He stirred.

"Are you feeling sick?"

He shook his head. "Just tired. I'm fine. I didn't sleep last night."

"Okay. Come here." She led him to the open door, thankful for the warm-for-January day. "Sit here." She pointed to the floor of the van.

He sat on the door jamb with his back to the passenger seat and held his arm outside the vehicle. Michelle removed the soiled bandage, and to her relief, the wound had stopped bleeding.

She opened the saline and made eye contact with Jonah. "This is gonna hurt."

He pulled away a bit. "Do you have to do it? I think the paramedics cleaned it out."

"It was still bleeding a lot then. I want to make sure it's clean before I wrap it again."

He scowled. "All right. Do it."

Jonah groaned through his teeth as she irrigated the gash. Once the bottle was empty, she retrieved some gauze to dry his arm after discovering she'd forgotten to buy paper towels.

She sensed someone watching her and looked up. Damien had twisted around in the passenger seat to see them. She met his eyes before focusing on Jonah's arm.

"Where did you learn how to do that?" Damien asked.

"I was almost a nurse." She opened the ointment and liberally applied it to the wound.

"Almost?"

"Yeah. When I became pregnant with my daughter, my husband insisted I quit school." Her breath caught.

She'd resented her husband for making her quit, especially so close to graduation, and she hadn't spoken of it before today. To her surprise, it felt good.

"Oh." Damien watched her for a minute before speaking again. "You're really good at it. Do you think you'll go back someday?"

She smiled. "Maybe." She packed gauze on the wound, wrapped the arm, and taped everything in place before she pulled the green souvenir shirt from the bag. She unfolded it for Jonah to see.

He chuckled. "That is so me."

"It's all they had." She handed him the shirt, and he put it on before she gave him the bottle of painkillers. He went back to his seat.

Michelle collected the bloody bandage and empty saline container in the grocery bag and placed the clean supplies in the storage area behind the passenger seat. She started to climb into the van and claim a seat in the middle row when a hand on her shoulder stopped her.

Damien stood outside the van, behind her. "Why don't you take the front? I'll sit in the back with him."

His hand was still on her shoulder. She nodded. "Okay." She pushed against him to get to the passenger door. He didn't seem to want to let her through.

After she claimed the seat, Alex ended his call. "I'm sorry I dragged you all into this."

She'd wondered if they should trust Alex to drive them around, looking for Sharon, since he worked with the kidnapper. But he was the one who called the police right away, so she dismissed her concern. If Alex meant to harm them, he probably would have done it by now. "I don't think anyone could have predicted what happened." Her imagination went to the nightmare that Sharon must be experiencing and tried in vain to force her mind elsewhere.

****

Jonah settled back into his seat, opened the painkillers, and popped two pills in spite of the fact that part of him didn't want to alleviate the pain. It kept him from ruminating on how his decision to rush the gunman nearly left Olivia alone and their child fatherless. He'd lied to Michelle. He did feel sick, but the gunshot wound had nothing to do with it.

What if Dave had been a better shot? Since learning about the baby, Jonah had decided he would be a different kind of father than his father was. He wouldn't assume his child was wasting time pursuing a passion. He wouldn't force his child to conform to his own expectations. And he wouldn't motivate his child to move so far away that visits came only a couple times a year. Jonah would be different – but only if he managed to not get himself killed.

Damien took the seat next to him in the back row. "You need to talk about anything?"

Jonah's eyes narrowed. "I don't think so. I know you're not the chatty type."

"Not usually. But you are, and I thought you might need to blow off some steam."

"Thanks, but I'll be all right." He glanced out the window and remembered something. "What happened to the map?"

"I have it." Damien pulled his wallet from his pocket, removed the map, unfolded it, and held it between himself and Jonah.

"This isn't very detailed," Jonah said.

"I know, but it must be clear enough for us to figure out, or our relatives wouldn't have left it with the jar." He paused. "What do you think this N and R mean?"

Jonah closed his eyes and inhaled as a wave of pain coursed through his arm.

"What does your tattoo mean?" Damien asked.

Jonah opened his eyes, thankful for the distraction. "It's Yiddish. It means 'God hears'. That's the meaning of my brother's name. Samuel."

"Yiddish?" Damien raised his eyebrows.

Jonah nodded. "Yeah, my mom's side of the family is Jewish. Plus, I thought the characters looked cool."

Damien grinned. "Why did you choose your brother's name as a tattoo?"

Jonah didn't like talking to anyone about Samuel, especially people he barely knew, but Damien seemed to genuinely care. "I got it on his twentieth birthday. The disorder he has... the doctors said he probably wouldn't live much past the age of twenty. So I got the tattoo as a way to remember him, both in life and…" He pursed his lips. "And after. He's twenty-four now."

"So he proved the doctors wrong."

"Yeah, he did." He brought his hand to the bandage. "Too bad I couldn't tackle that guy, huh?"

Damien leaned towards him. "He had a gun. Why did you even try?"

Because I thought I could stop him. "I guess I saw a chance, and I took it." He paused. "Next time, you jump him while his attention's on shooting me, okay?"

Damien laughed. "Sure, I'll get right on that."

The conversation brought Jonah's mind back to Olivia. He needed to do something that would occupy his thoughts. "Can I see that map again?"

****

Damien analyzed the map with Jonah for a few minutes, but he had trouble keeping his concentration on it. He willed his thoughts somewhere else, anywhere else, from where they wanted to go. They couldn't stay fixated on her. Talking to Jonah, worrying about Sharon, and looking at the map should have provided effective diversions.

Why had he put his hand on her shoulder – and worse – left it there?

He shook his head at the memory. What was he thinking? She's *married.* And it wasn't like he was looking to hook up with anyone.

He hated feeling so out of control of his emotions. He'd barely noticed Michelle before Dave pointed a gun at all of them, but watching her jump into action to care for Jonah and then hearing her admit she'd been forced away from a path where she had an obvious talent… her husband must be quite an ass.

Stop thinking like that.

Of course, his timing couldn't be worse. Sharon was kidnapped, Jonah was shot, and here he was, attracted to a woman he could never have. Perfect. He should have left the courthouse basement when he had the chance.

"I dunno. This isn't getting us anywhere." Jonah sat back in his seat.

Damien put the map back into his wallet.

"So what do you know about your relative? Any idea why he was involved with the jar?" Jonah asked.

Damien shook his head. "No idea. The only one who seemed to belong at the courthouse was your relative, if he helped build the thing."

"Yeah, and mine was the only one who didn't disappear." He glanced out the window. "Where are we going?"

"Back to the hotel, I think. Alex is still waiting to hear back from Bonnie about Sharon's brother."

"Seems like it shouldn't be that difficult." Jonah leaned towards the middle of the car and raised his voice. "Alex, don't we know Sharon's brother's name?"

Alex glanced in the rear-view mirror as he drove. "It's a common name. The phone number in public records is bad. Bonnie's checking state-by-state now. She has someone else tracking down Sharon's kids, in case we can get a number from them."

"They aren't telling her kids that she's been kidnapped, are they?" Damien asked.

"I'm not sure. They might want to know," Alex said.

Damien scowled. "Maybe we should try to find her first."

"That's what we're doing." Alex put his elbow on the door and rubbed his forehead with his thumb.

****

Sharon nearly cried at the indignity. She just wanted to go to the bathroom.

Dave stood in the single-stall restroom, watching over her as she used the facility. She tried to tell him that he could wait outside. What would she do, crawl through the ceiling tiles? He wouldn't have it.

After she finished, he pointed the gun at her, forcing her to stay in the corner while he had his turn. She closed her eyes and wished she could plug her ears without the risk of him screaming at her. As long as she stayed put, he wouldn't shoot her. He'd gone from nervous gunman to angry abductor since they left the courthouse. She couldn't decide which she preferred.

They walked back to his car, and he started the engine. "We're in West Virginia now. The heat should be off."

She thought about the jar behind her seat — that damn jar. Maybe she'd be able to understand this man's fanaticism if she knew what was in it. She put her elbow against the door and leaned into her hand.

"How old are you?" he asked.

"Sixty-six."

"Retired?"

She nodded.

"What did you do?"

"I was a dental assistant."

"That won't help anything."

Help with what? "What's in the jar?" She hadn't tried that question since just after he took her. Maybe he'd softened up.

"You'll find out soon enough."

"If you give me my phone, I'll call my brother. He can meet us somewhere with the other jar." Maybe the appearance of cooperation would work in her favor.

"Like hell that's happening. I'm starting to think you're as ballsy as your friend back there. What's his deal, anyway?"

"What do you mean?"

"Come on. There's you, dainty, skinny old lady; that Chinese woman; that tall, anal black guy; and… him?" He huffed. "I guess I don't get it."

"What's to get? Jonah's one of the descendants. I don't think his appearance has anything to do with it." After a pause, she added, "You didn't have to shoot him."

Dave checked his rear-view mirror before glancing at her. "If I let him jump me, I wouldn't have the jar." He scowled. "All I wanted to do was get the jar and leave. But then you said what you said about the other jar."

Could this all be the result of a robbery gone bad? It might not have even been a robbery. He worked for the historical society. He could have taken the jar and walked out the door without question.

"Who were you talking about?" she asked.

"Huh?"

"Back at the courthouse. You said something about 'they didn't believe me.' Who were you talking about?"

"You ask too many questions. Maybe you should take a nap."

She looked out the side window, unsure of how many more hours she had with this man before they reached her brother's house. Once he had the jar, then what? He had two choices: leave her there, where she could tell the cops everything she knew about him, or kill her.

Chapter Eight

Michelle stared out the windshield at the setting sun, trying to keep her mind from recalling the terror she'd felt when Dave pulled the gun on them. She'd screamed when he shot Jonah, and the sounds of the experience echoed in her consciousness. Treating Jonah's injury distracted her for the first few hours, but she didn't need to change the wrapping until the next day. Her hopes of finding Sharon soon waned with the daylight.

Wanting a distraction, she moved to the back row of the van to help Jonah and Damien figure out what the hand-drawn map showed. It was smaller than a standard piece of paper, which made sharing it with two other people difficult. She sat next to Jonah, who held it at an arm's distance with his good arm so it would be under the dome light, and Damien leaned around the seat in front of them.

She ran her finger on a curved line. "Is this a river? That could be what the R means."

"What are those upside-down V-looking things supposed to be?" Jonah asked without pointing.

Michelle squinted. "If that's a river, maybe those are supposed to be mountains. Or a forest."

"Okay." Damien shifted onto one knee, allowing him to lean towards them. "So the mountains would be on the eastern side. That line across the top must be the horizon."

"What if up isn't north?" Jonah asked.

"Let's assume it is for now. I bet that square is the target."

Michelle leaned closer to the map. "Mountains to the east, a river cutting through the southwest. I'm guessing the little lines around the square are supposed to be grass, like a field." She sat back. "This could be anywhere."

"Maybe one of our relatives had a cabin in the woods," Jonah said. "It's probably somewhere in the Appalachians, maybe even in Virginia. People didn't travel very far a hundred years ago unless they had a good reason."

"And if the R means River, we should figure out what the N means. That would help us," Damien added.

Michelle turned her attention to the front of the van. "Alex, can you take us to a library?"

****

Jonah watched the others enter the library without him; he wanted to call Olivia after spending hours trying to figure out how to tell her what happened. He'd considered keeping the whole ordeal from her, but his conscience wouldn't let him rest until he told her the truth.

He sat on a step outside the building, zipped up his coat in the near darkness, and took a visible breath as he waited to connect. The unseasonably warm day had given way to a bitterly cold night.

"Hey, baby," he said when she answered.

"Hey! I'm glad you called. I was just getting ready to fix dinner."

"It's good to hear your voice." He closed his eyes and imagined her twisting her long, black hair into a clip, which she did before performing any domestic task. The air around him felt warmer somehow.

He didn't want to tell her about his injury yet. Better to let her be oblivious for a little longer. "How are you doing with yesterday's news?"

"Really good." She told him about her phone call to the doctor, about her appointment scheduled a couple weeks out, and about her mother's reaction.

"You told your mom?" Heat rushed to his face, which surprised him.

She laughed. "Of course I did. Why wouldn't I?"

"I dunno, I guess I thought we weren't telling people yet."

She laughed again. He could listen to that sound all night.

She broached the subject he was avoiding. "Did you find out what was in the safe?"

The emotions of the day caught in his throat. "Yeah." His voice cracked.

"What's wrong?"

Just get through it. "It was a jar with some kind of powder in it. One of the historian guys stole it and kidnapped Sharon, another descendant. I tried to tackle him, and he shot at me." He swallowed, wishing he could protect her from the shock. Tears welled in his eyes.

"He shot you?"

"It just grazed my arm. I'm okay." A wave of pain in his arm made him grimace.

"Are you at the hospital?" She sniffed into the phone.

"No, it's not that bad." He moved his phone to his other ear when holding it with his left hand became too painful.

She was silent. He didn't wait for her to speak. "I thought I could stop the guy. His attention wasn't on me. I almost had him."

"You said you would take care of me."

He closed his eyes. "I know. And I will."

"How will that work if you get yourself killed?"

He rose to his feet and paced. "Olivia, listen. I obviously didn't think the whole thing through. I've only thought of you and the baby since it happened." He stopped pacing and looked at the sky as the stab of regret hit him square in the chest.

After several silent moments, she said, "I like hearing you say 'the baby'." Her tone had softened.

He smiled as relief covered him. "I'll need to stay with the others until we find Sharon. I don't think it will be too long. The police are looking for her too."

"Just try not to rush any more guys with guns, okay?"

He laughed. "I won't. I promise. I love you."

"I love you, too."

He started to jog up the stairs but slowed when the jarred landings sent shots of pain through his arm.

****

Damien and Michelle leaned over the large atlas that covered the table in the reference section. His job was to compare rivers and mountain arrangements on the left atlas page to those on the map. Michelle did the same with the page on the right.

"I think the N and R mean New River," he said.

She leaned towards his side. He ran his finger along the representation of the river, stopping it where the river curved the way it did on the map.

She held the map next to his finger. "That's possible."

Her hair smelled sweet, like a flower. While he wanted to close his eyes and inhale to fully appreciate the fragrance, he held his breath and tried to focus on the atlas.

"There are several places that have flat areas on the Northeast side, if we're assuming his map is oriented that way," she said.

Alex joined them, interrupting their conversation. "Bonnie called. She thinks Sharon's brother lives in their parents' old house in Indiana. She still doesn't have a phone number to verify that, though."

Michelle leaned towards Alex. "We should go there!"

Damien looked at her. "You want to go to Indiana? We don't know for sure that he's there."

"It's better than sitting here. Dave left the map in the basement, so he wouldn't take her to wherever it leads. Finding Sharon's brother is our best shot." She brushed her hair from the side of her face with her fingers.

Damien had to look back to the atlas. "Isn't Sharon's cousin a senator? Why don't we try to contact her?"

"I thought of that too, but I couldn't remember the name she said. Do you remember?"

Damien racked his brain but came up empty. Sharon had said the name once that morning, but Damien never had a gift for remembering names, even of new acquaintances who stood right in front of him.

Jonah joined them and stood next to the table while Alex sat in the chair across from Damien, clasping his hands. "I've asked the police in Indiana to check out the house and try to get us a phone number. In the meantime, I agree with Michelle. Going there is our only option. If we learn something different on the way, we can turn around. Let's check out the atlas so you guys can keep working with it, and we'll stop by the hotel to get your things and leave as soon as possible."

"Why don't we let the police handle it? They'll already be there," Damien said.

Michelle faced him with her hand on her hip. "We can't do that. If I were kidnapped, I would like to think the people who were with me at the time cared enough to come after me if they knew where I would end up."

Damien stared at her, speechless for a few seconds. "How far is it, Alex?"

"Almost ten hours. If that's where Dave's taking her, they have a six-hour head start on us."

"Okay, so he'll arrive in about four hours. Then what?" Damien had worried about Dave's next move all day.

"What do you mean?" Michelle asked.

"If the police aren't waiting for him, he'll have the other jar. What will he do with Sharon?"

The four looked at each other for a few silent moments.

"Let's worry about that when we get there," Jonah said.

Damien nodded, closed the atlas, and gave it to Alex to check out. Michelle was blocked into her place by Damien and the table next to her, so she put her hands on Damien's arms and squeezed between him and the chair to get out. His pulse quickened at her touch.

He closed his eyes and swore to himself.

****

"What do you know about your great-grandpa?"

Dave's voice woke Sharon from her shallow sleep. She blinked a few times. "What?"

"You heard me. Your great-grandpa. What do you know?"

"Not much more than what you told me. You seem to know a lot more about this than I do."

"We have two more hours until we reach your brother's house. I'll give you another chance to tell me. What I do with you hinges on your answers."

She tried to steady her shaking hands. "He disappeared around 1912, and he was a pharmaceutical researcher, since you told me about that."

"Any idea where he went?"

"No. My grandma was eight years old at the time. All we know is he disappeared one day." She stared out the side window to keep from looking at him, sure she wasn't giving him the answers he wanted.

"What if I told you he was part of the eugenics movement?"

Why was he talking to her at all? Because he was bored and planned to kill her anyway? "What do you mean?"

"Eugenics. Familiar with it?"

"No."

He glanced at her occasionally as he drove. "The idea was to create a better population of people by promoting fertility in desired groups and limiting it in undesirable groups."

What did this have to do with anything? Sharon kept her side of the conversation light in the hopes he would keep talking. "Okay."

"So in the early 1900s, my employer – your great-grandfather's employer – was charged with creating something that would render anyone who took it infertile, but without the patient knowing about it. The government didn't want a riot on their hands."

Her eyes widened. "That's horrible."

"Agreed. But that's the way it was. The developed product was prescribed to targeted groups – the mentally disabled and certain ethnic groups, primarily. It was sold as a supplement to treat a vitamin deficiency."

"Why are you telling me this?"

"Because I think you need to know what kinds of activities your great-grandfather participated in."

Her mind absorbed his words. "Which ethnic groups?"

"In his area of the country during his time, Blacks and Chinese."

"Oh my God." She brought her hand to her mouth. "That's why Michelle and Damien are part of this." Her mind spun at the idea that her family was connected to the attempted elimination – or limited procreation, at least – of entire groups of people. An image of marching Nazis flashed in her mind.

And Dave told her about it just to upset her. What other reason could there be?

Bastard.

She looked at him until his eyes met hers and gestured to the back seat with a head tilt. "That powder is it?"

He grinned.

"But we don't know what it is," she said.

"We knew you'd find out."

"Why did the men hide it?"

Dave clenched his jaw. "I called the company when Alex told me about the box and the keys. I knew this was it." He hit the steering wheel with the side of his fist. "After all that time pretending to give a crap about Virginia history. If that ass had just listened, none of this would have happened."

"That ass? Alex?"

"Alex is a harmless idiot. I'm talking about my boss, the guy who wanted to pull the whole project. He didn't think anyone would ever find the powder. We've been monitoring Richmond for a century to get it."

"So why are you doing all this, risking so much, for a company that didn't believe you?"

"Because I need to show them I was right! I knew it was there." He held a small grin on his face.

Sharon couldn't figure any of this out. Not only did her great-grandfather create this horrible powder, but he worked with the men who must have been damaged by it to hide it. Why would the other men do that? And where did they go?

"Did your company kill my great-grandfather and the other men?" She didn't have anything to lose from asking at this point. She already knew too much.

"Don't know about that."

"What about Jonah's relative? What does he have to do with it?"

"We're done."

She risked one more question. "What are you planning to do with me?"

"Keep you around for a little while."

What did that mean?

Her stomach turned when she considered both her situation and the historical implications of her great-grandfather's actions. How many more people might have existed if not for his creation? A pharmaceutical researcher should have been in the position to improve lives, to give people the chance to conquer disease and live longer than they otherwise would. Until now, she'd assumed her great-grandfather's position was exactly that.

Instead, he'd kept people from having children. He hadn't promoted and improved life; he'd prevented it. In her younger years, a couple of Sharon's friends had trouble conceiving. She'd witnessed the stress, turmoil, and blame that accompany those circumstances. To think that someone in her family purposely caused that to happen was unfathomable; it went against everything her family had done to better society throughout the years.

How did Dave know all this? There seemed to be a group at the drug company who knew about the powder, but the others hadn't believed Dave when he told them about the safe. She could assume that aside from herself, Dave was the only person who knew her family's tie to the eugenics movement.

But it wouldn't stay that way. It didn't matter if Dave let her live or not, he'd at least tell his company about the powder, and they'd make the connection.

She wished there was something she could do to keep the secret between the two of them.

Chapter Nine

Michelle woke with a start when her phone rang from her purse. "Oh, crap." She found it glowing in the darkness and dug it out.

"What's wrong?" Damien asked from the passenger seat.

She glanced at the clock on the dash. "It's only eight o'clock back home." She answered. "Hi! Sorry, I forgot to call."

Mark's voice boomed through the phone. She had to turn down the volume. "That's all right. The kids want to say goodnight."

A moment later, a tiny voice was on the line. "Hi, Mommy."

She smiled and turned the volume back up. "Hey, Sophie. How was your day?"

Sophie told her about her kindergarten activities, which included a project about Humpty Dumpty. She passed the phone to Grant, who declared he'd peed in his pants at preschool.

Michelle laughed and shook her head. That boy had no shame.

A minute later, Mark was back on the line. "Did you guys open the safe?"

"Yeah." She told him about the day's dramatic turns.

"Wait, a guy pointed a gun at you?"

She imagined him scowling at her from California. Maybe she should have omitted that part. "Yes, but I'm fine. I took care of Jonah's wound, which was pretty minor."

"You're coming home. Now." Mark's footsteps were as loud as his voice. He must be walking across the tile in the hallway – probably to go outside, where he could be louder.

"I can't do that. We're trying to find Sharon, and I need to keep an eye on Jonah until he can get to his doctor. You weren't expecting me home yet anyway."

"Dammit, Michelle! Your place is here!"

She flinched and nearly dropped her phone. She curled in her lips and didn't wait for him to yell at her more. "I'll come home when we're done. Don't worry about me. Nothing's going to happen."

The call ended. She pulled her phone away from her ear. Full signal, so the call wasn't dropped. He'd hung up on her.

She shook her head as she slid the phone into her purse.

After this, Mark would do everything he could to effectively put her under his version of house arrest. He'd taken her keys from her in the past. If she didn't go home soon, she'd be lucky if he didn't sell her car.

****

"We're going to her brother's house. A cop in Indiana called while you were asleep. Alex called the brother." Jonah hoped the information would distract Michelle from her obviously unpleasant phone conversation. Olivia was supportive of Jonah helping to find Sharon. It seemed Michelle didn't have similar support coming from home.

"Oh. Okay." She looked out the window. "So Sharon and Dave should be getting there right about now, huh?"

The question went unanswered.

Michelle broke the silence. "If a cop called with the number, won't they wait there?"

Alex answered as he drove. "No. They said there wasn't enough reason for them to stay. Everything looked fine when they were there earlier, and they said they weren't sure Dave was going there. They told her brother to call them if Dave and Sharon showed up."

She huffed. "That's ridiculous. The guy pulled a gun on us, and there's plenty of reason to think they'll go there."

"They didn't see it that way."

Jonah sighed. "Maybe we shouldn't think about it." He said the words in an effort to keep potential outcomes out of his own mind. He didn't want to imagine arriving at a murder scene.

Silence filled the car for a few minutes.

"Okay, so let's talk about something else." Michelle turned around to face Jonah. The streetlights provided regular flashes of illumination; it was enough to see her pursed lips. "I'm sure we all have our theories about how our relatives were involved with the box and the keys. What's yours, Jonah?"

He tilted his head, trying to decide how to respond to her snippy tone. "I think my guy being there was a coincidence. But I don't know why the others would let him have a key."

"If he installed the safe, maybe that was his payment," Damien said.

Payment would mean the contents of the safe were valuable, which Jonah couldn't see. "Maybe. What do you guys think about yours?"

"I don't know. What would our relatives have had in common a hundred years ago?" Michelle asked in Damien's direction.

Damien twisted around to face her. "Well, geography." He paused. "That's all I've got."

"Not even that, though. My uncle said my relative lived among the other Chinese. What reason would our people have had to interact? Society was a lot more segregated back then."

"The missing variable," Damien said.

Michelle sat sideways in her seat and leaned against the door. "What?"

"The missing piece. The one thing we haven't talked about is probably what brought them together. Sharon's relative."

"All right. What did he do?" Jonah asked.

"He was a pharmaceutical researcher," Alex interjected.

"How do you know that?" Jonah leaned forward in his seat.

"We did some digging into your families before I called all of you."

"Oh." Jonah scowled. "Anything else you haven't bothered to mention that could help us here?"

"No, you pretty much have it figured out. We couldn't deduce the connection between your relatives either. That's the primary reason we wanted you to come out here."

"So you knew he was a pharmaceutical researcher, Sharon said she saw another jar of powder at her brother's house, and you still have no idea what happened?" Jonah couldn't believe an historian would be so ignorant of history.

"How could I? We didn't know what was in the safe until you opened it. Sharon's ancestor probably had something to do with the powder, but unless we get it back from Dave, we won't be able to find out what."

"And Dave didn't say anything? He seemed to know it would be there. How long did he work for you?"

Alex sighed. "Six years. I admit, there was more to Dave's story than I realized. I never imagined having to deal with a double agent in the historical society."

Jonah chuckled to himself. What a dorky suspense movie that would be.

"So why would a pharmaceutical guy talk to our relatives?" Michelle asked.

"Maybe he was using our relatives for research, like human trials," Damien said.

Michelle shook her head. "Come on. That can't be it."

"Why not? The world was a different place. You said so yourself. It's no secret that the Chinese and Black populations weren't exactly favored for many years of our history."

Michelle crossed her legs. "If Sharon's relative used our relatives for research, wouldn't our relatives be kinda pissed about that? Why would they all work together in hiding that jar?"

Damien unbuckled his seat belt and moved to the seat across from Michelle, where he sat sideways. "They might have consented to participating. The company may have even paid them to be part of the research. Companies today do that all the time." He shook his head. "That doesn't explain why they would hide the jar and disappear, though."

Jonah remembered something. "Maybe they knew something about the med he was researching. Something shocking. What did the note say? The consequences were too severe for their time, right?" He didn't know if he was on the right track, but he sure felt like he was.

"How can we find out?" Michelle asked.

Damien sat back. "We need that jar."

****

After a restroom stop, Damien sat next to Jonah in the back row so they could study the atlas under the dome light without disrupting Alex's driving. Damien looked for any possible N and R combinations. He glanced at Jonah when Jonah's body jerked the atlas.

Jonah blinked and shook his head. "Sorry. Dozed off a little."

"You're on your second consecutive night of no sleep. Why don't you move to the middle and get some rest?"

"Good idea."

Damien lifted the atlas long enough for Jonah to move to the seat in front of him. Michelle surprised him by moving into Jonah's seat, next to him in the back row.

She put the page that Jonah had been looking at on her lap. "I can help you do this."

He tried to will his heart rate to slow. "Okay."

She moved her fingers along the page. She squinted and leaned closer at times, and he held his breath.

He hadn't been so drawn to a woman since college. Watching her, he regretted every past relationship decision he'd made, because they all brought him to this point. If he hadn't sworn off all women, he wouldn't be so emphatically driven to one he couldn't have.

He couldn't make his mind focus on the page.

His feelings for her were inevitable, he decided. He was almost thirty and could only speak of one serious past relationship. He'd planned to propose to his girlfriend on the Fourth of July following his undergrad graduation, but she broke up with him two weeks before that and moved to Oregon to be with an old boyfriend.

The experience left him so heartbroken he'd tried to convince himself he was one of those people who was destined to be alone. Maybe he wouldn't be entirely happy, but he would survive, not having to worry about another woman he loved nearly destroying him.

He subtly shook his head and stared at the atlas page. He was a man of science. This attraction was purely chemical, nothing more. There was something about Michelle that ignited the most primitive part of his brain, the part the earliest humans used to find mates and drag them to their caves. Damien was more evolved than that, evolved enough to rise above this draw to a married woman.

Still, she had a grace about her he couldn't ignore. Even now, as she ran her slender fingers along the winding representation of a river, she seemed to change the energy around her, making it something beautiful and feminine. She was quiet and reserved, and she watched the world instead of constantly trying to fill it with an exaggerated presence, as so many other women did. The way she'd cared for Jonah demonstrated how she cared for others without considering how it would benefit her.

He thought he should say something when he realized he was doing more staring at her than studying the map. "Everything okay at home?"

She glanced at him. "Oh. Yeah. It's fine. Or it will be, once I get back there."

"What does your husband do?"

"He's a financial consultant. A very busy one. He wanted to be sure that we'd have enough income for me to stay home with the kids."

Damien pretended to study the atlas. "I hope you can get back to doing what you want to do."

"Thanks. But it's okay. I enjoy being with my kids."

She didn't look away from him, drawing his attention. It took every muscle to keep from touching her face.

He exhaled a shallow breath and looked back to the page.

"I think I'll go try to sleep too," she said.

He nodded. "Okay."

She lifted the atlas and moved to her original seat, looking back to him one last time before facing the front.

Crap.

****

The house was dark when they pulled into Larry's driveway. How would this go down if he wasn't home?

"You didn't let me call him. How should I explain why I'm here?" Sharon asked.

Dave held her arm as he pulled her out the driver's side of the Explorer, and he pushed the gun barrel into her he side.

"You don't need to do that." She tried to make her voice sound steady.

"Let's go." He squeezed her arm as they walked to the door, and she rang the doorbell. She curled her shoulders towards Dave in an effort to relieve the pressure on her side from the gun.

After a minute, a light came on from inside the house and the door cracked open. Larry peeked out, glanced at Dave, then focused on her. "Hey Shar. Thought I might see you tonight."

Her pulse raced. Someone must have told him what happened.

"Why did you think that?" Dave pushed the gun into her side, as if Larry could see it. She winced.

Sharon stared into her brother's eyes. "Remember that jar I found in the basement? The one with that little bit of white powder in it?"

"Yeah. I remember."

"We need it. Dave needs it. Can you go get it?"

"Don't know that I should." Larry opened the door wide and raised a shotgun, pointing it at Dave.

"Don't even think about it, tough guy." He raised Sharon's arm and pressed the barrel further into her side, like he wanted to be sure Larry fully understood the situation.

"The police came by here. Said you were kidnapped. Wanted to make sure I was your brother. Josie's on the phone with the cops right now." He stepped to the side while keeping his gun on Dave. "Come inside, Shar."

Dave raised his voice. "Go get the jar, or I'll drop her right here."

She was sure the gun barrel was bruising her ribs. "Larry doesn't know where the jar is. I packed it away to keep the grandkids from getting to it. I can go get it in two minutes." Larry did know where it was, and there were no grandkids around, but she needed to get away from this guy.

Dave glared at her before focusing on Larry. "Drop the gun."

Larry didn't move.

Dave moved the gun to Sharon's head. "Do it!"

Larry set the shotgun on the floor.

Dave shoved Sharon through the door and grabbed Larry's collar, pointing the gun at his neck.

Sharon held her breath. Now Larry was the hostage.

"You have two minutes. You're not back, I'll put a bullet through his neck." He faced Larry. "Any funny business from you, and I'll make sure you watch me shoot her before I get you."

She ran up the stairs, trying to keep her panic at bay and hoping Larry wouldn't try to fight his way out of Dave's grasp. Both of their lives depended on it.

She rushed to the guest room. The jar was in a box in the closet. The jar containing the powder that her great-grandfather had created. The powder that irreparably damaged entire groups of people.

All she had to do was give Dave the jar.

She froze in place when she saw it.

If Dave took it back to his company, what would they do with the powder? Dispose of it? That seemed likely. They wouldn't want something that controversial on their record. But what if Dave didn't take it to them? He only wanted to show them he was right. Why would he hand it over?

Even if he was arrested tonight and didn't have the jars, he would talk about her great-grandfather to anyone who would listen. He'd proved that to her in the car.

As Dave drove her here, she'd considered how she could keep the secret between them. Her family name was in jeopardy. All of the accomplishments accumulated over the centuries – Jamestown, the city in Ohio, the war victories – would be tarnished because of this.

Her cousin's senatorial career increased the likelihood that the media would spread the story, if they linked Liz to the eugenics movement. It wouldn't matter that generations separated her from their great-grandfather. Anyone not on her side of the political spectrum would use this to damage Liz's career.

"What's keeping you?" Dave called from downstairs.

And Dave could still shoot her and Larry after he had the jar.

She knew exactly what she needed to do.

She retrieved the gun Larry kept in the nightstand and walked back down the stairs. Approaching sirens grew louder with every second. She had to hurry.

Josephine stood near the kitchen with her hand over her mouth. Dave held Larry on the porch, just outside the doorway.

Sharon saw her chance. Dave wouldn't see her until she was in his face.

She held her breath, raised the gun, and moved in front of the men. She analyzed Larry's position for half a second before she fired a shot and dropped the gun at the recoil.

The bullet hit Dave in his chest. His blood splattered on Larry's face.

"Shit!" Larry pulled away from Dave as he wiped his face with the sleeve of his flannel shirt. Dave stumbled back and leaned against the post at the edge of the patio. He lowered his gun and seemed to examine the bleeding wound.

Sharon couldn't hear anything through the ringing in her ears. Larry was saying something to her. Dave was still standing. He might survive.

She couldn't let him do that.

Before she could think about it, she picked up the gun and fired two more shots. One hit Dave in the neck and the other hit the pole behind him, splintering the wood. Dave collapsed on the porch.

Larry glared at her, wide-eyed. "You killed him!"

She handed Larry the gun, ran out the door, and retrieved the jar from Dave's Explorer. The sirens grew louder, adding to the high-pitched tinnitus already echoing in her head.

Larry followed her past Dave's bleeding form and up the stairs as she carried the jar, yelling towards her. "Shar, what the hell is going on? You're taking stuff from his car?"

"You don't understand!" Her heart pounded as the gravity of what she'd done settled on her. She rushed back to the guest room and put the jar in the box with the other one she'd found in the basement.

He grabbed her shoulder when she stood. "Did you kill him for that?" He pointed to the jars.

She couldn't make her hands stop shaking. "He was holding you hostage." The sirens stopped in front of the house.

"So what's with the jar?"

She looked towards the door. "This was an armed robbery, okay? He let me go inside to get money. I shot him to save you. We don't need to mention the jars. They don't need to know about them." She tried to convince herself with her words as much as her brother.

Voices carried up the stairs.

Sharon locked eyes with Larry. "We need to go."

Chapter Ten

"What happened here?" Michelle moved to the passenger side of the van to see the house clearly. The headlights of a police cruiser illuminated a perimeter of crime scene tape that surrounded an Explorer and the front porch. Officers and investigators walked between the car, the porch, and through the front door of the house.

Michelle's stomach sank. Dave must have killed Sharon and her brother. She didn't want to leave the van and have someone confirm her fear.

Alex parked the van in the street. They put on their coats, left the van, and walked towards the house. When they were halfway up the long driveway, an older man in a heavy coat exited an old Ford pickup and intercepted them. "You the others?"

Alex stepped towards the man. "Yes. Are you Sharon's brother?"

"Yessir. Larry." He held out a hand for Alex to shake.

Michelle exhaled. At least one of them was still alive, and Larry didn't look upset. "Is Sharon here?" she asked.

He shook his head. "Cops needed to complete a report. Had to after she shot the guy. Once in the chest and once in the neck. Never stood a chance."

"Sharon shot Dave?" Damien asked.

"Yessir. Fool let her go inside," he paused, "for money. He was holding me at gunpoint. She came back downstairs with the gun."

He seemed calm for a guy who had been held at gunpoint. "Are you okay?" Michelle analyzed his face for signs of distress.

Larry nodded. "Yeah, that asshole wasn't gonna do anything. He was scared of his own shadow. It's why Sharon shooting him surprised me."

Larry hadn't seen Dave as a threat, in spite of the gun. So why did Sharon shoot him? "We know Dave didn't want her to get money," Michelle said. The jars had to have something to do with it.

He leaned towards her, positioning his face close enough to hers that she could smell his onion breath, and dropped his voice to a whisper. "I know you know. It sounded better than he wanted an almost-empty jar." He stood up straight. "What's the deal with that jar?"

"We don't know." Damien said as he put a hand on Michelle's shoulder. A gentle nervousness settled in her stomach.

The way he'd looked at her back in the van hadn't been her imagination.

Her heart raced when she realized he made her feel safe. A man hadn't done that for as long as she could remember. She tried to push the thought from her mind. He didn't move his hand.

Needing to break the connection, she stepped away from him and towards the yellow tape, like she wanted to see the scene for herself, but not far enough away that she couldn't hear the conversation. She imagined she could still feel his hand on her shoulder.

"What happened to the jars?" Jonah asked. Michelle turned back to face the group.

Larry walked down the driveway towards the street and gestured for them to follow. He quietly spoke again after several steps. "Sharon said the guy dumped the first one in a river. She flushed the powder from the other one down the toilet before the cops got here."

"What? Why would she do that?" Damien asked.

Larry stopped them from walking and faced them. "I have no earthly idea. Was hoping you'd know. The cop didn't arrest her. He took her to the station, though. She was too upset here to tell what happened. I'll call ya' when I pick her up."

Alex handed Larry a business card, and the group walked back to the van.

****

Jonah and the others slept in the van for a few hours after Alex parked it in front a small restaurant. As soon as it opened for breakfast, everyone went inside except for Alex. They let him continue to sleep. He'd sulked since learning the powder was destroyed, as if that would somehow magically bring it back. Alex's moodiness was wearing on Jonah's nerves.

Jonah wished his busy mind would allow him to comprehend what the menu said. He finally gave up, closed it, set it on the table, and looked at the two who sat across from him at the booth. "I don't get it."

Damien looked up from his menu. "Get what?"

"What Sharon's brother said about the jars. Why would Dave dump the powder? And then Sharon dumps the rest? It makes no sense."

"That's what I thought." Michelle looked over the top of her menu at him. "Do you think that's really what happened?"

Jonah stared at the table. "If it is, we're done."

The situation frustrated him. His father would try to use their lack of success as evidence supporting his belief that Jonah never finished what he started. It didn't matter that Jonah finished enough school to work in IT; he hadn't made progress with his music career. It didn't matter that he had a long-term girlfriend; he hadn't discussed marriage, though his father didn't know about the baby. If Jonah and the others only found a jar that was stolen, and they never learned why their ancestors worked together to hide it, the safe would have been buried for nothing. Jonah's father would add this to the list of Jonah's failures.

The three sat in silence for the few minutes before the waiter returned and took their orders.

Damien broke the silence after the waiter left them alone. "We still have the map."

"What good will that do?" Michelle asked.

"Our relatives left it in the safe for some reason."

Jonah leaned into the table. "Yeah. There must be something else there for us to find."

An alert sounded on Michelle's phone. She checked it and scowled before putting it back into her purse. "We have no idea where that map is supposed to lead us. The closest we've come to figuring it out is New River, and that might not even be right."

"Any ideas how we can find out?" Damien asked.

Jonah grinned. "Yeah. We can run the river."

"What do you mean?" Michelle asked.

"Rafting. My roommate's a river guide during the summers. I bet he can study the river and take us out on it." Jonah sat up straighter, filled with renewed hope.

"It's January. The water will be freezing." Michelle tilted her head towards him.

He raised his eyebrows. "I know that. We'll go in the summer. The map's been hidden for a century. A few more months won't make a difference. I'll talk to Chris."

Damien dumped a sugar packet into his coffee. "Do you think we'll find something?"

Jonah shrugged. "If we don't, at least we'll have a fun rafting trip." He smiled. It felt good to have a plan, and something told him their trip wouldn't be fruitless.

****

After breakfast, Damien walked with Michelle to the neighboring grocery store. He figured that being around her was less risky now, since they all planned to fly home the next day and not see each other for five months. Surely, his feelings would have dissipated by then.

"What was that on your phone back there?" he asked.

She glanced at her purse. "My husband texted me."

He nodded and waited to see if she would elaborate.

"He wants me to come home immediately. He's just worried about me." She looked at the floor.

He breathed through the urge to put his arm around her shoulders. "Tell me about your kids."

Her demeanor improved as she talked to him about her children. By the time she finished picking out snacks and drinks for the ride back to Richmond, she was smiling and laughing again. Damien partially listened. He focused on her voice and her shiny black hair, imagined how she would be around her kids, and wished there was a way he could instantly make her not married.

"Do you have a girlfriend?"

Her question pulled him from his trance and caught him off guard. He glanced at his feet. "Oh. No."

"Maybe you should find one."

He blinked at her, speechless.

She looked at him for a few moments, pursed her lips, and walked towards the register.

He stood in place until she finished her purchases, looked back at him, and left the store. He picked up his pace to follow her, and he put his hand on the back of her arm, stopping her on the sidewalk in front of the building. She turned and faced him.

It took a moment for him to figure out what to say. "Look..." He peered towards the sky. "I know you're married, and I know my attraction to you is completely inappropriate. I can't help that, but I can help acting on it or not. And I won't." He closed his eyes and swallowed. Saying those last three words hurt.

"Damien?"

He opened his eyes.

"You're a good man." She stretched up and kissed him on the cheek, turned, and walked towards the van.

He put his hand on his cheek.

Damn his luck.

****

Sharon sat on a bench and examined the reflection of the lights on the tile floor of the police station lobby. She listened to the sounds of the station – a ringing phone, voices, footsteps – anything to drown out her own thoughts.

She'd killed a man. She'd persuaded her brother to lie for her. She hid some kind of substance in his house, knowing the power it could potentially wield. And for what?

To keep her family clean? For self-protection?

Maybe.

She stood and paced in front of the reception desk in an effort to squelch her anxiety.

It was a self-defense case, the officer had said. He'd believed her. Her kidnapper tried to rob them and held her brother at gunpoint. What other explanation could there be? The officer didn't even arrest her.

She'd never believed Dave would shoot Larry. He'd accidentally shot Jonah. Dave had only wanted the powder, and he did what he thought he needed to do to meet that end. Now, everyone thought Sharon was a hero for saving her brother. A few cops had shaken her hand because of her actions. They'd be less grateful if they knew the real reason she'd pulled the trigger.

She wanted to get back to Larry's house to hide the jars somewhere more secure than the closet. Hopefully, the other descendants believed Larry's story that the powder was destroyed. They wouldn't look for it. They would forget about her. They had to.

She blinked slowly. When was the last time she'd slept? It must have been the night before they opened the safe. Every time she started to doze, images of Dave shooting Jonah entered her mind. Images of Dave grabbing her arm and pulling her into the hall.

Images of him collapsing on the porch.

She returned to the bench and leaned against the window. Maybe she *should* destroy the powder, just to keep anyone else from getting it.

Her phone rang from her purse. She retrieved it and answered.

"Sharon?" a woman's voice asked.

"Yeah. Who's this?"

"Michelle. Larry gave me your number."

"Oh. Okay." She stared at the floor again.

"How are you doing?"

"I'm waiting for Larry to pick me up."

After a moment of silence, Michelle spoke again. "Larry told us what happened with the powder."

"Okay."

"Did Dave tell you what it was?"

She swallowed. "No. He destroyed it and told me he would kill Larry if I didn't get rid of the rest." She was getting pretty good at lying.

"Okay. Well, we're planning a trip to find what was on the map. It won't be until June, though." She told Sharon they were all flying home the next day and about the rafting idea.

"I'm not going rafting." Why couldn't this just be over?

"I figured. I'm not sure I will either. Jonah will call us if he finds anything."

"All right."

"Are you coming back to Richmond with us, to catch our flights?"

She glanced at the opening front door. Larry entered the station.

"No. The cops asked me to stay here for a little while." She looked at her brother. "I need to go. Larry's here."

"Okay. Call me if you want to talk about it."

She ended the call and left the station with Larry.

Why couldn't they just leave the whole thing alone? They had no idea what they were getting into.

They'd better not find anything on that river.

Part Two: The River
Chapter Eleven

After sitting down on the playground bench, Michelle retrieved her phone from her pocket and read the text.

A developer accepted my project.

Damien had been so nervous about presenting his project. Michelle suppressed a smile, fearing Anna would get suspicious. She'd already been careless in reading his texts with other people around.

Michelle and Damien had been texting almost daily since they'd left Virginia, and she told herself it was harmless because they only discussed things she felt she could show her husband.

That didn't stop her from deleting a few of the messages, though.

Back in January, Mark had been so furious after she returned from the Richmond trip that he ignored her. He saved that particular punishment for the most serious offenses; lesser ones resulted in verbal arguments. Silence showed she wasn't worth the effort of a confrontation. Michelle had started texting Damien during this time, just so she'd have another adult to talk to.

After deciding to wait until she was alone to return the text, she pocketed her phone and looked at her cousin. "Ready to head back?"

Anna nodded and hollered for the children. Britney and Sophie ran from the playground. Grant stood on a plastic bridge and picked his nose.

Michelle shook her head. “Come on, mister. It’s time to go. And get your finger out of there.”

He laughed and ran to the slide. She pulled a wet wipe from her bag and met him to clean his fingers.

They walked towards Anna’s house, and Michelle let Anna do most of the talking. Michelle couldn’t keep her mind off Damien’s text.

She tried to suppress another smile.

“What are you smiling about?” Anna asked.

She glanced at the ground. “Oh, it’s nothing. I was just remembering something funny.” She recounted part of Jimmy Fallon’s lip synching act from the night before.

She supposed she could have told Anna the truth.

It wasn’t like this with Mark, who’d blown into Michelle’s life with the intensity of a hurricane, full of charm and interest in her. He gave her cards full of flower petals, surprised her with fancy dinners, and seemed to only want to talk about her. He was naturally outgoing, a foreign idea to Michelle, but she figured opposite personalities often made relationships work. Intimidated by his forwardness, she’d nearly broken up with him before he proposed one month after they started dating.

In hindsight, she should have seen that as a problem. Why was he in such a hurry to get married? With Mark, she’d never experienced what she was now experiencing with Damien – the anticipation, the inability to suppress her joy, the nervous energy that insisted on occupying her stomach.

But she did marry Mark, and they had two beautiful children together, though their schedules overlapped so infrequently that any occasions they were together felt odd. He’d started to drift shortly after the wedding: the gifts and flattery stopped, and he impressed his expectations of what a wife should be onto her. Six months later, Michelle was pregnant with Sophie. She hadn’t wanted a baby so soon, but Mark did, and Michelle learned there was little she could say in the matter. If she’d known he’d force her to quit nursing school, to walk away from her dream and not look back, she would have been more firm in her argument for birth control.

Mark’s behavior aside, Michelle felt guilty about her feelings for Damien, but not because they dishonored her husband. In a way, the choices she made outside Mark's knowledge were liberating. She assumed she felt guilty because societal norms told her she should. Every time Damien sent her a text, her guilt melted away.

Ten minutes after they'd left the park, they arrived at Anna's house, and Michelle stole away to the bathroom to type a response to Damien. *That's so great!* She sighed.

His message came a minute later. *Yeah. It's a relief.*

She wiggled her thumbs over the keys, contemplating what to say when another text appeared.

Jonah's heading to Virginia on the tenth.

It was about time someone talked about that. Jonah had said he'd arrange for the rafting trip to happen in June, and June was just three days away. She typed a response. *Okay. Are you going?*

I think so.

After a short pause, another text appeared. *Are you?*

She swallowed. She wanted more than anything to spend a week on the river with Damien, but she needed to figure out how to make it work. *Not sure. I'll text you tonight. Congrats on your project.*

She flushed the toilet and washed her hands to give the illusion she was in the bathroom for its intended purpose. Her phone chimed again as she walked back to the kitchen.

Thanks. Looking forward to tonight.

She smiled and deleted his last message.

****

"There! Did you feel that?" Olivia moved Jonah's hand around her belly, trying to chase the elusive baby-foot-created lump.

He laughed. "I caught the edge of it that time."

She grabbed both of his hands and covered her belly with them. "Just wait. He's doing somersaults in there, I know it."

She rested against him as they sat sideways on the couch, and his hands covered the sphere her abdomen had become over the past five months. He leaned over to rest his chin on her shoulder, and she turned her head to face him. He had to remove his baseball cap before he could face her in such close proximity. After putting the hat on his knee, he replaced his hand onto her belly. "Did I miss anything?" He looked into her brown eyes.

"No. But you could have. Maybe you shouldn't insist on wearing that hat everywhere."

"I know. I'm just not used to having no weight up there yet."

"It's been two months."

"Has it?" He playfully smirked at her. Cutting off his dreads had been his surprise wedding present to her; his memory regularly replayed the look on her face when she saw his new hairstyle as she walked down the aisle. She'd touched his short hair before the minister had even started speaking.

"Yeah. Doesn't seem like it, huh?" she asked. "Do you miss the dreads?"

"Sometimes. Would it bother you if I grew them back?"

She laughed.

He closed the inches between them and kissed her. She inhaled, and he tried to move his hand to the back of her neck, but she pressed his hand against her belly. She giggled mid-kiss.

"You really want me to feel this, don't you?"

"It's like he knows those are your hands, and he's being a stinker." She pressed his fingers into her belly, and something pushed back against his right hand. "There! Finally!"

"It's so weird you can feel that from the other side." The lump slid across the length of his hand. "Wow."

"He's pretty strong." She sighed and leaned against him.

"Hmm." The lump pressed into his hand two more times. He closed his eyes and tried to imagine the coming September day when he would hold his son for the first time. The anticipation of that moment settled in his stomach. He kissed Olivia on the cheek, trying to comprehend how he could love someone as much as he loved her.

His phone chimed from the kitchen counter. "I'd better check that. Damien's supposed to get back to me about the trip." He slid out from behind her and walked to the kitchen, dropping his hat on the counter.

She sat against the back of the couch. "Do you really have to go on that trip?"

He read the text. *I'm in. Let me know which airport I should fly into.*

"He's coming." Jonah walked back to the couch and sat next to Olivia. "And no, I don't *have* to, but we want to see if we can find what's on that map. Our ancestors left it in the safe for some reason. It feels important, after what happened to Sharon–"

"And to you." She put her hand on his arm, where his sleeve covered the scar from the gunshot wound, and she looked into his eyes.

He cradled the side of her face with his palm. "Pretend it's just a rafting trip. The shooter is dead, and Alex doesn't even know about the trip, so if we do find something worth shooting people to get, he's out of the loop."

Alex was harmless, and Jonah had considered telling him about the trip but figured it would be easier to bring him in if they found something. Alex was too sulky for Jonah's taste, and he didn't want to volunteer to drag Eeyore around Virginia if they didn't find anything.

"Have you even been rafting?" she asked, apparently still trying to talk him out of going.

"Chris knows what he's doing on the river. We'll be fine." He kissed her. "I promise."

She moved her hand from his arm to the back of his neck and pulled him close. Her warm lips moving over his sent chills through his body, and he wrapped her in his arms while he still held his phone. She reached inside his shirt and gently ran her nails up his back, and he dropped his phone onto the couch.

Texting Damien back was going to have to wait.

****

Damien glanced away from the sizzling pork chop in the frying pan and to his phone, which rested on the counter near him. Michelle had said she would text him, and he grew more anxious about it as the hours passed.

The elation of having his water sanitation project accepted for development and corporate use – the very thing for which he'd been hoping – paled in comparison to the elation he'd felt when he told her about it. Corporate use meant something he'd created would directly impact how companies interact with the environment. It meant mass production, royalties, and perhaps a promotion. He hadn't told Michelle all those details. She only knew this was a major step in his career. He didn't want to say too much, fearing he'd subconsciously – or consciously – plan how to weave her into his future.

How could one woman turn his life upside down?

Back in Richmond, after Jonah told them his roommate could take them on the river, they all exchanged numbers. Damien had told himself he wouldn't use Michelle's unless he really needed to.

She ended up being the first to make contact. She'd wanted to tell him she was looking into nursing schools again.

That was all the encouragement he needed. They found some reason or other to text almost every day since, fueling his infatuation. Her messages revealed her feelings for him, and instead of his feelings dissipating with time, like he'd hoped they would, just the opposite occurred. He'd fallen in love with her.

He'd adopted new habits to keep his mind off her: starting a new project, working out more, and visiting his mother. He'd even tried to take Michelle's advice and find a girlfriend. He went out with his co-worker, Sydney, a few times in the hopes that being around another woman would help him forget Michelle. But Sydney was too much of a talker. She flicked the tips of her nails when she read the menu. She rolled her head back when she laughed.

She wasn't Michelle.

He grew tired of glancing at his silent phone. After seasoning the pork chop and inhaling its aroma, he grabbed his phone and sat at the table to text Jonah, having decided in that moment he was going on the rafting trip. It would take his mind somewhere else.

And there was the chance Michelle would be there.

He shook his head after he sent the text. What would happen if she was on that raft with them? Jonah and his roommate would be there too, so it wasn't like there would be an opportunity for Damien to be alone with her. At least not during the day. At night, when they camped, they could potentially sneak away. Maybe he should put a condom or two in his wallet, just in case.

Stop thinking like that. It can't happen.

There was only one way to handle this. He needed accountability, and that meant telling someone what he'd kept a deeply buried secret during the past four months. It had to be someone who would be on the trip with them.

He would tell Jonah. But only if Michelle was coming on the trip too. That felt reasonable.

He stared at his silent phone, planning what he would say to Jonah, until he smelled something burning. He jumped up and ran to the stove as the smoke detector sounded. Turning off the burner, he moved the pan before waving a dish towel around the alarm.

Damien was usually an attentive cook, so the sight of his pork chop, which was now charcoal on one side, was frustrating. He dumped it in the trash and fixed himself a bowl of cereal.

His phone sat on the table, silent.

****

"Mom, your phone's ringing."

Sharon looked up from the newspaper and squinted. "What?" She listened. A quiet ring tone came from the family room.

"I'll go get it for you."

Sharon's oldest daughter, Amelia, left Sharon alone in the dining room. Amelia had already stayed with Sharon for three days, and Sharon's son would likely appear shortly after Amelia's departure. Since Sharon had returned to Dallas three months ago, her kids were reluctant to leave her alone for more than a few days. She assumed Larry had said something to them that made them overly concerned about her.

She'd spent a month at Larry's house after the shooting. After she decided not to flush away the powder and to store the jars in a tightly-sealed cardboard box in Larry's basement, she had trouble leaving them. She'd killed a man because of those jars; she couldn't destroy their contents.

She left the table and went to the kitchen sink to wash her hands, which she felt compelled to do whenever she thought of the shooting. It didn't make sense, but it didn't hurt anything. All it cost her was a little soap, and it made her feel better for a short while.

As she dried her hands, she imagined the box in Larry's basement, wishing there was a way for her to get the jars back to Dallas without the extreme scrutiny two jars containing white powder would likely invite from airport security. She'd considered mailing them, but she worried any rough handling by postal workers would break them. That left driving them to Dallas, but Larry had protested when she'd told him she wanted to drive a thousand miles in February by herself. For now, Larry's basement was the most sensible place to leave them.

Amelia reappeared holding Sharon's cell phone. "I couldn't get to it before it went to voicemail."

"Oh, okay." She accessed the message.

Sharon, it's Jonah. We're heading back to Virginia on the tenth to run the river. I'm assuming you'd rather not come along, but I wanted to ask anyway. Call me back if you want the info.

Sharon disconnected. It was sweet that they wanted to include her. Naïve, but sweet.

She returned Jonah's call. After they exchanged greetings, she said, "I don't think I can handle a rafting trip, but will you call me if you find anything?" Like more jars?

"Yeah, I can do that."

"Thanks."

She ended the call, and her mind flashed back to the night she shot Dave.

His blood had spurted from his neck. She and Larry couldn't get the stains out of the porch and had to paint over them. The new coat of paint made the place look unblemished, but she knew what was under it; the image of the blood pool was burned into her brain.

She resisted the urge to wash her hands again, because Amelia had just seen her drying them.

What if the others found more powder? They would take it somewhere to learn what it was. And they would probably make the connection to her great-grandfather, linking her family to the eugenics movement.

She would have killed Dave for nothing.

"Are you okay?" Amelia broke her trance.

She forced a smile. "Yes, honey. I'm fine. Why don't you head home soon?"

"You were just staring at the wall, Mom. What's going on?"

"Nothing. I'm fine. I was just spacing out. Don't you do that?"

"Yeah, but it's usually from lack of sleep, not because I've been traumatized."

"Amelia, drop it. I don't need you and Zach to watch after me all the time, okay? I know how to handle this." Sharon hoped her tone was firm enough that Amelia would listen.

"Fine." Amelia picked up her purse from the counter and left the house. A moment later, her car pulled out of Sharon's driveway.

Sharon sighed, thankful for the solitude. She washed her hands again before she returned to the table, looked at the newspaper, and silently prayed she would never hear from Jonah again.

Chapter Twelve

"Absolutely not! You're not leaving again! Did you really think my answer would change?" Mark gripped Michelle's arm above the elbow as he looked down at her. She tried to step away, but he squeezed her arm tightly enough that she winced.

His dark eyes bore into hers. He didn't often get physical with her. In the past, he'd only done so when he had an especially stern point to make, a point that usually had something to do with Michelle wanting to do something on her own.

"The others will be there tomorrow. I can't stop thinking about it. I'm a part of this too." She considered jerking her arm away but decided against it, fearing that doing so would anger him more, and she'd have no chance of talking him into letting her go. "I can still get a ticket and meet them somewhere."

"Someone nearly shot you last time. You think I'll let you go back to that?"

"The shooter is dead. This is just a rafting trip."

He chuckled, released her arm, and stomped up the stairs. "Like you're an outdoorsy person."

She rubbed the place he had grabbed, sure he'd left a bruise, and followed him. "We need to find out what's on that map. Our families left it for some reason."

He snapped around to face her, causing her to nearly walk into him.

"Michelle, do you have any idea how worried I was last time? What if it was you who was shot, instead of that guy?" He stood two steps above her, making him tower over her more than he already did. "This family would fall apart without you. What would I tell the kids if something happened to you?"

For the first time, concern filled his eyes, in spite of the manipulation in his words. He didn't ask what he would do without her; he used the kids as leverage. For a few short moments, she considered relenting. As a dutiful wife, she should stay.

Then she imagined the map. In the days since she learned of the trip, she'd allowed herself to daydream what it would be like to find what their ancestors left for them. It would be a celebratory occasion, as there wouldn't be anyone there with a gun. "This is important to me, okay? Doesn't that count for anything?"

"You're not going. I suggest you get used to the idea." Mark continued up the stairs, went into the bathroom, and slammed the door.

She trudged back down the stairs.

Jonah and Damien would call her if they found something, which Michelle believed was likely. Their relatives wouldn't have hidden whatever it was so thoroughly that it would be impossible for her and the others to find it.

It wasn't just the unsolved mystery that drew her to the river, though. Damien would be crushed if she wasn't there, and she'd be lying to herself if she said she wouldn't be equally disappointed. She glanced at the closed bathroom door.

Going on the trip would be the ultimate betrayal. She'd be going to be with another man, a man who made her feel valued and appreciated.

She scowled, determined to go on the trip. Trying to get Mark's permission would have been the easiest way, but she hadn't thought it would be successful. Fortunately, she'd made a contingency plan that didn't involve him. She hoped her mother would loan her the money she needed.

****

Jonah peered out the window to the 4Runner in the street, from which Chris honked a distinct rhythm. He laughed when he recognized the beat of *Another One Bites the Dust*. The shrill horn just didn't have the same effect as a moving bass line.

"He's not coming inside? And why is he honking like that?" Olivia met Jonah in the living room, where he'd gathered his bag and camping supplies.

"He's a drummer. And he's in a hurry." Jonah opened the front door so Chris would stop honking. He turned back to Olivia, set his bag on the ground, and put his hand on her cheek. "I'll see you in a week." He leaned over to kiss her, then removed his hat and bent over to kiss her belly. "Bye, Jimmy."

"That's not his name."

He smiled, kissed her again, and put his hat back on. "I'll call you later. Love you." He picked up his supplies and walked to Chris's SUV while chuckling at his own wit. He'd pretended to name the baby after a famous guitarist every day since they learned they were having a boy.

Today, his name is Jimmy Page. Jimmy Page Ward. Has a nice ring to it, don't you think?

He remembered her scowl and laughed.

He opened the back of the 4-Runner to load his supplies. The folded rubber raft filled a third of the cargo area, and Chris's gear crowded much of the remaining space, so Jonah had to shove his items to make them fit. Once everything was stowed, Jonah sat in the passenger seat and looked at Chris. "Bring enough stuff?"

"Maybe. Was the keg in the way?"

"That suggests you buy your own beer."

Chris pulled the car into the street but glared at Jonah for a moment. "Funny guy."

Jonah pulled his phone from his pocket. "So how will we get the car after we've floated downstream?"

"Kind of depends on where we end up. I'm guessing someone will meet us if we find something. What are we looking for?"

"I don't know." Jonah unplugged Chris's phone from the stereo and plugged in his own before accessing a playlist. "We have a square on a map. So I guess we'll stop when we see something that could be what our relatives hid."

Chris bobbed his head to the beat of the new song and turned up the volume. "That'll slow us down getting to West Virginia. Do you really think you'll find something?"

"Don't know that either. Whatever it is was important enough for our ancestors to leave the map, so I'm hoping it won't be too difficult."

"Maybe it's like, buried treasure." Chris laughed.

"It's not a pirate map. There's no X marking any spot. I doubt we'll find a stash of doubloons in the middle of the Appalachians."

The music paused when his phone rang. Michelle's name lit the screen. "Hey, Michelle."

"Hey."

"Are you gonna be able to make it?"

"I think so, but I doubt I can get there by the time you start tomorrow. Can I meet you somewhere downstream?"

"Hold on." Jonah lowered his phone and repeated her question to Chris. After a brief discussion, Jonah brought the phone back to his ear. "We'll be getting to Claytor Lake sometime on Monday, depending on how much exploring we have to do."

"Okay. If I can get out there, I'll rent a car at the airport and meet you at the lake."

"Well, text me if you make it, and we'll look for you. I'm sure we'll have occasional cell reception."

"All right. Let me know if you find anything before I get there."

"Sure thing." He disconnected, and the music resumed.

Would they find something before Michelle arrived? Jonah tried to keep from becoming too hopeful. It had been a hundred years since their ancestors left the map, plenty of time for whatever they hid to be taken or destroyed. But the note Jonah had found in the safe said elapsed *centuries*, meaning the ancestors must have thought whatever they hid would have to stay hidden for much longer. They must have planned to keep it safe somehow.

Jonah allowed himself to feel a little hopeful.

****

After a long flight, bus trip, and taxi ride, Damien paced in front of the tiny cafe in Fries, Virginia, where he and Jonah had agreed to meet. The town was small and quiet enough to notice, and he squinted in the bright sunlight. He'd considered waiting inside the restaurant to escape the afternoon heat, but Jonah's last text indicated he and Chris would arrive any minute.

The last time Damien talked to her, Michelle still didn't know if she'd be able to make the trip. A sense of hope insisted on occupying his chest; he tried to squelch it in an effort to avoid later disappointment. The more realistic outcome was Michelle's husband would force her to stay home, and Damien would never see her again.

He couldn't stand that thought. He'd fantasized about seeing her countless times since Jonah scheduled the trip. Closing his eyes, he imagined what her face would look like the first time she saw him. Her eyes would widen, she would smile, and she would open her arms for him without hesitation.

His daydream only fed the hope he tried to suppress.

He opened his eyes at the sound of tires rolling over the gravel. A silver 4Runner pulled into the parking lot. Damien studied it for a moment and looked away when he didn't recognize the men inside. He removed his phone from his shorts pocket to see if he might have missed a text from Michelle, but he looked up again when a male voice said his name.

"Hey, Damien." A stocky, young guy wearing a baseball cap approached from the 4Runner. Had they not been at their specific meeting place, Damien wouldn't have recognized the man.

"Jonah? Wow, you look different."

Jonah grinned. "Yeah, had to clean up for the wife." He shook Damien's hand.

"Really? When did that happen?"

"A couple months ago. Olivia's having a boy." Jonah beamed.

"Congratulations." Envy rose from Damien's gut, which surprised him. He hadn't thought twice about Jonah's situation since Richmond. He tried to swallow the feeling.

"Thanks. You ready to go?"

"Yeah." He picked up the small bag that rested by his feet. When his phone chimed and he glanced at the text, he tried to keep from beaming as much as Jonah.

I'll be able to make it.

He waited until he sat in the back seat of the 4Runner to return the text. *I'm so happy to hear that. When do you think you'll get here?*

"Where are you from?" Chris asked after Jonah introduced them.

Damien looked up. "Tempe." He looked back to his phone, anxiously awaiting Michelle's reply.

"Bet it's hot there," Chris said.

"Oh. Yeah, it's toasty." He studied the three dots that indicated Michelle was typing.

"He's not a big talker," Jonah said.

Damien looked up again. "Sorry. I'm just distracted." Her reply arrived the same moment.

Monday. I'm meeting you guys at a lake.

Two days. He would see her in two days, a remarkable improvement from his earlier belief that he would never see her again. *Looking forward to it.*

"Who are you texting? You're smiling a lot at your phone." Jonah had twisted around to face him.

"Oh, um…" A stubborn grin took over his face; he'd have to make up a reasonable explanation. "I've been seeing someone." His nerves rushed to his stomach. It was fun to pretend that was true.

Jonah seemed surprised. "Really! What's her name?"

"M… Megan."

Jonah nodded and faced the front. "That's awesome. I guess you divorced yourself from your work."

Damien laughed through the discomfort that Jonah's use of the word "divorce" caused. He changed the subject to keep Jonah from asking more questions. "Does Alex know we're doing this?" Damien knew Jonah didn't have much use for Alex, so the question would be adequately distracting.

"No. Maybe we'll tell him if we find something. He still thinks the whole safe thing was a bust. If this doesn't pan out, I don't want to drag his mopey ass around the mountains." Jonah told him their plan to stop at anything that could be represented on the map.

"That doesn't sound promising," Damien said.

Jonah shrugged at the same time his text alert chimed. He checked it. "Michelle's in. She's meeting us at the lake."

Damien smiled and stared out the side window. She was smart to text Jonah as well, since he'd arranged the rafting trip; it would decrease any suspicion that would result from Damien receiving her news first.

He remembered the night he formed his accountability plan. "Jonah?"

"Yeah."

The words he'd practiced ran through his mind, but he was unable to voice them. *I'm in love with Michelle. Can you call me on my behavior if I'm not appropriate?*

A few silent moments passed. He had to say something. "When will Michelle get to the lake?"

"Monday."

"That's good." He clenched his jaw, frustrated with himself, until he realized why he couldn't ask Jonah to keep him accountable.

He didn't want accountability. He wanted to be with Michelle.

****

On the eleventh of June, Sharon shelved books at the library, a volunteer position she'd taken after returning to Dallas. She'd hoped staying busy would keep her thoughts off the shooting and the jars, but the silent environment only allowed her mind to wander. *Today. They're starting their search today.*

She had to look at the call number of the book she held three times before she comprehended it enough to know where to put it on the shelf.

What if they found something? They would call her, and then what?

She might have to meet them somewhere. If they found more jars, they would show them to her. They'd ask if she knew anything. And she would lie. Again.

"Are you okay?" A tall, skinny librarian stood at the end of the row, looking concerned.

Sharon rapidly nodded. "Oh. Yes, I'm fine. I'm just distracted."

"Anything I can help you with?"

Sure, I shot a man to death four months ago, and it's been eating at me ever since. "No. Thanks for asking. I'll finish shelving these and head home." She grinned, hoping the librarian would get the hint.

Some of the other shelvers listened to music while they worked. They would plug headphones into their phones, though Sharon had no idea how they managed to store music there. She made a mental note to have her daughter show her how to do that. If she listened to her phone as she worked, she wouldn't risk missing a call.

She shook her head, irritated with her inability to decide if she wanted Jonah to call or not.

She tried to imagine the conversation they would have if they found more powder. One of the others would insist on identifying it. Damien, probably. He seemed the most scientifically minded. Though Michelle was rather curious herself.

It wasn't just about the powder, though. What if they found something about their missing relatives?

What if her great-grandfather was responsible for that, too?

She swallowed the anxiety that thought created as she walked towards the front of the library, removing her cotton gloves and connecting with the tall librarian. "You know, I am feeling a bit under the weather. I think I'll head home, if that's all right."

The librarian agreed, as Sharon knew she would. No one questioned the physical condition of someone Sharon's age.

As she walked to her car, she found a name in her contact list, asking herself how far she would go to protect her family.

Chapter Thirteen

While she waited in her rental car for the rafters, Michelle watched the river. It cut through some of the greenest land she'd seen, contrasting sharply with her drought-stricken California home. Full trees lined the bank, though occasional gaps allowed her to see the rushing water.

She'd tried to read but couldn't keep her concentration, partly because she was excited to see Damien and partly because she had to squelch the guilt of leaving her kids with her mother and sneaking away against her husband's wishes. She was certain her kids were safe with her mother but worried what Mark would do when he discovered she was gone.

She grasped her necklace, the one the kids gave her on Mother's Day, with her mother's help. It depicted two connected silver hearts, each holding a birthstone: a ruby for Sophie and an amethyst for Grant. She almost left it at home to keep it safe from whatever elements she might encounter on the river, but she couldn't bear to leave behind something so special. As she followed through on her plan to escape to Virginia, she found herself running her fingers over it when her anxiety started to take hold.

The sun lowered over the horizon, but it was three hours earlier back home. Michelle imagined Mark at work during that day, talking to clients, completely oblivious to what she'd done. Her mother had never approved of Michelle's marriage to Mark, so she supported Michelle's decision to get away on her own.

I'm going on a trip with some friends, she'd told her mother. It was true; Jonah and Damien were friends. Not the kind of friends her mother probably assumed she was talking about, but friends nonetheless. Her mother had said she was happy to see Michelle doing something for herself for a change.

Of course, Mark would immediately see through that story. Thankfully, he hadn't talked to her about the rafting trip long enough to know which river she would be on; he'd been too busy hiding behind his laptop and dodging her attempts at conversation since she'd brought it up. It seemed he thought avoiding the subject would make her forget about it.

If he did a little digging on that laptop of his, he might find her confirmation email for her flight to Roanoke, but that's as far as he'd be able to get. She didn't want to imagine the fit he'd throw when he hit the dead end.

She sighed. There would be hell to pay when she got home, and it would take a miracle for her to fix it.

Maybe she wouldn't be able to fix it at all.

The epiphany struck her. In all the communication with Damien, she hadn't allowed herself to imagine that her marriage could be destroyed by this. The idea had felt just outside the realm of possibility. She and Mark had plenty of experience with conflict: she would do something to make him mad, he'd get mad, and she would smooth things over. His favorite form of penance was chocolate pie followed by an evening of make-up sex. He'd never offered anything in apology, because their difficulties were always her fault.

At least she knew for certain this transgression was her fault. The thought was oddly liberating.

Tired of thinking about Mark, she picked up her bag and left the car. She settled on the bank between two trees and leaned back on her elbows, feeling the warmth of the setting sun on her hair and skin and admiring the golden glow the low sunbeams produced. She closed her eyes for a few minutes to listen to the river.

She opened them again at the sound of distant, male voices. An orange raft floated towards her from the south. She stood and waited to see if the men in the raft were the ones looking for her.

****

Jonah squinted and pointed towards the shore. "Is that her?" He lifted his sunglasses to get a better look. He sat in the front of the raft, forward of where Chris sat and worked the oars.

"Yeah, I think so," Damien said from the back of the raft.

Chris steered towards the shore. Jonah waved and jumped out of the raft to pull it onto the bank.

Damien hopped over the side of the raft and into the water, darting past Jonah and towards Michelle. He hugged her like they were longtime friends finally reuniting.

That was weird. Jonah caught himself staring at them, wondering if he was seeing things.

Damien and Michelle walked back to the raft. Both of them were grinning, and Michelle might have been blushing.

It couldn't be how it looked. She was married and he had a girlfriend.

Still, Jonah was surprised they weren't holding hands.

"Hey, Michelle," Jonah said.

"Wow, you've changed!" She stepped closer to him and took off her sunglasses before giving him a hug – a friendly hug, not like the one she'd exchanged with Damien.

He smiled. "Yep. What do you think?"

"You look like you could be in a documentary."

Jonah groaned. No one had brought up the documentary story since the day they opened the safe, when Alex said he'd used the story to get them all to Virginia. Jonah had never wanted to be on film, but the subject remained an awkward undercurrent between them, because they'd all allowed Alex to dupe them.

"Have you guys found anything interesting?" Michelle asked.

"No, but at least all the stops are slowing us way down." Chris said from his place in the raft. He took off his sunglasses and looked at Michelle. "I'm Chris, and I'll be your guide through these wilds–"

"You knew we'd be stopping a lot," Jonah said, interrupting Chris's attempt at humor. "I don't know why you're acting all surprised."

"Hey, relax, bro. I'm just not used to it. But I'm afraid I'll have to charge you one beer per stop from here on."

"Well, I have about a five hundred stop credit, then." Jonah climbed back into the raft and faced the two still on the bank. "We're pretty close to where we want to camp tonight. Hop in."

They did, and together, they made their way to the back of the raft. Damien held a hovering hand near her back, occasionally making contact. Michelle seemed more at ease than Jonah had ever seen her. Jonah kept his eyes on them until they were seated.

Something was definitely going on there.

****

The sun had nearly set by the time the group found their camping spot, which was in a wide grassy area flanked by trees. Damien busied himself setting up the campsite and starting a fire, hoping to avoid any questions from Jonah. He had a feeling Jonah had picked up on whatever vibes he and Michelle were sending, and he mentally kicked himself for running out to her on the shore. If he wanted to keep his feelings for Michelle a secret, he'd have to do a better job of hiding them.

As Damien stoked the small flames in the fire pit, Jonah tapped him on the shoulder. "Let's collect more firewood. Michelle can keep an eye on this."

Michelle looked back at Jonah and then the fire. "I'll try. But I've never done this before."

"Ask Chris for help if it starts going out." Jonah turned to Damien. "Come on." He walked into the forest.

Damien followed. *Crap.*

Jonah picked up some small sticks as he walked. "So, tell me about Megan."

Damien's anxiety caught in his throat. Maybe he should just spill the truth. But if Jonah didn't know, he certainly didn't want to tell him. "Oh, she's great. She's smart, and–"

"Cut the crap, Damien." Jonah stopped walking and turned to face him.

Damien sighed. "Fine. There is no Megan. Michelle and I have been talking since January." An odd sense of relief covered him. Someone else knew about Michelle, making the relationship – if he could call it that – feel more real.

"You know she's married, right?" Jonah asked.

Damien brought his hand to the back of his neck. "Of course I know. Believe me, if I could just stop feeling what I feel, I would do it."

Jonah looked at him for a moment and resumed collecting small pieces of wood.

"That's it? I was expecting a lecture or something." Damien followed but didn't pick up anything.

"I'm not your father. You're a grown man." Jonah kept his eyes on the ground. "But don't you wonder about her husband? If Olivia was talking to someone behind my back like Michelle talks to you, it would kill me. And no one would be able to keep me from going after the guy."

Damien stopped in his tracks and tried to rationalize his behavior aloud, but he couldn't find the words. He wanted to say how awful Michelle's husband was to her, what she'd said about how Damien made her feel, all the reasons – or excuses – Damien had made for himself. But in the end, Jonah was right. Damien was pursuing another man's wife, and what would that man do if he found out?

Jonah silently picked up a few more sticks, walked past Damien, and returned to the campsite, leaving Damien standing alone in the forest.

Damien picked up some sticks so he wouldn't return empty-handed.

He wasn't worried about Mark coming after him. From what Michelle had said, the man was a fearful weasel, someone Damien could easily take out if needed. He worried about what Mark might do to Michelle and their kids.

But could Damien do anything about that? Whatever Mark did would happen after she returned home, and Damien would be back in Tempe, where he couldn't protect her. Even if Damien didn't continue pursuing Michelle, Mark would do something to send a message to her, a message that said he still ran the family, no matter how dysfunctional it was.

Damien grinded his teeth in frustration as he walked back to the camp.

Later that evening, after a modest meal of bratwurst, trail mix, and beer, the group sat on the ground around the fire. Damien made a point of not sitting next to Michelle. He hadn't told her what Jonah said, but only because he didn't want to give voice to something he thought neither of them wanted to admit.

He should have felt guilty for desiring her, but he didn't. He couldn't help but think he'd be a better match for her. With him, she could be her own person, not like a child he could control.

Had Michelle thought of leaving her husband? Damien couldn't imagine what made her stay. He had treated his ex-girlfriend with respect and consideration; she'd even told him as much, saying how grateful she was to have him. But in the end, she left for an ex-boyfriend who had treated her like crap.

Maybe women liked being treated like crap.

Damien chuckled to himself and shook his head at the thought as he leaned back on his elbows to take in his surroundings. This was the leanest camping experience he'd had. The group was severely limited in the amount of cargo they could take on the raft: a five-person tent, the sleeping bags, a small cooler, two water jugs, and their own personal bags comprised everything they owned here, so Damien was surprised when Jonah pulled a ukulele from his backpack.

Jonah sat with crossed legs on the ground, held the ukulele in front of him, and smirked. The instrument looked ridiculously small against his broad frame.

Michelle laughed. "I didn't know this was dinner and a show."

Jonah played through a chord progression, and after a few measures, Chris used sticks on the cooler to drum out an accompanying beat.

The song was some kind of island tune, and Jonah knew every word. Damien watched and listened, amazed by Jonah's talent. He wondered what the man could do with a real instrument and a real stage.

Damien glanced across the fire to Michelle, who met his eyes.

He tried to look away. At least, he thought he tried. The glow of the fire against her smooth skin and charcoal hair made her appear radiant, almost regal. Her dark eyes reflected the flames.

His longing for her filled him, and he found himself facing two choices: go to her, or walk alone into the woods until his desire to go to her ebbed.

He stood and walked until he could barely see the fire through the trees. He assumed the others would think he had to relieve himself and let him be, but after a few minutes, she was walking towards him.

Oh God, no! Don't come here!

He paced and wondered if he should venture farther into the dark forest. The music continued; it seemed Jonah and Chris were unaware of the situation. Damien decided to stay where he was rather than risk getting lost in the woods.

She walked into the trees and scanned the area. "Damien?"

"I'm over here." Maybe he should have stayed quiet.

She approached him, holding out an open hand. "I think we need to talk."

He looked at her hand. "I can't do that."

Her smile disappeared, and she lowered her arm. "I'm sorry."

He shook his head. "Don't be sorry. Please. It's just…" He brought his fingers to his forehead and closed his eyes. "If I touch you, I'm afraid I won't be able to stop myself." Needing to look anywhere but right at her, he glanced at the sky and moved his hand to his neck. "I don't want to be that guy who destroys a family." He squeezed his eyes closed again.

He opened them when she touched his arm. She gazed into his eyes. "You're not that guy." She didn't move her hand, and she didn't look away.

He couldn't pull his eyes away from hers, and he couldn't help himself. Framing her face in his hands, he kissed her. When she didn't stop him or pull away, he moved his fingers into her hair. Her soft lips moving against his sent electricity into every limb, and his heart pounded.

When he finally pulled back, he kept his hand on the back of her neck and rested his forehead against hers with his eyes closed. This would likely be his only chance to kiss her, and he didn't want to forget it. He inhaled, trying to breathe her in as the ukulele chords played in the distance.

"I think I'll head back," she said.

He wanted to say so many things to her: how much he loved her, how he would protect her, how he could be the man she deserved, but in the end, he only said, "Yeah."

She stepped away from him. He kept his hand on her arm so he touched every inch of it before she was out of range. She looked back to him before she stepped out of the trees.

He put his arms against a tree and leaned into them as he closed his eyes and took deep breaths.

****

Sharon kneeled next to the sealed cardboard box in Larry's basement. Running her hand across the top of it, she felt the cold tape and wondered if she should move the jars again. She pushed the box back to its original position, covered it with the other boxes, and went upstairs.

"How're ya doin'?" Larry asked.

She sat with him at the kitchen table and feigned a smile. "I'm okay."

"Are ya' ever gonna tell me about those jars?"

She sighed. "It's probably better if you don't know." *You don't want to know how our great-grandfather damaged whole populations of people. Trust me.*

"Maybe I can help, if ya' tell me."

She swallowed and stood. "I think I'll go upstairs."

She'd planned her trip back to Indiana the same day she left the library – the same day the others were to start their rafting trip – so she'd be closer if they found something. That was three days ago, and she hadn't heard anything. The silence didn't ease her anxiety.

She sat on the edge of her bed, and for the first time since she returned to her brother's house, she opened the drawer of the bedside table. The gun she'd used to shoot Dave was still there. She picked it up.

The rush of adrenaline returned, as strong as she'd felt it just before she entered the doorway that night.

That man had no idea she held his life in her hands – his ultimately meaningless life, as he couldn't accomplish the one thing he'd set out to do.

He'd failed because she decided he would fail.

She smirked.

The thought reached her conscience. She gasped, dropped the gun into the drawer, and slammed the drawer shut before rushing to the bathroom to wash her hands.

What the hell is wrong with me?

Chapter Fourteen

The cold night air cut through Michelle's sleeping bag. The ground was hard and bumpy, and her folded-sweatshirt pillow gave her a neck cramp. Those conditions didn't contribute to her inability to sleep, though.

Laying on her back and staring at the top of the tent, she studied the geometric patterns the seams in the fabric created, the only things she could see by the moonlight: triangle, square, another triangle. Her eyes traced the lines and angles as she listened to the river roar nearby.

Jonah and Chris breathed deeply as they slept. Chris snored a little. She couldn't tell if Damien was asleep, as he was on the opposite side of the tent, separated from her by the other men.

She closed her eyes and tried to squelch the discomfort in her gut, a discomfort she couldn't name. Guilt? Regret? Maybe. Those feelings would have made more sense if she didn't long for Damien's next kiss. She brought her fingers to her lips.

She tried to think of her husband, but doing so made her feel something she could name: animosity.

There was the regret, but it didn't stem from her behavior with Damien. It came from her inability to stand up for herself all these years. What if she had been firm when Mark made her quit nursing school just months before graduation? He would have either respected or resented her for doing it. At least she would know, and maybe she wouldn't resent him now.

Tired of analyzing the tent fabric, she sat up, put on the sweatshirt that was her pillow, collected her sleeping bag, and went outside. She settled next to the fire pit, which emitted a thin trail of smoke as the last embers burned away. A stale, smoky smell filled the air.

She climbed into her sleeping bag and looked at the stars, amazed at how many she could see this far away from a city. It was hard to comprehend their enormous number.

A rustling sound came from the tent a few minutes later. Damien emerged, carrying his own sleeping bag. "Mind if I join you?"

She looked at him, and her heart ached. "No."

He walked around her and settled with his head next to hers, but his legs pointed in the opposite direction. The position would make cuddling impossible, and for a moment, she felt slighted.

"Are you okay?" he whispered.

His breath brushed against her cheek, making her pulse quicken, but she tried to keep her voice steady. "I think so."

"I'm sorry about what happened."

She lifted herself onto her elbow. "Are you really?"

"Maybe not." He glanced up, like he was thinking. "I never thought I'd be the type to do this… you know, get involved with a married woman." He sighed. "I don't want to break up your family. My dad took off when I was ten, and I still can't talk to him about anything. I don't want that to happen between you and your kids." He closed his eyes.

Michelle shuffled in her sleeping bag as she lay back down. "I knew what I was doing when I came here. Mark didn't want me to come. I snuck away after he went to work yesterday." Was that just yesterday? It felt like an eternity ago. "Honestly, you're thinking about my family more than I am." There was the guilt.

He faced her, and she met his gaze as well as she could, as he appeared upside-down to her.

"Why did you come here?" he asked.

She hesitated before answering. "I wanted to be with you." She moved her hand to his cheek and stroked it.

He lifted onto his elbow, twisted around, and kissed her. Unlike the passionate intensity of their kiss in the woods, this kiss was gentle and light. His lips barely touched hers, sending chills across her skin. She brought her hand to his jawline, feeling the stubble from a few unshaven days.

He pulled back. "I'm not sure what you want, but I can't just have a fling with you. I'm way past that." He stroked her cheek with his finger. "I love you, Michelle. And I think you need to go home to your family." He kissed her forehead, climbed out of his sleeping bag, gathered his things, and re-entered the tent.

Wishing she could tell him to stay, she grasped her necklace, stared at the stars, and wiped away her tears as she silently cried.

****

Jonah sat up in the tent and squinted as he looked around. The sun was up, but Damien and Chris were still asleep. The place where Michelle had been the night before was empty.

He climbed out of his sleeping bag and opened the zipper of the tent to peek outside. Michelle slept on the ground, near the fire pit. Her nose was red from the cold, and her skin appeared paler than normal.

He left the tent, constructed a teepee of sticks in the middle of their makeshift fire pit, and placed the rest of the flammable garbage from last night's dinner under the teepee before finding the matches in his backpack. Soon, he had the fire going, and he added two larger pieces of wood to it. He frequently glanced at Michelle to see if she would respond to the warmth.

She took a long breath in her sleep. He approached her and put the backs of two fingers on her cheek; it felt cold, almost clammy. But she wasn't shivering, so he guessed she wasn't too cold. He kept a close eye on her as he arranged the supplies and placed foil-wrapped breakfast burritos near the fire.

He watched the flames and wondered if he and the others were wasting their time on the river. His hope of finding anything related to the safe in Richmond faded a little more at the end of each day, and it seemed Damien and Michelle tagged along just to see each other. In any case, they had two more days before they reached West Virginia, where Chris had said the real rapids started. At least they could look forward to that. It was a mild consolation.

Jonah's father had been critical when Jonah told him about the trip. Jonah's desire to find the map's target grew after that, if only to show his father that something he wanted to do mattered. After the conversation, Jonah remembered why he'd moved so far away. His father had one son who was physically incapable of achieving anything he'd hoped for his children, and he seemed determined to make sure the other one – Jonah – was just as unlikely to accomplish anything. His father's weapon of choice was constant discouragement.

Back in February, when Jonah told his father about the baby, his father had scolded him, shaming him for behaving in a way that resulted in an unplanned pregnancy. Jonah bit his tongue to keep from reminding the man that an unplanned pregnancy was the reason Jonah existed. The only reason Jonah didn't lash out was doing so would make it more difficult for him to see his mother and Samuel.

While Jonah stoked the fire, Damien emerged from the tent. He looked at Jonah, who put a finger to his lips and pointed at Michelle. Damien sat next to him.

"What happened last night?" Jonah asked in a whisper.

Damien kept his eyes on the ground. "I told her she should go home."

Jonah leaned forward to turn the burritos. "You know, you're the first person I told about Olivia being pregnant, back in Richmond. I didn't even tell my mom for a week."

"Really? Why?"

Jonah tried to remember that January morning. "I think because I knew you wouldn't be judgmental. And you're easy to talk to, even though it's not your favorite thing to do."

Damien grinned. "Thanks. I think."

"I'm sorry things can't be the way you want them to be." He gestured with a head tilt towards Michelle.

"So am I." Damien clenched his jaw.

"Can I ask you a personal question?"

Damien nodded.

"Why her?"

Damien's eyes narrowed. "What do you mean?"

Michelle rolled over in her sleeping bag, and Jonah's pulse quickened, hoping she hadn't heard his question. She took another deep breath.

He released the breath he'd been holding. "I mean, there are plenty of single girls out there. Why go after a married one?"

Damien stared at Jonah without answering for a few moments. "You've never had a crush on someone you shouldn't?"

Jonah chuckled and raised his hands to his face, as if surrendering. "Hey, this is about your unhealthy attractions, not mine."

Damien threw a stick into the fire. "I don't know. There was just something about her, when I watched her take care of you back in Richmond. And then learning how her husband treats her…" He shook his head.

Jonah turned the burritos and added a small log to the fire. "Well, if you like nurses, maybe you should go hang out at hospitals. Go find yourself a single one. I can hit you with a rock or something, if you want."

Damien laughed. "Maybe it'll come to that." He looked at Michelle before facing Jonah. "So, are you excited to be a father?"

Jonah smiled, remembering the night he felt the baby kick against his hand. "Yeah. Really excited. And terrified."

"Terrified?"

"Yeah, it's like this huge thing, you know? I'm responsible for this little person. My dad's always been distant towards me, and I don't want to be like that with my own kid." He picked up some wood chips and threw them into the fire. "I just want to do it right, I guess. And I'm not sure how." Jonah had kept these thoughts buried until now; what was it about Damien that made him spill his guts? He almost laughed at the realization.

"Well, maybe if you know that going in, you can choose not to be like your dad."

Jonah nodded. "Yeah. You're right. Keep an eye on these burritos for a little bit. I'll be right back." He stood and walked into the forest.

****

In the ten minutes Jonah was hidden in the trees, both Michelle and Chris woke. Chris got right to work rolling the bags, collapsing the tent, and replacing everything into their large, waterproof bags. This guy was all business, at least when it came to rafting.

Damien turned the burritos and watched Michelle dig her phone from her backpack. She glared at it.

"What's going on?" he asked, thankful to have the silence broken.

"I have a bunch of messages, but the signal's too bad here to check them."

"We have to portage around the dam and stop in the next town we float by to refill our water. You'll probably get a signal in one of those places," Chris said as he packed the tent.

"Yeah." She slid her phone back into her backpack and walked into the forest with it.

Despair draped her, and it crushed Damien to see it. This was the exact opposite of how he wanted her to feel.

Jonah returned, and Damien remembered to check the burritos. They were hot, so he used his sweatshirt sleeve to remove them from the pit. The three men ate their breakfast, and Michelle still hadn't returned by the time they finished.

Damien stood. "I'll be right back." If Michelle had found a signal wherever she ended up, Mark could be chewing her out right now.

He walked through the trees but didn't see her. He veered to the left and proceeded farther into the forest while scratching an itch on his jaw.

He needed a shave.

The thought made him stop in his tracks.

Most men wouldn't be bothered by a little stubble, but until now, Damien had been meticulous in his personal grooming. The fact that it took him three days to realize he needed to shave astounded him. His mind was obviously preoccupied.

He shook his head and resumed his walk, making a mental note to clean up when he returned to the campsite.

Five minutes later, he found Michelle wearing different clothes – Bermuda shorts and her sweatshirt, which probably covered a lighter-weight shirt. It would be too hot that day to stay in a hoodie. She sat on a boulder, scrolling through her phone and crying.

A knot formed in his stomach. He sat next to her on the rock, and she wiped her face with her sweatshirt sleeve.

"There's a weak signal up here. Mark's livid. He left twelve voicemails and thirty texts." She held her phone towards him so he could read the messages.

Is there another guy?

I don't know what I've done to deserve this. I've always taken care of you.

You know what? Don't answer. I'll take the kids and disappear too, since that's how we're doing things now.

Damien balled his fist and clenched his jaw again.

"I don't think he'll take the kids." She sniffed. "He threatens a lot of things but doesn't follow through. I thought about telling my mom he might try to take them."

"Why didn't you?"

"He's just mad that I left. The kids will still be there when I get home." She grabbed her necklace. "He doesn't know about you."

Damien didn't care if Mark knew about him. Men who bullied women usually didn't want to start fights with other men; the fight would be too even. His worry for Michelle increased, though. What would Mark do to her if she didn't return soon? He resisted the urge to take her hand. "We're still close to your rental car. Do you want to bail?"

She shook her head. "It'll be a nightmare no matter when I go home. I'll call him and my mom when I have a good signal. I still want to see if we find something."

"Okay." He suppressed a grin as relief covered him. He hadn't been lying when he told her she should go home, but that didn't mean he wanted her to go.

He felt like he needed to do or say something before he returned to the camp. He put his arm around the back of her shoulders and gave her a gentle squeeze, stood, and left her alone.

****

Five days after the others were to start their river trip, Sharon finally felt a sense of relief. No one had called her, and they must be close to the end by now.

She stood on the porch of Larry's house with her coffee, looking out at the bright, late-afternoon glow around her. This place was so much quieter than her home in Dallas. Maybe she should move here, as she'd considered several times since Larry offered it. She could live the rest of her days in the house where she grew up, with the history of her family – both the good and the bad – packed safely away in the basement.

She sighed and sipped her coffee. She hadn't realized how anxious she was about the river trip before now. All her worries about the trip – and what the others might find – had fallen away over the past few days. She could breathe again.

An image flashed in her mind.

She tried to suppress the memories of the vivid dreams she'd had since she saw the gun in the drawer two days ago, dreams where she was about to shoot someone – the person changed in each version. She clearly remembered the dreams because she'd wake the moment she was about to pull the trigger.

Her pulse quickened, and the corners of her mouth turned up into a small grin.

She shook her head and took another sip. So much for enjoying the peaceful evening.

She set her cup on the rail and rubbed her hands; they were chapped from washing them after every dream and memory of the dreams. The washing habit wasn't normal, but it stopped the adrenaline rushes she experienced when she thought of shooting someone.

The front storm door creaked open, and Josephine joined her. "Beautiful day."

"Gorgeous."

"I was just upstairs, and I heard your phone ringing. I thought you might like to know."

Sharon's anxiety took hold in her stomach, and she tried to push it away. "Okay. I think I'll go check, in case one of the kids needs something." A sense of dread she couldn't explain covered her.

Once in her room, she retrieved her phone from the dresser and looked at the screen: one missed call.

She held her breath and accessed the voicemail.

Chapter Fifteen

Michelle sat alone in the back of the raft. She'd hoped to enjoy the cool spray from the rapids to break the near-summer heat, but here, the river was calm. Chris had to use the oars to keep them moving at a faster clip. She dipped her hand into the water occasionally and spritzed her neck with her fingers.

They'd reached the town at nine o'clock, meaning it was six o'clock at home. Michelle had a brief conversation with her mother, but she sent a text to her husband in the hopes she wouldn't wake him; she didn't need to give him another reason to be mad at her.

I'm not ignoring you. In the middle of nowhere. There isn't another guy.

Mark hadn't responded before they floated out of signal again; she couldn't decide if she was disappointed or relieved. She hadn't directly lied about her feelings for Damien before today.

An hour later, Jonah pointed ahead and to the right. She squinted, trying to make it out what he saw. Chris steered the raft to the shore, where Jonah jumped out and pulled the raft onto the land between two of the full trees that lined the river.

Chris waited while Michelle climbed out with Jonah and Damien. They took off their life jackets and left them in the raft. Michelle was thankful her floral-patterned tankini hid any sweat spots the life jacket had created; the men had large, wet patches on their tank tops. Maybe Jonah wanted to stop just to get into the shade and out of the life jacket for a few minutes.

Jonah led the way through a wide field bordered by a forest on the far end. Damien followed him, and Michelle brought up the rear.

As they walked, Michelle's eyes were drawn to the well-defined musculature of Damien's arms and shoulders; she'd only seen him in short-sleeved shirts before today. The moisture on his brown skin glistened in the sunlight, and she stood in awe when he stopped walking and arched his back to swig from a water bottle.

He wasn't just attractive. He was *gorgeous.*

She shook her head and forced herself to look for the reason they stopped. Jonah walked ahead and drifted to the left, and Damien followed. She veered to the right.

There was nothing but nature in front of her, nothing that could be a buried secret. What if the target was literally buried? How would they have any idea where to dig?

No, it couldn't be that complicated. Whatever they looked for had to be above ground. Their ancestors would have known the limited information they'd left on the map, so the target should be relatively easy to spot. Maybe it was something other people would see too, but only she and the other descendants would understand its meaning. But what could that be?

More jars? Would those last above ground for a century? Not likely. Someone would have walked away with them or shot them to pieces long ago. Maybe it was something more permanent, like a structure.

Michelle scanned the area for buildings or building remains, but only grass and trees were within sight.

Soft footsteps sounded from behind her, and she turned around. Damien approached, holding the water bottle out to her. "I thought you might need a drink. It's pretty hot around here today."

Yeah it is. She took a drink to keep from laughing out loud and gave the bottle back to him. "Thanks."

She resumed her walk, and he walked alongside her.

"Do you know why Jonah wanted to stop?" she asked.

"Before we picked you up yesterday, we were stopping whenever the river turned to the northwest. We're trying to match the layout of the map. The most interesting thing we found was a deserted cabin. There was still some furniture inside."

"Are you sure it was deserted?"

He chuckled. “Yeah. Part of the roof was caved in. The furniture looked like it was from the fifties.”

“What do you think we’re looking for? Do you think it’s a building?”

He shrugged. “It must be something that could last centuries, or they wouldn’t have said so in the note.”

She walked in silence as she peered into the distance.

“Did you reach your family?” he asked.

She glanced at her feet, mourning the brief respite from her worry. “I talked to my mom. Mark didn’t pick up the kids, so she still has them.”

“That’s good, right?”

“Yeah. I guess.” Mark had probably been too angry to deal with the kids the previous night, and he’d had the whole night to decide what to do about her leaving. She kept reminding herself that Mark didn’t know about Damien, because if he did know, he would take the kids somewhere, just to spite her. She’d go home to an empty house and have no idea where they were.

She squeezed her eyes closed and held her necklace, trying to keep her imagination from going there. Even Mark wouldn’t do something that awful.

After a minute, Damien asked, “Did you talk to your husband?”

She stopped walking and turned to face him, unable to stop the tears she’d managed to hold back for the last hour. “I texted him.”

He kept his eyes on her.

She glanced at the single cloud that covered the sun and wiped her face with her open hands, wanting to talk about anything besides the possible repercussions of her actions. “Why do you have to be such a good guy?”

His eyes narrowed. “I’m sorry?”

She laughed through her tears and turned to walk towards the raft.

“You’re just… so different from how Mark is. I’ve already known you longer than my entire courtship with Mark lasted.”

“Really?”

She nodded. “We were only together for three months before we got married.”

"Can I ask why?"

"He wanted to get married. He was very charming." She felt foolish telling the story. In fact, everyone, including her mother and her friends, had told her she was foolish for marrying Mark so quickly. They'd said he must have had reasons to want to rein her in. She remembered thinking she was lucky for finding a guy who knew he wanted her right away. She shook her head at the memory, regretting that she hadn't listened to anyone.

Damien sighed. "Maybe we shouldn't talk about this."

"I know." She looked across the field. Jonah walked towards the raft from the opposite direction. He apparently didn't find anything either. "Do you know much about Jonah?"

Damien nodded. "We get along all right."

"I feel like I hardly know him at all. Just that he's a musician. Do you know why he cut off his dreads?"

"Yeah, I know. But maybe you should ask him. He might not like me talking about him."

She admired his decision to keep his friend's confidence and looked at him long enough for him to lock eyes with her. "It's funny; when all this started, you were the quiet one. But now you seem to know everyone in the group better than anyone."

He grinned. "Everyone except for Sharon, I guess."

"Hmm." Michelle thought about her own relationship with Sharon. None of them seemed to know much about her, and she'd barely spoken to any of them since the night she killed Dave. Michelle had even tried to make contact a few times.

It seemed Sharon had gone the direction opposite of Damien: she had gone from friendly and open to secretive.

Maybe she had a reason.

****

Halfway into the fourth day of rafting, Jonah felt anxious due to his growing belief that they wouldn't find anything on the river. It would be nice if they found *something*, even if it was a ruin, just so they would know why their relatives left the map in the safe. Maybe they should have explored that abandoned cabin more thoroughly, in case whatever they looked for was in there. It seemed this trip would be a complete bust. He doubted riding the coming rapids would ease his disappointment.

As the river started to bend and Jonah directed Chris to another landing spot on the northeast side, Jonah saw the last thing he thought he'd see in this remote area: a man, fishing from a small ramshackle dock. He seemed oblivious to the approaching raft.

In a few minutes, they floated close enough to the man to make out his details. He appeared Asian and middle aged, and he was dressed in old coveralls and a straw hat, like a 1930's farmer. As the raft approached him, he gathered his things and walked away from the river carrying a metal bucket and a fishing rod.

Jonah had to find out where this guy came from. He looked like a recluse who might have thorough knowledge of the area, and he happened to be on the northeast side of the river, matching their target on the map. Maybe the guy could help them identify something.

"Chris, take us over there." Jonah pointed towards the dock. The man continued walking away from them and into a wide, grassy field. "Hurry."

Chris steered the raft to the shore. Jonah removed his life jacket and hopped out to pull the raft onto the land, and he jogged into the field. The man continued on without looking back. Something told Jonah that talking to this guy was important, so he sped his jog. When he felt he was close enough for the man to hear him, he yelled, "Sir! Wait, please!"

The man stopped and turned.

****

Damien jogged to catch up with Jonah. He couldn't figure out why Jonah thought talking to this man was important; the man looked like he'd been plucked from a history book. He was likely a hermit, sheltered from society and certainly not in a position to help them.

Jonah caught up to the man, but it took a minute for Damien and Michelle to reach them. Michelle squinted as they approached. "He looks familiar."

"How is that possible?" Damien asked.

"I don't know." She studied the stranger like she was trying to solve a puzzle.

Jonah took the map from his pocket and showed it to the man, whose eyes widened and jaw dropped upon seeing it. His attention moved from person to person as he seemed to lose his balance, and Jonah put a hand on his back to catch him.

What was that about?

The man approached Michelle and silently stared at her long enough for the pause to become awkward. Damien was about to step between them when the man finally turned and led them away from the river. "Please, come with me," he said with a slight accent.

He led them through the field and to a rustic cabin at the edge of the forest. Aside from the intact roof, the cabin looked the same as the abandoned one they'd found three days ago. The man leaned his fishing rod near the door, held the bucket, and entered the cabin. He turned back when no one followed him. "Come on."

He held the door open for them.

This was weird.

Jonah climbed the two steps to the porch, and Michelle followed him.

Damien kept his place. "Wait a second. We're not just going in there."

Jonah looked back. "Why not? He knows about the map."

"We know about the safe and the powder, too," the man said.

Jonah raised his eyebrows at Damien. "Convinced?" He walked into the cabin, and the man closed the door.

"Let's go. He's okay," Michelle said. She held her hand out to Damien.

He took it, and she squeezed before letting go and entering the cabin. He followed, more to make sure she would be okay than to satisfy his curiosity. Nothing about this felt right.

They entered a small space, and Damien looked all around it in surprise. Unlike the rustic appearance of the man and the cabin's exterior, the interior of the cabin was completely modern: a flat-screened TV tuned to a news network was mounted above the fireplace, and a tablet sat on an ottoman in front of a leather couch. Another middle aged man, this one white with thinning blond hair, sat at a desk and used a laptop. Like the Asian man, he was dressed in old-fashioned clothing. He looked up at them.

"Robert, they have the map," the Asian man said to the white man.

Robert's jaw dropped. "Where is Elroy?"

"He went to town. I'll clean these before he gets back." The Asian man entered the kitchen, removed the day's catch from the bucket, and put the fish on a cutting board set on the counter. A loud whack filled the room when he chopped off a trout's head, startling Damien.

Robert used a remote to turn off the TV. He rose from his desk chair and walked towards the group, standing across from Jonah when he reached them. Something about Robert's eyes was familiar, but Damien couldn't decide what it was.

"Son, are you familiar with your heritage?" Robert asked.

Jonah leaned slightly away from him. "Uh, yeah. A lot of my family is Irish."

Robert nodded. "You are descended from William." He scanned the group. "Is there not another?"

Damien blinked. "Another person in our group, you mean?"

"Yes. There were meant to be four."

Damien's pulse quickened. "You mean four descendants? You were expecting us?"

A rumbling motorcycle engine sounded through the open windows.

"Elroy is back," the Asian man said from the kitchen as he wrapped the fillets in foil.

A minute later, an older, black man holding a helmet entered the cabin. He tossed a set of keys into a bowl on a small table near the door. Unlike the other two men, he wore modern clothing: jeans and a golf shirt. His thin beard and hair were almost completely gray. He scrunched his eyebrows upon seeing the group.

"Elroy, it seems these young people discovered the safe," Robert said.

Elroy approached the group and stopped in front of Damien. After staring at him for a few seconds, he shook his head and walked down a short hallway, entering another room.

Robert's attention followed Elroy into the room before going back to Damien. "Elroy thought he would not see this day. He will come around."

"Come around to what? What's going on here?" Damien asked.

"Perhaps you should all have a seat, for this will take some time to explain. May I fetch you a drink?" He gestured to the small room where he'd been sitting.

After a few moments of hesitation, Jonah walked into the room and sat on the leather couch. Michelle sat in a neighboring recliner, and Damien settled on the floor and leaned against her chair, next to her legs. Elroy returned wearing old-fashioned clothing. The Asian man had finished cleaning the fish and put the fillets into a stainless-steel refrigerator. He washed his hands before joining the others in the living room.

Robert sat in the desk chair and turned it to face the group. "We've been waiting for this day for quite some time. May I ask your names?" After they introduced themselves, he continued. "My name is Robert." He gestured to Elroy, who stood in the space between the living room and the kitchen. "This is Elroy, and this is Gao," he said while gesturing to the Asian man.

Michelle gasped. Damien looked at her. She'd sat up straighter and stared towards the kitchen.

"I take it from your reaction that you've recognized Gao," Robert said to Michelle. "Am I correct in my perception?"

Michelle looked from Gao to Robert and back to Gao in quick succession. "My great-great-grandfather's name was Gao. I saw a picture of him. He looked like you. It just surprised me."

"And surprised you should be. Gao is the man you describe," Robert said.

"What?" Damien asked. This just took a sharp, right turn into bizarre. "How is that possible? He would be somewhere around a hundred thirty years old now."

"Indeed." Robert rose from the chair, walked into the kitchen, opened a cabinet, and removed a large Mason jar full of white powder. He carried it into the room and reclaimed his seat. "Does this look familiar to you?"

"It's like the one we found in the safe," Jonah said.

"Precisely." He glanced at the jar before looking back to Jonah. "Your relative, William, installed the safe in the courthouse for us. In fact, he had a hand in designing it. We offered to let him leave with us, but he only wanted a key for his family."

"What are you talking about?" Damien wasn't accustomed to being confused and wished Robert would get to the point.

Robert sighed. "Allow me to start at the beginning. Long ago, I worked for a pharmaceutical company. I was charged with the task of developing a medication that would establish infertility in anyone who consumed it. I'd believed the company was taking the lead in establishing a contraceptive for family planning, a largely non-existent concept at that time. I learned later that the purpose was to slowly eliminate certain groups of people." He shook his head.

"How long ago?" Jonah asked with a scowl.

"I'll answer your question, but allow me to finish." Robert went back to scanning the group. "Gao and Elroy were part of my experimental groups, though they and the other subjects believed they were receiving a vitamin supplement designed to boost immunity."

He stood and handed the jar to Gao, who returned it to the cabinet. Robert remained standing and faced Damien's group. "The powder, which I call Deinix, worked as intended, but there was a side effect. I'd dispensed it to animals before it was distributed to the targeted populations, so I could fully understand its effects. I discovered that the medication not only halted fertility, but it greatly slowed the process of aging. My guinea pigs, which should only have lived four years or so, were still youthful twelve years after I began my study."

"Wait, so you're saying this medication kept people young?" Damien asked.

"Exactly. I had no way of knowing the degree to which the aging process slowed. I told Gao and Elroy about this effect, as they had become my friends over the years I treated them with Deinix. Even after I told them the initial intention of my company in creating it, they wanted to participate in this next stage of my own research, if you will. I also started taking it at that time."

"What next stage?" Jonah asked.

"To see how long we could live if we continued to take it. The one guinea pig I kept with us finally died of age-related illness in 1940 at the age of forty."

Damien quickly did the math. "So at the same rate of aging, you could live –"

"You're saying that you're really our relatives? The ones who disappeared?" Michelle interrupted.

Eight hundred to a thousand years, Damien thought.

Gao took over the explanation. "Yes. Robert said that we could go with him and live a long time, but we couldn't see our families anymore."

"Why not? Why couldn't you just keep taking the powder and live your lives?" Michelle asked in a louder voice.

"Because I stole it," Robert said.

Silence covered the group for a few moments before Robert continued speaking. "The company knew what I had created, and they wanted to destroy it. There's no money in keeping people young and healthy. Pharmaceutical companies need people to age, get sick. I couldn't let them have it, not when it could be used for the greater good." He sighed. "Deinix comes from the Latin for 'God's snow'. We have to believe there's a divine purpose in it, greater than any of us, or staying hidden away as we have would be unbearable. It can save people, but it must be used judiciously. We've stayed hidden to protect it for the time being."

"Protect it? So why did you keep some in the safe for anyone to find?" Damien asked. He frequently looked at Elroy, trying to grasp the idea that the man was his supposedly-dead great-great-grandfather. Why did he appear so much older than the others?

"We didn't leave it for anyone to find. We left it for our families to find, though we'd predicted it would take much longer – centuries – for that to happen. We'd hoped society would evolve to a state where long life would be desirable, and we wanted our families to benefit from having and selling Deinix." Robert looked at his long-time research companions. "We traveled from New York with the jars, unsure of where we would settle. When we saw the construction site at the courthouse, Gao had the idea of hiding one of the jars. William was there, and we explained the situation. He agreed to help us, in exchange for a key to the safe." Robert stood. "I'm sure you have more questions. However, there is something I'd like to show you."

****

Sharon listened to the voicemail twice, trying to discern any hesitation in Jonah's voice.

Sharon, it's Jonah. You need to come to Virginia. We found something you have to see.

He sounded out of breath.

Call me, and I'll tell you where we are.

There was no hesitation. Sharon stared at her phone and tried not to panic.

She closed her eyes and quietly swore before she returned the call.

Chapter Sixteen

Robert lit a gas camping lantern inside the doorway of a storm cellar under the cabin, and the group followed him inside. Michelle gasped.

The flickering light illuminated dozens of powder-filled jars, placed on five levels of shelves that surrounded the space. A couple dozen more jars covered half the floor.

Robert faced the group. "There are one hundred fifteen jars left. I spent our first few years here acquiring ingredients and creating as much Deinix as I could, unsure of how long we would take it. At one point we were storing nearly three hundred jars. I slowed production when I concluded we each needed only two grams per day to maintain its effects."

"How long will this last you?" Michelle asked after failing to figure the answer in her head.

"The twenty jars I took from the company lasted ten years. If Gao and I continue to take it as we are now, there is enough here and in the cabin to last ninety more years."

"Only you and Gao are taking it?" Damien asked.

Robert leaned, as if trying to look past the group and out the door, and continued speaking in a softer voice. "Elroy chose to stop taking it in 1968, when the Reverend Martin Luther King, Jr. was killed. I suggest you ask him if you'd like more details."

Michelle tried to comprehend the amount of powder before her, wondering if Sharon would try to dump all this into the river. But wasn't dumping it Dave's idea?

As if reading her mind, Robert asked, "Do you still have the jar from the safe?"

She looked at Damien, who said, "You asked earlier about the fourth person. Sharon is the fourth person. She said her family came from Jamestown."

Robert nodded. "Then she would be my…" He squinted. "How old is she?"

"Older than us. In her sixties, I think," Michelle said.

"My great-granddaughter then, I suppose."

Damien recounted Sharon's kidnapping and the steps he and the others took to find her. He ended with, "She said Dave dumped the powder from the safe in the river, and she flushed what was at her brother's house."

Robert shook his head. "That makes no sense. Who is this Dave person?" He walked towards the door of the shelter.

"You mean who was he. Sharon killed him." Michelle followed Robert out the door. "He *was* an historian. He was with us when we opened the safe."

Robert turned and stood outside the shelter with the still-lit lantern in hand. "She killed this man? For what purpose?"

"Self-defense. He took Sharon's brother hostage until she got the jar. She came downstairs with the gun instead." Michelle tried to ignore the nagging in her gut that said there was more to the story.

Robert extinguished the lantern and walked to the shelter door to place it inside. "I'll wager that man was more than a simple historian. He would have already had reason to know about Deinix, if he wanted it so badly." Robert pulled the door closed and locked it. "He likely worked for my former employer." He closed his eyes and sighed. "If not for my pride." Stepping through the group, he walked up the small hill that led to the front door of the cabin.

If not for his pride? What did that mean? Michelle could hardly manage the number of thoughts bouncing around in her head.

"Why are you telling us all this? Aren't you worried we'll take the powder or tell someone about you?" Damien asked as they walked.

Robert stopped walking and faced them again. "We knew our secret would either die with us or our descendants would find it in the safe. The three of us decided that if you arrived, we would pass along everything we know about it. You must decide what you will do with the information. I will say it would not be in your best interest to release it to anyone." He resumed his walk to the front door.

"Wait, what does that mean?" Michelle asked.

Robert answered without stopping or looking back. "There are powerful people, corporations, that will do anything to get their hands on Deinix. They already know what it does. They *don't* know where it is. I strongly suggest you don't place yourself between these powers and the medication."

He entered the cabin, leaving the other three standing on the grass to digest Robert's words.

"He found Gilgamesh's plant," Damien said while staring at the cabin door.

Michelle scrunched her eyebrows. "What?"

He faced her. "Gilgamesh. He was a Sumerian king. Legend says after his friend died, he became obsessed with avoiding death himself and traveled to the underworld, where he received a plant that would make him immortal. But a serpent stole it. Some say mankind has been searching for the plant ever since."

Michelle tried to discern the meaning of his reference. "So what if everyone is looking for something to make them immortal, and not only does it exist, but we control it?"

"What do you mean?" Jonah asked.

"Robert said the drug companies wouldn't want it out, because their business depends on people getting old and sick. But what if only one drug company controlled it? They'd be the only corporation with the ability to sell a "fountain of youth" formula. And beauty companies wouldn't like it either, unless they could market it in a way that would benefit them. That would only work if one company had it."

"Do you want to sell it to one company? Because that's a horrible idea," Damien said.

Michelle shook her head as her anxiety rose. "Damien, you said people have been searching for the plant for what, thousands of years?"

He nodded.

"If word gets out that we found it, there won't be any more searching. There will be fighting – fighting to determine which company would be the sole provider of the 'miracle drug' to the masses. Unless two companies are fighting over it, one company will be fighting *us* for it. Even if we tried to sell it, they would have no reason to believe we didn't keep some hidden somewhere. They wouldn't leave us alone."

Michelle suddenly wished to get the powder as far away from her as possible. If those companies connected it to her, they could come after her children. She wouldn't put it past a greedy company to use her children as leverage.

"So what should we do with it?" Damien asked.

The three stared at each other.

Jonah broke the silence. "I'll go call Sharon. She needs to be a part of this." He turned and walked through the field and towards the river.

****

Jonah stopped by the raft and found Chris asleep. He kicked Chris's shoes.

"Come on, man, wake up. You won't believe what we found." Jonah debated how much to say. Robert had just said not to release the powder to anyone; was telling Chris about it releasing it?

Jonah didn't think so. Chris was his friend, and if Jonah told him to keep their discovery quiet, he would. And he couldn't leave Chris waiting in the raft forever.

Chris sat up in the raft. "Well, what?"

Jonah tapped his fingers on his legs in an effort to calm his nerves. "We found the ancestors."

Chris scrunched his nose. "Ew. Like, dead?"

"No. They're alive."

"Ha ha. You don't have to be such a smartass all the time."

"I'm not. This is serious." Jonah told Chris about the jars and what Robert told them. "We need to keep this quiet, okay?"

"Seriously? Man, that stuff could be worth millions!"

"Exactly. I don't want rich guys trying to kill me to get it." Jonah picked up a water bottle. "I have to walk upstream a ways to make a call." He pointed towards the cabin and told Chris to meet the others there.

Jonah jogged on the nearly-flat, grassy bank alongside the river and traveled for just over an hour before he found a cell signal. He pressed Sharon's name in his contact list: after five rings, it went to voicemail. He left a message for her to call him so he could tell her where they were before he realized he'd have to stay where he was if he wanted to receive her call.

He sat on the river bank to catch his breath and took a few swigs from the water bottle.

Watching the river flow over a boulder, he wondered how much it had shrunk in the last century. Would he be able to live here in solitude for a hundred years, as those men had done? Jonah didn't think he'd last more than a year or two without going completely stir-crazy. Plus, those men had left their families, an idea that Jonah found incomprehensible. He planned to be a husband and father, and not even the promise of immortality would change that.

Maybe that was why his great-great-grandfather didn't join the others, hiding out, waiting for society to evolve to a point where having the powder wouldn't be disastrous. But would society ever reach that point? Whoever controlled the powder – and the formula for it – could potentially decide the fate of mankind. They would decide who deserved to live forever, and by default, who didn't.

Jonah shuddered as he imagined having such a responsibility.

Robert had said there were powerful corporations who knew about Deinix. What would they do if they found out he and the others had it? Jonah wouldn't just hand it over to them; they were the last ones who should be deciding who lives or dies, and Michelle was right about corporations fighting for it. But if one company had the powder, they would be able to buy corrupt politicians with it – politicians who would suddenly stop dying.

Eventually, one corporation would control everything.

Just as Jonah was deciding he and the others had to do whatever they could to keep Deinix a secret, his phone rang. He sighed with relief at not having to wait hours for Sharon's call.

"What did you find?" she asked without offering a greeting.

Jonah tried to form a sentence when he realized his turn to speak arrived more quickly than he expected. "Oh… well, you need to see for yourself. There's a town upstream." He told her the name of the town. "Go there, and I'll find you and bring you to where we are."

She was quiet. He wondered if the call dropped.

"I'll be there in the morning." She disconnected.

Jonah scowled at his phone. Sharon hadn't been that rude to him before. He'd thought she'd be happy to hear they'd found something.

He put his phone into his pocket and walked towards the raft.

****

Damien found Elroy crouched and tinkering with the motorcycle, and he considered leaving the man alone. Elroy hadn't seemed at all interested in interacting with Damien from the moment he returned to the cabin.

Damien approached from Elroy's side, making enough noise with his feet on the dirt for Elroy to notice and look up.

Elroy stared at Damien without saying anything.

Damien's flight instinct kicked in, and he nearly walked away. "What kind of bike is that?" he asked, hoping to cut through the tension.

Elroy turned the wrench in his hand, working to tighten a nut. "1981 Goldwing, ten eighty-four ccs, four-cylinder boxer," he said with a deep, gritty voice.

That meant nothing to Damien. He jumped to the reason he had approached Elroy in the first place. "I was wondering if I could ask you some questions."

Elroy tossed the wrench into a tool box next to him, took a dirty, white rag from his pocket, wiped his hands with it, and stood as he returned the rag to his pocket. He approached Damien. "Okay. Ask."

His tone and demeanor made Damien wish he had left him alone to work on the motorcycle. Elroy's face held a scowl. He was a few inches shorter than Damien but somehow made Damien feel small.

Damien blinked twice, trying to figure out what to ask. He suspected Elroy would allow only a few questions. "How old are you?"

"One hundred twenty-seven."

"Why do you look older than the others?"

Elroy tipped his head up. "Let's walk." He tore away, and Damien had to jog a bit to catch up.

"I quit takin' the powder in '68, when King was shot," Elroy said while staring at the ground.

"Why then?"

Elroy glanced at him. "Was then I knew. The world was goin' to hell at lightnin' speed. That man didn't want nothin' other than peace an' hope. And he got killed for it." He put his hands in his pockets. "I didn' want to keep waitin. Nothin's gettin' better."

Limited questions, Damien reminded himself. "Did you ever wonder about your family? The one you left behind?"

Elroy stopped walking to face Damien again. "What're you to me?"

Damien stood up a bit straighter. "I'm your great-great-grandson."

"Hmm." He turned and walked towards the motorcycle.

"Aren't you going to answer my question?"

"Nope." He quickened his pace and pulled in front of Damien.

"Your wife made your son keep an empty plot next to hers at the cemetery, hoping you'd come back one day." Damien stopped walking and let his words hang in the air.

Elroy walked a few more steps, and his shoulders slumped. "Shit." He turned around and stomped back to Damien. "You think you know everythin', huh? You know she cried every night when we couldn' have more babies? She blamed me!" By now he was inches from Damien's face.

"Then why did you go with Robert? It was his fault. He gave you the powder."

The man scowled. "The hell you know." He turned and tromped towards the cabin. "It was supposed to help!" He entered the cabin without looking back.

Damien stood in place and listened to the sound of slamming doors carrying through the open windows.

****

Sharon sat in the driver's seat of Josephine's Altima, tapping her fingers on the steering wheel. She was still in Larry's driveway, where she'd been for the past twenty minutes, arguing with herself.

Jonah hadn't said anything about what they found. It had to be something important or serious, or he wouldn't have told her to go out there. What if it was something she needed to hide?

She should get the gun. She could keep it under the driver's seat, just in case.

Just in case of what? In case she needed to shoot one of those lovely people who likely had no clue about her great-grandfather or the eugenics movement?

They'd had no clue before this rafting trip, at least. If they found more powder, they'd have it analyzed and make the connection.

This had to stay her secret. Her family's legacy and her cousin's political presence depended on it. She'd already killed one man to meet that end.

She left the car, re-entered the house, and removed the gun from the bedside table drawer in the guest room. She felt the weight of the handle, remembered what it felt like to fire it at Dave, winced when she remembered dropping it.

Don't bring it. You killed Jonah in last night's dream, remember?

For a few moments, she stared at the gun, and for the first time in months, she didn't want to wash her hands at the thought of it.

She checked the magazine for ammo, tucked the gun into the top of her capris, and covered it with her shirt, unsure of why she felt the need to hide it. Larry and Josephine weren't home.

Upon returning to the car, she stashed the weapon under the driver's seat.

Chapter Seventeen

Michelle stayed on the porch after she decided not to follow Jonah in his search for cell coverage. Mark probably hadn't tried to contact her. At last check, her mother still had the kids, and they sounded happy enough when she spoke to them. They'd told her about going to the park and the movies. Sophie asked where Daddy was and seemed satisfied with Michelle's explanation that he was busy with work.

She hoped it was an accurate explanation. What on earth was Mark doing? He hadn't even called her mother's house to check on them.

As time passed, the kids would become more anxious. Michelle wished she could rush to her babies and wrap them in her arms, apologizing for what was likely a scary experience. They knew Michelle would be gone for a week; she'd prepared them for the separation. Eventually, Mark ignoring them would make them wonder if he was coming back.

What kind of father would do that to a four- and five-year-old?

On the other hand, Grant had told her more than once that Daddy scared him. A few weeks before Michelle left for Virginia, Mark had yelled at her for forgetting to pay a bill and stormed out of the house. As soon as Mark was gone, Grant had curled up in her lap and cried, saying how he wished Daddy was nice.

Her hand went to her necklace.

Maybe it wasn't such a bad thing for the kids to have a break from him.

Wishing she hadn't had the thought, she entered the cabin. Gao was busy at the counter, working to prepare a chicken dish.

"Can I help?" she asked.

He twisted around and looked at her. "You can…" He surveyed the room. "Salad. Make salad." He pointed to a pile of vegetables on the far end of the counter, nodded, and focused on the chicken.

"How do you guys pay for what you need here?" It was one of Michelle's burning questions since they arrived.

"Robert writes many books. Since we came here. Under eight different names. I help with some." He poured a creamy sauce from a pot over the chicken breasts in the baking pan.

Michelle stopped tearing lettuce for a moment and scanned the cabin again, wondering if she'd read any of Robert's books. They must do well, if the ancestors could afford all this. "What kind of books?"

"History books. Some fiction. He always writes. Gets what we need. I think he feels guilty." He covered the pan with foil and put it into the oven.

"Guilty? About the powder?"

He set the timer and faced Michelle. "My wife only had a daughter. We wanted more children. It was the powder." He looked at the floor and shook his head before turning to get plates from a cabinet.

"Why did you leave your family? Didn't you think they needed you?" The irony struck her. She'd sneaked away and left her family behind, but she reminded herself Gao's story was different. She wasn't leaving her family forever.

Gao set the plates on the counter and stared at them as he spoke. "I was ashamed. Business was bad. I couldn't make my wife happy." He picked up the plates and walked towards the table with them. "Do you know when she died?"

He asked as he set the table, the question rolling off his tongue as smoothly as it would had he asked about the weather.

"No. I don't." Michelle started slicing a cucumber. "Your daughter – my great-grandmother – was very beautiful. I saw a picture of her."

Silence followed, and she looked at him. He was wiping tears from his face with the back of one hand.

What kinds of wounds had this man been keeping for a hundred years? And why would he choose to live for hundreds more with this pain? Was he afraid of dying? Or did he think he deserved to suffer?

Michelle tried to imagine being faced with his choice. She already missed her children to the point of distraction; how could she live somewhere away from them, knowing they would grow up, graduate, get married, have their own kids, and she wouldn't be a part of it? The idea seemed impossible, yet the evidence that it was stood before her now, in the form of her great-great-grandfather.

He stood up straight and exhaled. "I joined Robert to do something that mattered. Deinix can save people. I'm proof." He walked to a drawer and retrieved silverware.

His answer sounded rehearsed. "Do you really believe that?" she asked.

"Yes. I failed my family. Leaving was my only choice." He set the silverware around the plates with no further hint of emotion, then gestured to his surroundings. "This is my legacy now."

"I doubt your family thought you failed them." She turned back to the cutting board.

He didn't respond.

****

The table was too small to seat everyone, so Jonah leaned against the counter and held his plate. Chris stood next to him, obviously uncomfortable with their current setting. He stared at his food as he ate, pushing it around with his fork in between bites. It was a sharp contrast to his usual practice of shoving food into his mouth as though trying to beat a speed eating record.

The meal was quiet in spite of the number of people present. There seemed to be tension between Michelle, Damien, and their respective relatives. Jonah finally broke the silence ten minutes into the meal. "Sharon will be here in the morning. I'm going to the town upstream to pick her up."

"How will you do that? We don't have a car here," Michelle said.

"I was hoping to borrow the motorcycle." Jonah took a bite of salad and didn't make eye contact with anyone, hoping one of the centenarians would offer the use of the bike.

Elroy scowled at him. "You ever ride before?"

Jonah nodded. It had been a while since he rode his high school buddy's motorcycle, but Jonah wasn't about to share that information.

Elroy shook his head and looked at his food. "It's a bad idea."

"What do you suggest?" Robert asked in Elroy's direction.

Elroy glared at Robert. "You go get her."

"Be reasonable, Elroy. She won't know me, and she'd be a fool to accept a ride from a stranger. The motorcycle belongs to all of us." He looked at Jonah. "You may take the bike. Of course."

Elroy grumbled.

"Thanks." Jonah hoped he'd be able to start the thing and ride away without looking like an amateur.

"Can I ask a question?" Chris asked.

Jonah glanced at him in surprise. Chris hadn't seemed interested in interacting with the men. He'd seemed to be scared of them.

"Certainly," Robert answered. "What is it?"

"Why do you guys wear old clothes? It doesn't really, you know…" He gestured to the rooms. "Fit."

Robert sipped his water. "It is how we are most comfortable. We tried to keep up with present fashion for a while, and we wear modern clothes when we go into town. This keeps us in touch with who we were when we came here."

"How do you keep them from falling apart?" Damien asked.

"Gentle cycle, gentle soap." Elroy said the words without looking up from his plate.

Jonah chuckled quietly at Elroy's uncharacteristic response.

"You have a washing machine?" Michelle asked.

Robert rose from the table and walked to a closet at the end of the hallway nearest the kitchen. He opened the door, revealing a small, stackable washer and dryer set.

"Would you mind if we used that?" Michelle asked.

"No. In fact, I would encourage you to do so." Robert grinned at Jonah.

Jonah laughed, this time aloud. These guys were capable of humor after all.

****

In addition to the use of the laundry appliances, their relatives had offered the use of their shower. Damien was amazed at how energizing a shower felt after five hot days on the river. He felt like he could conquer the world.

He sat on the front porch while his clothes finished drying, thankful he had one pair of clean shorts to wear while he waited. All of his shirts were dirty, and he'd decided going shirtless for a couple hours wouldn't hurt anything. The cool evening air felt good against his skin.

Michelle joined him on the porch and sat in the chair opposite him. She looked at him without saying anything and smiled before putting her elbow on the arm of the chair and hiding her eyes with her hand.

Damien laughed. "What?"

"You look really good," she said without moving her hand. "Are your shirts almost clean?"

"Wanna go for a walk? I promise, I won't make you look at me."

"Yeah. Let's go." She left the porch and walked towards the river.

He laughed again and ran up beside her, and she glanced up at him.

"Made you look."

She elbowed him. "You don't know how torturous this is."

Oh, I know, he thought. Time to bring this somewhere appropriate. "Have you talked to your husband?"

She shook her head. "I haven't had a signal since around noon, though."

"Let's walk until we find one. I think Jonah walked this way to call Sharon."

"Okay." She took his hand as they walked.

His heart rate tripled. "Is this a good idea?"

"Please. I need this. Okay?"

He couldn't argue with that. "Sure." Gently squeezing her hand, he allowed the energy her touch created to course through him. He closed his eyes for a few moments, trying to absorb the sound and smell of the river and the feel of her skin.

They walked for a few minutes before either of them said anything.

"Did you mean what you said on that first night?" she asked.

"What do you mean? I think I said a lot of things."

She looked up at him. "You said you love me."

He stopped her from walking and faced her, their fingers still intertwined. "Michelle, I love you more than I thought I would ever love another person." He considered continuing but chose to walk again, only making it a few steps before she pulled on his arm to stop him.

She stretched up to reach him, but he closed the remaining inches between them. She released his hand and wrapped her arms around his bare torso as they kissed, and he enveloped her small frame in his arms. All of his senses focused on her: her soft lips, her sweet, clean smell, the sound of her breathing. He lifted her up.

When she pulled back, the running of the river re-entered his consciousness. He sighed and lowered her to her feet.

She took his hand again. "Can I ask you a question?"

Whatever it is, the answer is yes. "Sure."

She resumed their walk. "Mark hasn't returned my calls or texts for three days, and he hasn't even checked on the kids."

"Okay." This wasn't going where he hoped it would go.

"I have a feeling he's gone somewhere, maybe for good. I knew he'd be mad about me leaving, but I never thought he'd ignore the kids like this."

He walked silently.

"If he did leave, and we file for divorce…" She looked at him for a few moments before glancing at the ground. "Never mind. Forget I said anything."

"I would be with you. I'd go wherever you want. I'll help raise your kids. Anything." The words were out of his mouth before he could stop them.

She stopped walking and faced him, her mouth agape. "What?"

He placed his hand on her cheek. “I mean it. I don’t want to just date you. I want to be with you.” Keeping his hand in place, he gently kissed her.

Damien couldn’t get over how much his life had changed since November, and it all started with Alex’s call. Damien had almost turned down the trip or left before opening the safe several times, irritated that Alex’s project took precious time away from work and his life of solitude. If Sharon hadn’t talked him back into the renovated office back at the courthouse, if he’d left her his key and abandoned the group, Damien would never have become attracted to Michelle. He wouldn’t be here now, holding her hand and imagining a future with her, a possibility he hadn’t dared entertain before tonight.

She’d said Mark might have left her. That had to be difficult, but she’d nearly asked Damien to stay with her in the same breath. He was the one she wanted.

I hope Mark doesn’t call.

****

Sharon drove into the small lot on the edge of the town. She parked the car and stepped outside, looking at the river. The sun had risen just an hour earlier, making everything around her glow. She sighed, enjoying the beauty before she remembered why she was here.

She didn’t know when Jonah might arrive. There was a small café across the street; she collected her bag and left the car but paused when she was a few steps from it.

What about the gun?

She could come back if she needed it.

Shaking her head, she stomped towards the café. Why would she need it? The whole idea was ridiculous. So what if the group found more jars? Would she kill all three of them to keep the powder a secret?

She paused with her fingers on the café’s door handle.

Would she?

She tried to push the thought from her mind as she found a table near the window and placed her order. She could watch for Jonah while she ate.

The gun was right there. In her car. Under the driver’s seat.

And no one else knew about it. She grinned at the thought.

She shook her head again. Maybe she should take up hunting, since she seemed to get an odd thrill from shooting people. Shooting animals could have the same effect, and maybe it would take her mind away from the night she killed Dave.

But it wouldn't be the same. Animals were just animals. They weren't capable of making life-altering decisions or consciously acting in a way that could forever change the life of another person. They didn't offer her the same power.

She gasped at the thought and tried to remember the last song that played on the radio in an effort to give her mind something else to do.

After an hour and a half, a man on a motorcycle stopped in the parking lot. He wore a baseball hat instead of a helmet. Sharon didn't recognize him. She kept an eye on him, though, because he got off the bike and examined her car before turning towards the café.

Wait, she did recognize him. She stood, left the café, and approached him. "Jonah?"

He smiled. "Hey, Sharon."

"You cut your hair!" She said the words before she realized they were obvious. "But you probably know that."

He laughed. "Yeah, a little. Are you ready to go?"

She looked at the bike. "On this?"

"Basically." He remounted the bike and started the engine. "There isn't a road to the cabin, and it's not close to here."

The cabin? "Okay." She pulled the strap of her bag over her head so it crossed her body and looked back at the car.

"Did you forget something?"

She couldn't get it now. "No. I have everything. Let's go."

Chapter Eighteen

Michelle sat on the porch, listening to the distant river and glancing at the tent she and the others had set up next to the cabin the previous night. Jonah rode away on the motorcycle about ten minutes ago, but the noise of the engine didn't wake Damien and Chris as it had awakened her. She absorbed the calm around her, knowing her days here were numbered.

Her mind kept flashing back to last night's kiss with Damien. He'd literally lifted her off her feet. His strong arms embracing her told her that as long as he was there, nothing bad would happen to her. She closed her eyes and smiled at the memory, wondering if she should feel guilty about her joy.

Would she feel guilty if Mark knew about Damien? He couldn't know, could he?

It would explain why he hadn't even tried to contact her. It wouldn't explain why he didn't see the kids, though, unless he no longer wanted to see anything that reminded him of her and her disobedience. The kids looked more like her than him, and that could give him reason enough to avoid them, even if it was a despicable reason.

Tired of chasing her thoughts, she stood and walked towards the river. Gao was standing on the dock, facing the water.

When she stood next to him, he looked at her. "Good morning."

"Good morning." She glanced at the river then back to him. "What are you doing?"

"I watch the river. Every morning."

She let a few silent seconds pass before she asked, "Why?"

"It's peaceful."

He was a man of few words, which she could appreciate. Many members of her family seemed to prefer mutual quiet in place of obligatory conversation. She had trouble remembering he was her great-great-grandfather, as he appeared younger than her Uncle Li.

"That man, Elroy's descendant. He is your husband?"

She tried to keep the panic his question caused under the surface. "Um, no. Why do you ask?"

"I saw you. Last night, walking by the river."

She kept her eyes on the water, mortified she'd been caught and unable to find a response.

"You wear a ring. I thought it was…" He paused. "A coincidence."

The fleeting moment she'd considered removing her ring after she arrived in Virginia flashed in her memory. "He's not my husband," was all she could think to say.

"I see."

She felt cornered even though Gao didn't press the issue. Maybe he wanted to see if she would confess to something.

Gao had seen them. There was no use in denying anything. She could go on the defensive and explain her crappy marriage to him, but would that matter? It would have been better for her to divorce Mark first and then pursue a relationship with Damien. But that's not the way it had worked out.

"Do you have children?" Gao's question broke her trance.

His question puzzled her. "Yes. A son and a daughter. Grant is four, and Sophie is five."

He faced her. "You should stay with them." He turned and walked towards the cabin.

She stayed in place, staring at the water.

****

Jonah parked the motorcycle behind the cabin. Sharon climbed off from behind him and seemed to analyze the log walls.

"This is it?" she asked.

"No, this isn't it." He dismounted the bike. "Well, I guess this is part of it. Come on." He led her around the cabin to the front door.

Damien sat on the porch. "Hey, Sharon."

"Hi." She scanned the porch. "Didn't Michelle raft with you?"

"Yeah. She was gone when I woke up. I think she went down to the river."

"Why don't you go look for her? We should probably all be here for… later." Jonah wasn't sure how Sharon would receive the information about the relatives and the multitude of jars. If she was struggling with the kidnapping and shooting, having Michelle and her medical background nearby would be a wise move.

Damien grinned and walked towards the river.

Jonah watched him for a few moments before facing Sharon again. "Let's wait out here for them to get back." He gestured to the seat Damien had vacated.

Sharon looked puzzled. "Is whatever you found out here?"

Jonah shook his head. "It's inside. But I think we should all be here when you find out."

"Why?" She grasped the strap of her bag and twisted it.

Glancing towards the river, Jonah tried to think of an explanation that would keep her out of the cabin. "It's pretty huge, Sharon. I know you can't understand, but you have to trust me. It'll be better if we're all here."

She glanced at the door, then at Jonah, before she opened the door and stomped inside.

"Crap." Jonah rushed to follow her.

Sharon stopped just inside the cabin. Robert sat at the desk and worked at the laptop, and Gao sat at the kitchen table, reading a book and drinking from a cup of coffee. Elroy sat at the table with Gao and stared at the wall. All three men looked at Jonah when he and Sharon entered.

Jonah gestured to the men. "This is Robert, Gao, and Elroy." He turned to the men. "This is Sharon." He locked eyes with Robert. "She's the fourth descendant."

Robert rose from his chair and approached her. He held out his hand in greeting, and she took it. "It's such a pleasure to meet you."

Sharon scrunched her eyebrows and tilted her head.

Robert released her hand and held out his arm to the living room. "Please, make yourself comfortable."

"I'm sorry, what's going on here?" she asked before turning to Jonah. "You found strangers in a cabin in the woods? This is why you called me?"

"It's a long story, Sharon. Let Robert tell you." Jonah glanced towards the closed front door, wondering if Damien had found Michelle.

Sharon sat on the couch, and Robert sat in the chair facing her. "I hear your family originated in Jamestown. That's impressive."

She sat up straighter. "Oh. Yes. We did."

"I have a special interest in history. I'd like to know more about your family, if you don't mind sharing," Robert said.

Sharon maintained a tense posture with her bag still over her shoulder, like she was ready to leave at a moment's notice. "Okay." She told Robert how her family in America originated in Jamestown and described a few later generations. Robert asked follow-up questions, which softened her demeanor. When she told about her great-grandfather, she included her involvement with the group of key-finding descendants but didn't talk about the kidnapping or the jars.

Robert was smart to have her talk about herself and her family first. It would put her at ease and hopefully give Damien and Michelle more time to return. Jonah regretted sending Damien away. He couldn't ignore the nagging in his gut that told him something would go wrong.

"Do you know anything of your great-grandfather, other than his disappearance?" Robert asked.

She scooted closer to the edge of the couch and wrung her hands. "He was a pharmaceutical researcher."

Robert nodded, stood, and walked into the kitchen. Like he had done when Jonah and the others arrived yesterday, he removed the jar from the cabinet.

Jonah felt an urgency he couldn't explain. He wished Damien and Michelle would hurry and get back here; Damien must have left half an hour ago. Jonah cracked open the front door and peered outside. There was no sign of them. He closed the door.

Sharon stood near the couch with her arms crossed, glaring at Robert, who held the jar in front of him.

"Where did you get that?" Her eyes were wide.

"I created it," Robert said.

"That's impossible. My great-grandfather made the powder."

Jonah gave up hope that anyone else from his group would join them. "You're right. Robert, tell her how old you are."

Robert sighed. "One hundred thirty-four."

Sharon rapidly shook her head. "No. I can't… this can't…" She moved her hands near her face and walked towards the front door. Jonah put his hand on her shoulder when she reached him.

"Do you need to sit down?" he asked. Her face had become ghostly white.

"No. Let me go." She pushed past him and left the cabin. He hurried to follow her.

She walked several steps before she turned and walked back towards Jonah. "You're saying those guys are the real ancestors? The ones who buried the box and left us the keys?" She pointed at the cabin.

He stood in place and let her reach him. "Yeah."

"Then how did our families get the keys from them? And there were only three in there. Where's your guy?"

"Please, go back inside. Robert will answer all of your questions." He tipped his head towards the door, hoping she'd listen. He almost told her he was concerned about her but thought it might anger her more.

She shifted her feet and glanced at the cabin before walking towards it.

He exhaled the breath he'd been holding and followed her.

Where the hell are Michelle and Damien?

****

Ten minutes after Damien started looking, he found Michelle sitting on the sloped riverbank downstream from the raft, hidden from immediate view by the native shrubs. He sat next to her. She took his hand and glanced at him before facing the water.

"I have to go home today," she said.

He closed his eyes. Their separation had to happen eventually, but he wished there was a way to prolong the inevitable. He squeezed her hand. "Why?"

"Gao knows about us. And I need to be with my kids." She faced him. "I love you. No matter what happens, I'll never forget this."

His heart raced, but he tried to appear as calm as he'd been before she said those words. He released her hand and opened his arms. "Come here."

She scooted next to him, and he wrapped her in his arms before lying back on the bank. While resting her head on his shoulder, she draped her arm over his chest.

The clouds drifted across the bright, blue sky. Damien watched them as he held Michelle, wishing he could make this moment last forever.

Eventually, he remembered why he was looking for her in the first place. "Sharon's here. Jonah sent me to come find you."

"Hmmm." She breathed deeply.

He closed his eyes and enjoyed her warmth against him before anxiety took hold in his gut.

She wasn't really his, no matter how much he fantasized that she was. She still wore the ring another man had placed on her finger. And she planned to go home today, to return to that man. She could be resting against that man's chest tonight.

He pushed the thought away.

She said she loved him. Those words were all that mattered. He replayed them in his mind as he inhaled the flowery scent of her hair, and when she sighed and moved her hand to his jawline, gently stroking it, his body responded. He closed his eyes in an effort to squelch the urge to roll her onto her back and make love to her the way he'd dreamed of doing, sure she would let him.

"Your heart is pounding," she said.

He took a long breath. "I know." He kissed her forehead, trying to keep his impulses under control. "We should head back. Jonah will wonder what happened to us." He had to force himself to say the words. Everything within him wanted to stay here with her.

She gazed at him for a few silent moments. "Let him wonder." She stretched up and kissed him as she moved her hand into his shirt, tracing the edge of his ribcage with her fingernails and sending chills up his spine to the top of his head. Without releasing their kiss, she lifted herself and covered his body with hers.

He couldn't remember why he'd wanted to leave. Sliding his hands into her shirt, he explored her body as they kissed, feeling as much of her soft skin as he could and tracing every contour he could reach. When his wanting became unbearable, he rolled her onto the grass and retrieved the protection he'd only hoped he'd need from his wallet. They undressed each other just enough to join together and in the minutes that followed, his fantasy morphed into blissful reality.

Afterwards, they held each other on the riverbank as they let their breathing slow. Damien closed his eyes and listened to her, allowing his love for her to wash over him and wondering if he should feel guilty.

His hormones no longer demanding his full attention, the reality of his situation took over.

Michelle would have to face her husband eventually. Even if Damien didn't feel guilty, she might, She'd made a promise to that man to be his, forever. Damien couldn't even begin to guess what was going through her mind.

"Are you okay?" he asked.

She lifted herself to face him. "I'm more than okay. Why wouldn't I be?"

He wasn't sure he wanted to know how her husband fit into this, but he had to know, for her sake. "Just… you'll have to go home to him, after this. I know that won't be easy."

She kissed him. "Don't worry about me. I can handle it. I don't think my marriage was supposed to happen. You're the one I want to be with."

"So you'll ask for the divorce?" He tried to keep his excitement from being too obvious.

She nodded. "If Mark doesn't. It'll probably be ugly. I hope he can be civil, for the kids."

Damien swallowed, hoping she was wrong about the divorce being ugly. Maybe her husband would just surrender, if he knew he couldn't control Michelle any longer. Damien didn't want to be the reason for one of those nightmarish divorce cases he'd heard about on the news.

But he had to face the truth: even if the divorce went smoothly, he *was* the reason for it. Michelle's marriage wasn't healthy and possibly would have ended eventually, but Damien's actions certainly hastened its decline. They hadn't done anything the way they should until now, but that didn't mean they couldn't change course a little.

Michelle had rested her head against his chest again and sounded like she might have fallen asleep. "Michelle?"

"Hmm?"

"I don't…" He sighed, trying to figure out how to form the words he needed. "I love that we did this, and I love you more than I can tell you. But I don't want to do this again until we can be together freely."

She sat up, wrapped her arms around her knees, and twisted around to see him. "You're right. I don't want to hide anymore."

He sat up and kissed her one last time before they stood and adjusted their clothing.

Of all the choices he'd made in the last week, this one felt the most right. The next time they came together, there would be nothing scandalous about it.

They walked towards the cabin, and when it came into view, Damien released Michelle's hand.

Sharon was yelling at Jonah while pointing at the cabin. Jonah said something to her, and she stomped through the cabin door. He followed her.

"What's going on here?" Damien quickened his pace towards them.

****

Sharon re-entered the cabin at Jonah's insistence, feeling like she'd entered a crazy dream since he picked her up on that motorcycle.

The others must be fools to think these men in the forest could really be their ancestors. Someone must have been tracking their phone calls to create such a ruse. They even had a jar of powder identical to the one she pulled from the safe.

Jonah entered a few moments later, followed by Damien and Michelle, who smiled at her. Sharon didn't have it in her to make pleasantries. She wanted answers.

Robert sat in the desk chair. He'd place the jar on the desk, like it belonged there. If this was real, he'd know what the powder did and not leave it sitting just anywhere.

"I'm pleased you came back," he said.

"How did you get the keys to our families, if you all left New York to come here?" She dropped to her place on the couch, eager to start poking holes in Robert's story. Jonah sat on the opposite end of it, and Damien and Michelle stood by the door.

"We mailed the keys with instructions to keep them safe and to pass them down through the generations until our descendants knew what to do with them." Robert looked at Jonah. "I must say, we didn't predict it would be successful."

Sharon clenched her jaw, refusing to believe this man's story. He could have deduced the key story by listening to a phone conversation, or maybe he was working with Alex. "Do you even know what that powder does?"

"I created it. I know what it does."

Sharon looked at the other three descendants, sure they didn't know what it did. They weren't about to find out, either, because there was no way this man knew. She couldn't wait to call him on his bluff. "Tell me."

Robert clasped his hands in front of him. "You must understand; the world was very different when I created this powder." He told her its effect on fertility and aging and his tie to the eugenics movement.

Panic rose from her gut. Everyone in the room knew the secret she'd kept since Dave told her about it, the secret she'd killed to keep. The added piece about slowed aging did little to quell her anxiety. She simply couldn't accept that Robert was her great-grandfather, or that any of this was real.

She could no longer make sense of his words. They sounded muffled, like he spoke into a pillow. The people in front of her vanished. She stood, paced near the couch, and whispered to herself. "Can't be, it's all wrong, they can't know, they can't, it's not right…"

She startled when someone placed a hand on her arm. It was Robert's hand. "Are you okay, dear?"

She stormed away from him and out the front door, shoving Damien and Michelle out of the way. She had to get to her car. To her gun. She'd make Robert take it all back and tell her the truth, whatever truth didn't involve a horrible Nazi powder.

She walked on the grassy bank of the river. Following the river would take her back to her car.

Get to the car. Just get to the car.

Someone approached from behind her. She glanced back but didn't stop walking. Jonah caught up a moment later.

"What's going on? What's wrong?" He kept up with her quickened pace.

"Everything. It's all wrong. All of it. You shouldn't know anything. You shouldn't be here."

Jonah ran in front of her and grabbed her shoulders. "Sharon, stop!"

His yell made her stop walking. She shook her head. "Let me go. I have to go."

"You're not okay. Come back to the cabin."

"No! I need to get back to my car!" She wriggled from his grasp and continued her walk.

He left her. A few minutes later, he pulled up next to her on the motorcycle. "Get on. I'll give you a ride."

She stared at him as she continued walking towards the town. She didn't need his help. Jonah left the bike next to the river and walked behind her.

"Leave me alone, Jonah."

He kept following her.

Maybe there was a reason he was the last person she shot in her dream.

Chapter Nineteen

"Has she always behaved that way?" Robert asked as they stood on the porch and watched Sharon and Jonah walk away from them.

"No. Something's wrong." Michelle tried to piece together what had happened inside. Sharon seemed to have pulled inside her own head, pacing and chanting nonsensical words, like she'd lost sense of where she was. When Michelle was in nursing school, she'd seen similar behaviors, usually from people detoxing or who had experienced an emotional trauma. She doubted Sharon was on drugs, so trauma was the more likely culprit; Sharon must have had trouble coping with the kidnapping and shooting. Michelle wished she'd done a better job of connecting with her. "I hope Jonah can talk her into coming back."

"What do you think happened to her?" Damien asked.

"I don't know. She didn't get upset until she saw the powder. I don't think she's been telling us the truth." Michelle sighed. "It's a good thing she didn't see all those jars in the storm cellar." If seeing one jar made Sharon react the way she did, what effect would seeing over a hundred jars have?

Damien leaned on the rail. "What do you think she lied about?"

"About destroying the powder. Her story never made sense. I think she told us that so we wouldn't look for it." She turned to Robert. "The man back in Richmond, the one who took Sharon, seemed to know what it was. Do you know why?"

"Yes." Robert put his hands in his pockets and focused on the ground. "When we mailed the keys to our families, I also mailed a letter to my former employer." He closed his eyes and shook his head.

Michelle had a talent for getting these men to dig up their past regrets. In this case, she needed him to keep digging. "What was the letter about?"

"I boasted about how I'd taken Deinix from under their noses, and I shamed them for wanting to eliminate entire populations. I told them I hid a jar somewhere in Richmond, but they would never know where. I said when the jar was discovered by our descendants, the true nature of their atrocities would be revealed."

"Couldn't the company have made more of it? Weren't there papers with the formula?" Damien asked.

"No. Fortunately, electronic tracking did not exist then. I was able to take everything related to Deinix rather easily. I also left some paperwork containing false formulas."

"So why did you send the letter? You could have just left, and they wouldn't have known where to look for you or for the powder," Michelle said.

"I wanted to make them fear justice, even if the safe was never discovered. It was my way to make amends for creating the medication in the first place." He shook his head. "I never imagined they would station people in Richmond for countless years, waiting to take the jar."

Damien faced Robert. "It's worth millions to them. It makes sense that they wouldn't give up on it."

Robert nodded. "It's a fact I should have realized. And now you and your families may all be in danger."

"What do you mean?" Michelle held her necklace; hearing someone else say aloud what she'd feared – that a company could come after her children – almost sent her into a panic. She kept her anxiety buried so Robert would continue talking.

Robert walked to the patio chairs and sat in the one nearest the front door. Michelle followed and sat in the other chair, and Damien leaned against the rail behind her. She resisted the urge to look at him and take his hand, though doing so after she'd given herself to him was ridiculous. Their relationship felt like universal knowledge now, and she had to remind herself that they technically still had to hide it.

Robert continued his explanation. "If the company finds out Sharon has been hiding Deinix, they will come after her. If the man she killed worked for my company, as I suspect, they will likely know where to find her." He sighed. "And they may connect you to her."

He silently stared in the direction Sharon and Jonah had walked.

"I'm so sorry we left that jar in Richmond. You were better off not knowing about it." Robert stood and entered the cabin.

Michelle watched him until he was out of sight, then she looked at Damien.

He locked eyes with her. "I'm not sorry they hid the jar."

Aware of Damien's meaning, Michelle grinned, though the images of her children's faces flashed in her mind. She hoped Robert was wrong about the company coming after her and her family, but she started brainstorming places she could take the kids, just in case.

****

Jonah followed Sharon on the grassy riverbank for at least an hour before she stopped for a break. She stood in place, bent over with her hands on her thighs, and took slow breaths. Her endurance amazed him. He wished he had a water bottle to give her.

Nothing she'd done since arriving at the cabin made sense, and Jonah used the walking time trying to figure out her behavior. Perhaps Dave did something to her, something that shamed her enough to never talk about it. But she'd flipped out when Robert told her what the powder did: there was something about that powder that pushed her to the edge of her sanity.

She resumed her walk, though at a slower pace, and she surprised Jonah by snapping around and stomping towards him. "Why are you still here?"

He didn't move. "I'm not leaving you like this."

"Why not? I killed a man, remember?" Her shouting echoed across the quiet landscape.

"No one thinks you did anything wrong."

She turned away from him. “Yeah, *I* didn’t do anything wrong.” She continued walking. “To think I was protecting him.”

What did that mean?

They walked in silence, Jonah behind Sharon, for another hour. Jonah felt a little tired, but Sharon developed a limp that grew steadily worse as she walked. Finally, the town came into view. Sharon picked up her pace in spite of her limp.

She approached her car and retrieved keys from her bag. Jonah quickened his pace to catch up to her before she reached the car. “Let me drive. I’ll take you somewhere to get help.”

She unlocked the door, fell into the driver’s seat, shut the door, and leaned forward, like she was reaching for something under the seat. After a few moments, she sat up again, looked at Jonah, and drove away.

He looked at the license plate: Indiana.

At least he knew where she was going.

****

“Where did Robert go? I can’t find him inside.” Damien joined Michelle on the porch, where she’d stayed since Sharon and Jonah left almost three hours ago.

“He took the motorcycle to look for them. I think he’s upset that Sharon wasn’t more…” Her eyes narrowed.

“Stable?”

“Yeah. Maybe. Are you worried about what Robert said? About the drug company coming after us?”

“Not really. I think they would have done something by now.” In spite of his words, Damien found himself worrying about Michelle and her kids. He started thinking of places he could take them, if the company became a danger.

“I wish I knew what happened to her. She changed after Dave kidnapped her.”

Damien sat in the chair across from her. “Maybe she didn’t, though. We only knew her for a day before that.”

Michelle seemed to think about it and shook her head. “She was friendly when we met. She talked about her grandkids and wondered who was watching my kids. I’d like to think I’m a good judge of character.” She laughed.

“What’s so funny?”

"The second I said 'good judge of character', I remembered what I first thought of Jonah."

Damien grinned, remembering how he thought Jonah was a drug user at first sight. Now, he envied Jonah's life.

The sound of an approaching motor intruded on their conversation. Robert drove the motorcycle with Jonah sitting on the seat behind him.

Where was Sharon?

As soon as Robert stopped the bike, Jonah hopped off and stomped to the cabin. "She's going to Indiana. Probably back to her brother's house."

"She told you that?" Michelle asked.

Jonah entered the cabin, looked around it, then walked back out. "Where's Chris?"

"Down at the raft, I think," Damien said.

Jonah walked towards the river. Michelle and Damien followed.

"What's going on?" Michelle asked.

"We have to find her. She said something about protecting Robert. I think she has more of that powder, and something made her snap."

"So what if she has more powder? She's obviously been hiding it. She won't start telling people about it now," Damien said.

Jonah stopped walking and faced him. "Haven't you been thinking about this? It basically makes people immortal, and anyone who wants something with that kind of power certainly shouldn't have it. They would decide who lives or dies. Do you want that responsibility?"

Damien didn't have an answer.

"And what if Sharon decides who gets it? If she sells it or gives it to the wrong people, it would be a disaster." Jonah resumed his walk towards the river.

"Sharon wanted to keep it a secret, if she lied about destroying it," Michelle said.

"Exactly. Why would she do that? I think she wants the control. Maybe she was keeping it until we figured out what it did. She couldn't have known about the anti-aging part of it, but she does now. We need to get the powder and make sure Robert has it all. We know he won't do anything dangerous with it."

The raft came into view. Chris lay inside it, reading. He looked up when they approached.

"We have to leave. We'll take the motorcycle back to get your car. Grab your bag." Jonah turned to Damien and Michelle. "You two wait here. We'll be back this evening. Chris can drop us off by Michelle's rental car. We'll take that to Indiana."

"Do you remember where her brother lives?" Damien asked.

Jonah scowled. "Not exactly. When I have a signal, I'll call Alex and get an address."

****

When she reached West Virginia, the speedometer showed twenty over the speed limit. Sharon let up on the gas pedal and shifted in her seat to relieve the aching in her hip. That damn walk hadn't done her joints any good, but what choice did she have? She couldn't allow Jonah to give her a ride on the motorcycle. He was working with Robert, who certainly couldn't be trusted.

She couldn't make herself believe Robert's story, though it did explain why the ancestors disappeared. But why would Michelle's and Damien's ancestors hide out with him, if Robert had all but destroyed their families? Had he threatened them?

Michelle and Damien were lucky to have been born.

To think the man she'd blamed for blemishing her family's legacy – a man she'd thought was dead – was alive and youthful was too much for her mind to handle. If he was who he claimed to be, he didn't match the mental image Sharon had created of him. He was kind, articulate, and obviously intelligent. He didn't seem to harbor a desire to harm anyone – something she couldn't say about herself.

She glanced at her bag, where she'd placed the gun after she nearly pulled it on Jonah. Her heart beat so quickly in that moment she'd thought it might stop.

What made her leave it under the seat? That adrenaline rush she felt when she shot Dave returned when she wrapped her fingers around the barrel and slid the weapon out to her feet. What would it have felt like to raise the weapon, to see the shock on Jonah's face?

Jonah had stood outside her car, watching. He must have seen her reach for it, but he had no idea what she was reaching for. She could have so easily aimed it, and – pow.

She smirked, then shook her head, disgusted with herself.

In an effort to refocus her energy, she tried to remember her life before Dave kidnapped her. She'd donated money to help the poor. She'd volunteered at the local blood bank. She'd recycled. She wouldn't have dreamed of taking someone's life to protect a secret – or because she liked the power it gave her. Her life had been a simple one; some would say it was unremarkable. But it had worked for her.

She wished she could remember what her old life felt like.

Chapter Twenty

He wasn't at the house. His car was gone last night.

Michelle's mother's words echoed through her mind. She stood in the field where she'd found cell reception, staring at her phone and wishing Mark would answer just one of her calls. Where on earth was he? And what was he doing? Hiring a divorce attorney? Drinking himself to death? The few fleeting thoughts she'd had during the first days of this trip came rushing back – thoughts of running back to him and begging for forgiveness, as she had done after many of her prior offenses.

She scrunched her nose in disgust.

Before she met Damien, she'd wanted to keep the family complete for the children. Even if Mark was upset for something ridiculous, she'd claim responsibility to keep him from leaving, as he threatened to do so many times. Because of the children, she'd thought having him around was preferable to separating, no matter how unhappy she was or what kind of example he set for the kids.

Her nagging worry returned: would it be preferable for Grant to become the kind of man Mark was, or for Sophie to marry someone like him?

It had taken a century-old mystery and an affair for her to make up her mind. She should have never married Mark, but it wasn't too late to do something about it. She'd wanted to go home that day, get the kids, and start planning how to support them on her own, but she decided to stay at the cabin after Sharon stormed off. She didn't feel right leaving Jonah and Damien behind to deal with Sharon on their own.

She walked back to the cabin and found Robert sitting in one of the chairs on the porch. He leaned forward with his elbows on his knees, looking towards Michelle but not at her, like he was lost in thought.

She sat in the adjacent chair, anxious for him to start a conversation.

"You and Gao have much in common," he said after several silent minutes.

That was the last thing she thought he'd say. "You think so?"

"Yes. You have similar mannerisms and expressions, including the way you sat next to me and waited for me to speak. Gao often does that. I must remind myself that you and he have only just met."

"Huh." She listened to the silence for a few moments before continuing. "I'm sorry about what happened with Sharon."

He expressed a long sigh. "I suppose I shouldn't be surprised. What we told her must have been quite a shock."

"You told us the same thing, though." She almost said something about how they hadn't lost their composure but thought better of it. The man seemed disturbed enough about his great-granddaughter's behavior.

"We should have come here without hiding Deinix in the safe. It would have been better for you all to remain unaware of our truth."

She tried not to think about his warning. "I don't know about that." She remembered her life before Alex's call. "It's probably the coolest thing that's happened to me. How many people can say they've visited with 130-year-old men?"

He chuckled. "Everyone in the town could say that, if they knew."

"How does that work? Don't people figure out after a while that you don't age?"

He shook his head. "We move. When I drew the map, I only had the river in mind. We built our first cabin on the northeast side of the river in the southern part of Virginia. Every thirty years or so, we moved upstream and found a place to build on the northeast side, in case our descendants came looking for us."

She remembered something. "The guys found an abandoned cabin right after they started rafting. Was that yours?"

"I can't say for sure. What did it look like?"

"I didn't see it. Damien said the roof was caved in and it had furniture inside from the fifties."

Robert smiled. "Yes, I believe that was ours. It's a shame it's fallen into that condition. We've built these cabins ourselves, adding modern amenities as we go along, of course. No sense in living like rustics."

She laughed. "But why go to all that trouble? You said you didn't think leaving the keys would work. You could have moved anywhere and bought houses."

"It was important to keep hoping you would find us, for Gao more than for me and Elroy, I believe. He struggled the most with leaving his family. He needed the possibility that our relatives would find us one day."

Robert's words struck Michelle as odd, since Gao hadn't spoken much to her since they arrived. "Maybe I should go talk to him."

"It's a good idea. You and the others will be leaving soon. It will likely be your last chance."

Michelle stood and entered the cabin. Gao was sleeping on the couch.

She approached him, and the floor creaked. He stirred and looked at her.

"Can we go for a walk?" she asked.

He squinted. "What for?"

"I want to tell you about our family."

He shook his head rapidly. "No, I don't need to know –"

"I have to leave soon. I'd like to know more about you, and I want to tell you about your great-great-great grandchildren."

He grinned, rose from the couch, walked to the front door, and held it open for her.

****

"Alex, it's Jonah Ward." He'd stopped the motorcycle in the first town he and Chris reached to make the call.

"Jonah? I wasn't expecting to hear from you."

"Yeah, I know. Listen, I need a favor." He told Alex about Sharon's erratic behavior and his theory about her hiding the jar from the safe but not about the other jars or the ancestors. "We need to know where her brother lives. Do you have his address?"

"I do. Hold on."

Jonah waited for a few minutes before Alex came back on the line. "Okay, do you have something to write on?"

That would have been a good thing to look for while he was waiting. "Um, yeah. Hold on a sec." He hopped off the bike and grabbed a stick. "Go ahead."

Alex recited the address, and Jonah wrote it in the dirt with the stick.

"I'll head out there too, if you think she still has the jar. I can be there tomorrow," Alex said.

Jonah silently groaned. He'd hoped Alex would let him handle Sharon and stay out of it. "All right. See you then." Jonah disconnected and opened the map application on his phone to enter Larry's address.

Sharon would be surprised to see Alex arrive at her brother's house, especially if he beat Jonah and the others there.

Would Alex want to take the jar with him? He'd sounded excited when Jonah told him the powder wasn't destroyed. Maybe he just wanted it for historical purposes.

Jonah doubted it was that simple. Alex would want to identify the powder; it wouldn't make sense to lock it away, still a mystery to him. What if he found out everything the powder did? Alex liked to make up stories about documentaries to get people to do what he wanted – did that relatively minor lie mean he couldn't be trusted with something this huge?

Jonah shook his head and finished entering the address into his phone as he regretted calling Alex.

****

By the time Jonah and Chris returned to the cabin that evening, Jonah on the motorcycle and Chris in his 4Runner, Damien had packed up the tent, deflated the raft, and had all their supplies ready to go. Michelle and Gao had left hours ago, and since Elroy didn't want to talk to him, Damien needed a way to pass the time.

After the group finished loading the 4Runner, Damien found Elroy sitting by the river. Though his past interactions with the man had been contentious, it didn't feel right to leave without saying goodbye.

Damien stood behind Elroy and cleared his throat.

Elroy twisted around."You about ready to leave?"

Damien nodded and sat next to him. "Can I ask you a question?"

Elroy scoffed. "Sure. Go for it."

"What should I tell our family? About you?"

"Tell 'em you didn't find anything." He picked up the nearest rock and threw it into the river.

Damien watched the resulting splash. "How can I do that?"

Elroy scowled at Damien. "Look, boy. Tell 'em what you want. Tell 'em you found me alive in Virginia. See how that goes over." He tossed another rock.

Good point. "Maybe you can come back with me. We'll bring some of the powder and tell them the truth."

Elroy laughed. "Shit, and I thought you were smart." He faced Damien. "We agreed a long time ago that Deinix would have to die with us. Can you imagine if some moron gets hold of it and sells it for millions? Suddenly the government or whoever decides who gets to live for a thousand years. And I bet it would be the rich assholes who would get it. I don't want any part of that."

"What about giving it to a hospital that treats sick kids? I don't think anyone would argue with that."

"You got the wrong idea. It just slows aging. We could still die of infection or somethin'. Gao almost died of the flu back in '57. It won't help sick kids."

"So why are Robert and Gao still taking it, if they won't do anything with it?"

Elroy shrugged. "Damned if I know."

"What about you? Will you ever start taking it again? I mean, things have changed since '68."

Elroy glared at Damien. "No. I'm done. I'm not doing anythin' worth stickin' around for that long."

Damien nodded, stood, and waited for Elroy to do the same. He didn't.

"Well, I need to go. Everyone's waiting for me." Damien stood in place.

Elroy looked up and casually saluted.

Damien waited a few seconds more before walking away. He hadn't received so much as a handshake from the man.

It seemed bitter and distant was how the men in his family wanted to live. Though his father wasn't related to Elroy, both men had similar attitudes about the world. Until four months ago, Damien was on the same path.

Damien walked to the car, vowing to set a different example for his future sons.

****

On the way back to Indiana, Sharon decided there was one way to end the nightmare that began when she pulled the second jar from the safe. One way to feel like her former, sane self. She had to flush away all of the powder at Larry's house. She wouldn't feel compelled to protect it any longer, and she could pretend there weren't any jars or ancestors in Virginia. They'd hidden from society for a century. Why would they make themselves known now?

Once she arrived at the house, though, she stashed the gun in the nightstand and collapsed onto her bed, letting her exhaustion overtake her. After driving fourteen hours in a day with a long walk in between, she decided the powder could wait until the next day to be flushed.

After what felt like a few minutes, a knock on the front door woke her.

She opened her eyes; she'd been asleep for more than a few minutes. The orange sunrise invaded her room through the windows. It was too early for visitors. Maybe she'd dreamt the knock.

Two more knocks sounded. She sighed and rose from her bed.

She met Larry in the hallway. "When did you get back?" he asked.

"Last night. Late." She led the way down the stairs and peered through the peep hole. A slightly overweight man with short, brown hair and glasses stood on the porch. "Alex?" She opened the door enough to poke her head out.

"Hi Sharon. Are you doing okay?"

"What are you doing here?" She scowled at him and didn't let him in.

"Jonah called me yesterday." He stretched up, as if he wanted to see over her. "I apologize for arriving so early. Can I come in?"

"Last time you were involved in my life, I was kidnapped at gunpoint." She was past any use for manners and started to shut the door in Alex's face.

"Wait, Sharon, I had nothing to do with–"

"Geez, Shar, what's the matter with you? He drove the other three here looking for you that night. Would he do that if he was dangerous?" Larry said from behind her before she had the door shut all the way.

"But he could–"

"I didn't know about Dave, Sharon. I feel terrible about what happened. Let me try to make it right," Alex said.

Sharon glared at him. Why did Jonah call him? What did he know? She stepped back and let him enter, only because she wanted answers to her questions.

Larry led Alex to the kitchen and started a pot of coffee. Sharon and Alex sat at the table as Alex began explaining. "Jonah was concerned about you. That's why I came here. I knew I would get here before they could."

It was a ten-hour drive from Richmond to Larry's house; the drive took seven hours from the cabin. Maybe he was counting on the time the group needed to pack the rafting supplies. "So they should be here any time, right?" she asked.

"I think so."

"What else did Jonah tell you?"

Alex stared at her for a few moments. "I'd rather talk to you about that when they get here."

Jonah must have told him about her nervous breakdown. She shook her leg under the table, wondering if Jonah also told him about the powder and the still-living ancestors. Nothing about Alex's presence felt right. "I think you should leave."

Alex's mouth hung open for a second before he responded. "I thought we'd discussed this already."

"This has nothing to do with you. They'll be here soon. You don't need to be here. I think you should leave."

"It has nothing to do with me? I'm the one who started all this. If I hadn't called you–"

"If you hadn't called me, there wouldn't be a life-destroying powder out there, I wouldn't have been kidnapped, and I wouldn't have killed a man!"

Larry turned and faced her from the kitchen. "Shar, stop it." He placed slices of banana bread in front of her and Alex. "Let's pretend we're having a normal breakfast with a guest. Okay? You mind? Everyone knows about this guy but me. I'd like to find out."

Sharon spent the next hour watching Alex and Larry make small talk over coffee and Josephine's banana bread; the real purpose for Alex's visit remained an unspoken undercurrent. She started to wonder if the others would ever show up and help her remove Alex from the situation, since Larry wouldn't. Finally, another knock sounded from the front door.

Larry answered it and escorted Michelle, Damien, Jonah, and Robert into the kitchen.

Robert?

Sharon stood. "What are you doing here?" Robert wore jeans and a green button-down shirt, unlike the old clothes she'd seen him wear earlier. He could have been any middle-aged guy off the street and not her 134-year-old great-grandfather.

Robert approached her. "I didn't like the way you left yesterday. I feel responsible for what happened, and I want to make sure you're all right."

She took a few steps back but kept her eyes on him.

"Can we sit down?" Jonah asked.

"Yeah, please." Larry gestured, and he offered coffee to the guests.

They sat around the table, and Sharon eventually joined them. Everything about this felt wrong. She kept her eyes on Robert and didn't touch her coffee or bread again.

Alex reached a hand across the table towards Robert. "I'm Alex."

"Robert. Pleasure to meet you. You must be the historian."

They shook hands. Sharon pinched her arm to make sure she wasn't dreaming.

"I am. What is your connection to the group, if you don't mind my asking?" Alex asked.

Sharon held her breath.

"Well, you could say I'm a fellow historian. I write history books. These young people encountered me as they were searching for information relating to a map they found in a safe in a Richmond courthouse."

What was Robert getting at? He must know that Alex was behind the whole safe-opening operation. Sharon squinted at the men.

Alex looked at Jonah. "Oh yes, I was hoping you still had the map. To be honest, I forgot about it after the powder was destroyed. I'm a little embarrassed to say so."

Robert chuckled. "Do you know about the powder, then?"

"I wish I did. We traced Dave's information back to a drug company in New York, so I think the powder was connected to that." He picked at his bread. "I wish we had just a little of it, so we could have it analyzed."

Sharon stared at her bread, willing the men to stop talking.

"I know I asked you this before, Sharon, but did Dave say anything to you about the powder? Maybe you've remembered something since then?" Alex asked.

She looked up. "Oh. No. He didn't." Her focus returned to her bread.

"You said you found the first jar here. Do you mind if we look around where you found it, in case there's more powder here that you aren't aware of?"

Why was Alex being so pushy? Sharon had to concentrate on her breathing to hide her panic. If she agreed, they might find the jars. If she protested, they would know she'd been lying since January.

A chair scooted on the linoleum, bringing Sharon's attention back to Alex, who left the table. He turned to Larry, who leaned against the kitchen counter. "May we look around, in case Sharon missed something? This may be our only chance to learn the truth."

Larry looked at her but asked Alex, "You know what the powder does?"

"No. I don't think anyone knows." He turned to Robert. "Do you?"

"Stop! Everyone stop talking!" Sharon bolted up from her seat, banging the table with her leg and spilling her coffee in the process.

Everyone stared at her.

"No one's looking around. For anything. Got it?" She glared at Larry.

Jonah held out a hand towards her. "Sharon, you don't know what else–"

"Shut up, Jonah! Your guy shouldn't have even had a key! You shouldn't be here!" She faced the other side of the table, where Damien and Michelle sat next to each other. "And aren't you two pissed off that this guy," she pointed at Robert, "irreparably damaged your families?"

"That guy is your family," Michelle said.

"Your family? What does she mean?" Larry asked.

Sharon's mind was spinning. No single thought landed long enough for her to voice it. "No! Stop! Just… leave. I have to leave." She stomped away from the table, up the stairs, entered her room, and slammed the door.

Chapter Twenty-One

Michelle followed Larry and the others into the basement, which was cleaner and brighter than she'd expected. It wasn't finished, but long, fluorescent lights ran down the middle of the ceiling, illuminating the concrete walls and floor. Open shelving containing a variety of objects filled most of the space. A cookie jar shaped like a tan cat caught her eye. It was just like her grandmother's.

"These have been nothin' but trouble since Sharon shot that guy. I'm happy to get them out of here." Larry led the group between the shelves to a stack of boxes on the opposite wall. "She'll never forgive me, but," he sighed, "she hasn't been herself."

He moved four boxes and reached the bottom of the stack. He picked up a cardboard box slightly smaller than a laundry basket and taped closed.

He set the box in an empty space on one of the shelves, pulled a small knife from his pocket, flicked it open, and ran the blade along the tape.

Michelle held her breath when he removed the gallon-sized jars from the box and set them on the shelf. The cause of Sharon's unraveling was now on display before them.

"Okay. I showed you where the jars were. Now, tell me what you meant about this guy being my family." Larry gestured to Robert, who stood next to him, while looking at Michelle through the shelves.

Michelle glanced at Robert, who peered over the jars at Alex. "Would you mind waiting for us upstairs?"

Alex scowled. "Why should I do that? Can I not hear this?"

"It is a personal matter."

Alex reached through the shelves and grabbed both jars, holding one in each arm. "Actually, I do mind. If it weren't for me, you wouldn't have any of this." Pushing his way past Michelle, he backed away from the group and towards the stairs.

Larry walked in the same direction on the other side of the shelves.

Jonah squeezed himself between Michelle and shelving, moving towards Alex. "What the hell do you think you're doing?"

Alex turned and darted to the staircase. Larry reached it a second after Alex and grabbed his shoulder. Alex twisted back and elbowed Larry in the nose, sending a disturbing crunch into the room. Alex ran up the stairs and shut the door behind him. A scooting sound, like furniture on linoleum, came through the door.

Larry cupped his bleeding nose with both hands. Jonah, Damien, and Robert ran up the stairs.

Jonah tried the door. "He put something in front of it." He pressed his shoulder into the door and shoved until he moved whatever blocked it.

Michelle stayed at the stairs' base to tend to Larry.

"No! Go get him! Before he drives off!" Larry said through his hands.

She was sure his nose was broken, but she didn't argue with him. She ran up the stairs.

****

"Come on! We can catch up to him!" Jonah fell into the back seat of Michelle's rental car, frustrated at the sight of Alex's silver Camry disappearing down the street. He'd almost caught up to Alex before he got to his car. Jonah cursed at himself for not figuring out a way to keep Alex from going into the basement with them.

Damien and Robert followed close behind Jonah. Robert joined him in the back seat, while Damien reclaimed his place in the passenger seat. A minute later, Michelle left the house. Sharon was with her.

Jonah groaned. The loose ends that insisted on complicating what should have been the simple task of getting the jars from Larry's house kept multiplying. Who could tell what Alex would do with the powder? And if they managed to get it back, what would Sharon do? For half a second, Jonah wondered if Michelle's medical background gave her access to tranquilizer darts.

After Robert squeezed into the middle of the back seat, Sharon joined them. She clutched her purse on her lap like she was worried it could escape.

Michelle started the engine and pulled out of the driveway as soon as Sharon closed the door. She reached an intersection before asking, "Which way should I go?"

"Go back towards the interstate. He's either going to Richmond or New York." Jonah focused on the rushing traffic, seeing an upcoming break.

"New York? Why there?" Michelle turned left onto the busy street.

"I don't think he'd steal it to keep it locked in a display case in Richmond. I'll bet he's going to Dave's company." Jonah leaned slightly over Robert and looked for Alex's car through the windshield.

"But he doesn't know what the powder does. We made a point of not telling him." Michelle shifted into the left lane and passed a slow truck.

On the way to Indiana, Jonah and the others had discussed how much to say in front of Alex once they arrived at Larry's house. They'd agreed to say as little as possible, though that became trickier when Larry led them to the basement. Maybe Jonah should have punched Alex's lights out, like he'd wanted to do since January. It would have solved a lot of problems.

"He said they tracked Dave to the drug company. They might have told him why Dave wanted the powder and offered him something for it," Damien said. He pulled his phone from his pocket. "I'll try to track down Bonnie. Maybe she can give us an address."

"Bonnie's working with Alex. How can we trust her?" Michelle asked.

"Look up Flag Pharmaceuticals. The name of my company hasn't changed," Robert said.

"Should we call the cops? We can report this as a robbery," Michelle said.

Jonah shook his head. "They'll take the jars if we do that. They might think it's drugs or something."

"He's right." Damien searched on his phone. "I'll get an address for the company."

Sharon stared at the back of the driver's seat. Jonah wondered if she would jump out of the car. He wouldn't have put it past her after her behavior at the river and at Larry's house.

"I see Alex's car." Michelle jerked into the right lane and accelerated past three cars. She positioned her car behind the Subaru that was behind Alex's Camry. Damien entered an address into the dash GPS.

She followed Alex's car for five minutes, but Alex must have noticed because he pulled into the left lane and accelerated.

"Crap." She changed lanes and followed. Jonah glanced at the speedometer: after twenty seconds, she was twenty-five over the limit. She clenched the wheel in her fists, and the engine screamed in response until it finally shifted. Jonah pulled on his seatbelt to make sure it caught.

After weaving through traffic while racing towards the interstate for ten minutes, Alex slowed, though they still traveled fifteen over the limit.

Michelle checked the rear-view mirror. "Dammit!" She pulled over.

Jonah looked out the back window to see why. The cop car stopped behind Michelle's.

The state patrolman approached Michelle's window as Alex's Camry shrank in the distance.

****

Damien focused out the windshield, willing Alex's car to get a flat tire, until the car was out of sight. After the cop took Michelle's papers and walked back to his car, Damien glanced at her, and she locked eyes with him. He wished he could take her hand.

By the time the officer finished writing Michelle's ticket and let them leave, Alex was long gone.

Michelle accelerated onto the highway, though she maintained a slower speed.

Sharon broke the silence that followed. "We should just let him have the jars."

Damien twisted around. Sharon stared straight ahead at the driver's seat and hugged her purse against her body. Her demeanor was cold, almost robotic.

"Why should we do that?" Jonah asked.

"It doesn't matter now. Everyone will know." She kept her attention on the seat.

"Everyone will know what?"

"What the powder does. And that Robert made it." She looked at Robert. "How could you?"

"I'm sorry?" Robert leaned away from her, invading Jonah's space in the small back seat.

"Do you have any idea what our family has done? Over centuries? We came from Jamestown! What you've done tarnishes our entire legacy!"

Robert sighed. "You believe I created Deinix with malicious intent." He shook his head.

"Why else would you have created it? The whole point was to keep people from having kids when they wanted them! Did you choose which groups to target?" Sharon's eyes were wide, like she was trying to impale Robert's skull with them.

"I believed I was creating it for people who wanted to control the size of their families purposefully, much like the hormonal methods of birth control today. My company and the government perverted Deinix's use. By the time the trials started, I was too involved. They said if I left the company or told anyone about the targeted groups, my family would be in danger." He didn't look away from the windshield.

"That's why you left," Damien said.

Robert turned to Damien. "Yes. I sent my family to live with my wife's sister in Pennsylvania, and I left in the middle of the night." He looked at his lap. "Gao and Elroy suffered greatly from the powder's effects. They told me personally. I offered them the chance to create a new legacy. If we knew how long the powder allowed us to live, we could use that knowledge to benefit mankind. I loaded all the Deinix I'd created until then into a buggy

– twenty jars – along with all of my notes and paperwork related to it. I met Gao and Elroy in front of a grocery.

"We didn't have a plan until we reached Richmond. Gao saw the courthouse under construction and shared his idea of hiding a jar for our families to find." Robert faced Jonah. "We would not have been able to do it without William's help. What was his relationship to you?"

"He was my great-great grandpa."

Robert nodded. "He was a good man."

Jonah didn't respond.

Damien didn't yet have a family of his own, but he couldn't help but place himself in Robert's situation. If he had a wife and kids, would he be able to leave them behind if he believed they were in danger and his absence was the only way to protect them? There was a real possibility that Damien would raise Michelle's kids with her, and they would likely have their own child one day.

The thought sent chills of excitement through Damien's body, surprising him. He hadn't entertained the thought of fatherhood before today, and he found himself completely consumed by the idea. For a distraction, he looked at the GPS. "We'll be there in ten hours, if we don't stop." He thought for a moment. "It'll be after business hours by then. Alex will probably wait until morning to bring the powder there."

"Then what?" Jonah asked.

Damien twisted around to see the back seat. "What do you mean?"

"How will we get the jars from him? We didn't do a very good job in the basement."

The car was silent for a few seconds.

"We need to meet him outside the building. If he gets inside, there's no way we'll get the jars," Damien said. "Maybe he'll give them up if we surround him."

Jonah looked out his window. "He's already risked his career for them. Whatever the company is offering must be pretty huge."

Damien faced the front, agreeing with Jonah. "Alex won't give up the jars easily."

****

Sharon wrapped her purse in her arms, unwilling to risk anyone accidentally discovering what she'd put in it. Having it close made her feel more secure, likely the same reason her grandson took his blanket with him everywhere. Not having the gun with her simply felt wrong.

"So, I'm confused. Why is it bad for Alex to give the powder to the drug company? Maybe we should just let him. They might just destroy it," Michelle said.

"They won't destroy it. They know what Deinix does. They've known from the beginning," Robert said. "If they control it, they also control who receives it."

"You didn't have a problem deciding for yourselves who should receive it." Sharon glared at Robert.

"You're right. The three of us –"

"You abandoned your families! And for what? To see if it works?" She couldn't believe this man was her great-grandfather. Surely, he could have figured a better plan for the powder than to hide in the woods with it.

"It works. There is no question about that."

"So why have you been hiding it? You could have saved people!"

"Saved them from what? A natural death?"

She scowled at him.

"Who should get it?" Robert asked.

"What?" she asked.

"I want you to tell me. One name. Tell me one person you think is deserving of Deinix. It will have to be someone innocent of wrongdoing, yes? Perhaps this person is a great humanitarian. Or maybe an inventor? Give them more time to create? Or a doctor?

"Remember that in choosing who receives the powder, you are also choosing who does not receive it. You're deciding who is not worthy. I believe most people would broaden the scope of recipients to avoid making such a choice. So should all doctors receive it? All artists? Say people had children and then started taking Deinix. What will happen to the world then, if no one dies?"

Damien answered. "We would suffocate it."

"Precisely." Robert sat back in his seat. "And do you trust the company or the government to answer the questions I just asked you?"

Jonah scoffed.

"We cannot allow the company to get Deinix. The risk is too great," Robert said.

Sharon pulled her purse closer to her body, knowing she could take out Alex and get the jars back in a matter of seconds if she wanted to. She wondered if that would make her a hero in the eyes of her companions.

Chapter Twenty-Two

Michelle pulled in front of an opulent five-story office building set behind a couple acres of landscaping. "You worked here, Robert?" She studied the reflective windows and pristine grounds illuminated by path and parking lot lights. Though the address matched the one Damien found, the name of the company was not apparent on the building.

"I assure you, it looked nothing like this in my day."

"Anyone see Alex's car?" Jonah asked.

Michelle lowered her gaze to the parking lot. "I don't see it."

"He wouldn't bring the jars here now. Everyone's probably gone home for the night," Damien said. "How about you and Sharon stay in a hotel? We'll stay here and keep watch, in case he comes here before the office opens."

"No, I'm staying right here," Sharon said.

Michelle drove away from the building as she tried to ignore her developing fatigue headache. "I'm too trashed to stay up, Sharon. I'm going to a hotel. The guys want to take turns keeping watch. I think we have the better end of this deal."

"When did you discuss this?"

"You were asleep." Michelle had been thankful for the reprieve from Sharon's attention while she made a plan with the others. Sharon hadn't been fit to make any decisions since she left the cabin back at the river. Michelle wished Sharon hadn't seen her leaving Larry's house. They might have been able to go after Alex without her.

Sharon sighed. "All right, but can we come back early tomorrow, before they open?"

"Yeah. We'll come pick you up." Jonah said.

After Michelle and Sharon settled into a shared hotel room, Michelle sat on the edge of her bed and called Mark. No answer. She called her mother.

"Hello?"

"Hey, Mom."

"Michelle." Her mother was quiet, odd for her.

"How are things there? How are the kids?" Michelle asked.

"Mark came by today."

Her heart rate skyrocketed. "Okay. I haven't been able to reach him. Did he take the kids?" She closed her eyes, silently begging her mother to say no.

"No, he didn't."

Michelle exhaled.

"He came to say goodbye to them. He told them he had to leave for a while."

"What? Where is he going?"

"I don't know. He barely spoke to me, dear."

Images of her children flashed through her mind: Grant building a block tower and knocking it down, Sophie helping to make pancakes. The image of their smiles and their young giggles filled her memory. She grasped her necklace.

Having discussed the possibility, Michelle couldn't help but imagine the worst case scenario. She had been so distracted, first by the key, then by her relationship with Damien, that she hadn't given the children the attention they deserved. What if Mark had taken them and kept them from her? What would they think of her as they grew up? Mark would tell them she was selfish, that she liked to leave them while she went away to be with a man who wasn't Daddy. Would they understand why she left?

Should they?

Michelle's mother's voice interrupted her thoughts. "Is there anything you want to tell me?"

Her heart ached, wishing she could rush home and wrap them in her arms. "Um, not right now. Are the kids okay?"

"They're upset. Do you think you'll be home soon? You should be with them."

She remembered Gao saying the same thing to her. "Yeah. Tomorrow or the next day."

"Okay. Call me when you leave." Her mother ended the call.

Michelle pulled the phone away from her ear and looked at it. She opened her text messages and wiggled her thumbs over the letters before deciding to send the message she had in her mind.

Mark left.

She imagined Damien sitting behind the wheel of the rental outside the office building. *Do you want me to come back?*

She wanted to say yes. *No. I'll keep an eye on Sharon.*

Sharon left the bathroom and walked to her bed.

Damien's response appeared in the same moment. *Okay. I'll be up most of the night if you need to talk.*

Michelle closed her eyes, allowing herself to feel the conflicting emotions all the conversations in the last fifteen minutes produced. She was about to type a response when another message appeared.

I love you.

She smiled. Tonight, she'd learned that her husband left her, and she was smiling. That couldn't be normal.

I love you, too.

Sharon climbed into her double bed wearing the long, New York souvenir shirt she'd bought at the gift shop. She put her purse under the covers on the empty side of the bed.

Michelle scrunched her eyebrows. What was up with that purse? Sharon hadn't put it down for even a second since they left Indiana.

Michelle sat on her own bed and played on her phone until she was sure Sharon was asleep, as she told the men in the car she would do, before she entered the bathroom to take a shower.

****

After calling Olivia, Jonah beamed as he reclaimed the passenger seat. Damien had parked the car down the street from the office building, where night security likely wouldn't see them. Damien looked towards the building through a pair of binoculars.

"You must have received good news," Robert said from the back seat.

Jonah remembered Olivia's words. "My wife's having a baby and had a checkup today. She said the kid didn't want to hold still long enough for the nurse to get his heartbeat." His smile seemed permanently affixed to his face.

Robert laughed. "That's wonderful. They didn't have such technology when my daughter was born. You're obviously looking forward to fatherhood."

"Yeah, I am. We weren't planning on a baby so soon, but it's been amazing."

"Do you guys have a name picked out?" Damien asked.

Jonah remembered the last name he'd given the baby. "Not really. I've been messing with Olivia and giving the baby guitarist names. The last one was Jimmy Page."

Damien laughed. "Think it'll stick?"

"Absolutely not. So no, we don't have a name yet." For the first time, Jonah seriously thought about what name he and Olivia should give their son. They'd casually discussed naming him after her grandfather or even after Samuel. The meaning of Samuel's name was tattooed on Jonah's chest; it meant something, if only to Jonah. He had to make sure his child had a name just as meaningful.

It was an overwhelmingly important assignment, and he promised himself he'd talk to Olivia about it as soon as he arrived back home.

Jonah glanced at the office building. "Robert, how do you keep the company from tracking you? They must know you're still alive."

"I don't believe they do. I use aliases. My books are published under eight different names. All of our accounts are under a false name, though I'm not sure such steps were necessary. I think the company stopped trying to find me shortly after I disappeared."

"Why would they do that? Aren't you still a threat to them?"

"I've kept quiet about Deinix for a century out of necessity. I stole it and everything related to it before the company could patent it, which was in violation of my contract with them. They knew I wouldn't try to patent it on my own or release information about it because they would have grounds to sue me. I suspect only a few at the company know about Deinix and about me. They likely think I'm dead. They don't know the degree to which the powder slows aging, as I didn't know it myself when I left."

Jonah turned to face Robert. "Can I ask you a personal question?"

"Sure."

"Do you regret leaving your family behind?"

Robert nodded. "Yes. Often. But I believed my presence would put them at risk, so I tell myself I was protecting them by leaving." He looked out the side window. "I did my best to keep track of them. It was different for Gao and Elroy. I thought Elroy might return to his family a few times in the early years."

"Did he say why he didn't?" Damien asked.

"In a way. He said he couldn't give his wife what she wanted. I think he believed he was doing her a favor by staying away."

"Hmmm." Damien stared out the windshield, seemingly unconvinced by the explanation.

"What was my great-great-grandpa like?" Jonah asked, hoping to relieve the tension that settled on them.

Robert smiled. "He was a gifted craftsman, so confident he was almost cocky, and rightfully so. If he wasn't an Irish immigrant and had standing in society, he probably could have made a living as an engineer." He laughed. "William's accent was so thick I could hardly understand him. But he was funny. He would have made a welcome addition to our group." Robert's eyes met Jonah's. "But he never considered it. He said his place was at home. His family meant everything to him."

Jonah smiled and faced the windshield, hoping he'd be the kind of father his great-great-grandfather was.

****

Damien started his watch shift at three AM, after Jonah woke him. He looked at the grounds around the building while glancing at his phone. He kept going back to his texts to read Michelle's last message.

I love you, too.

He loved a woman, and she loved him back. He felt a little guilty for delighting in her news that Mark left, but he couldn't keep from imagining the new possibilities. Maybe Mark would insist on a quick divorce. For the second time that day, Damien dreamt of building a life with Michelle, raising her kids, and having one or two kids of their own. He smiled when he tried to picture a young boy whose appearance was the combination of her Asian features and his African ones.

But maybe her husband wasn't leaving for good. Maybe he was just taking a break. Damien told himself he shouldn't get his hopes up, just in case.

He sipped the soda he'd bought to help him stay awake. The sun started to rise earlier than he expected, and he focused more intently on the parking lot. He didn't want to risk missing Alex's arrival.

At six-thirty, Jonah took the car to the hotel to pick up Michelle and Sharon. Damien and Robert ducked into a drugstore, but Damien hoped Jonah wouldn't be long. They couldn't see the building well from the store.

Jonah returned with the women thirty minutes later. Robert and Damien loaded into the car, and Jonah parked it in the back corner of the drug company's visitors' lot.

"What time do they open?" Jonah asked.

"Nine o'clock. But Alex might get here early," Damien said. He sat in the middle of the back seat, next to Michelle. They locked their index fingers in the small space between their legs. Robert, who sat on Damien's other side, might have noticed, but Damien didn't care. With Michelle was the only place he wanted to be.

****

Nine o'clock came and went. Sharon hadn't slept well during the night, and she nodded off in the passenger seat a few times while they waited for Alex.

"They opened an hour ago. Do you think he's coming?" Michelle asked.

Sharon jerked her eyes open upon hearing Michelle's voice. She looked out the windshield and scowled, frustrated with herself. She would have missed Alex's arrival if it had occurred in the last half hour. Here she was, with the means to get the jars back in a matter of seconds, and she couldn't stay awake.

To keep her mind focused, she imagined what she would do once she had the jars back. She didn't doubt the others would let her have them, especially if she had to shoot Alex, but then what?

How would she get away? This was Michelle's car… should she steal it?

She'd have to figure out a way to get the keys from Jonah. The gun ought to work for that too. Jonah wasn't even supposed to be part of this group; his ancestor had been included by coincidence. If she made him believe he never belonged here and would shoot him because of that, he'd give her the keys.

"Maybe we got it wrong." Jonah leaned on his arm that he propped against the door. "What do you guys want to do?"

"We've only been waiting an hour. Let's give it more time," Damien said.

It didn't matter how long it took for Alex to arrive. The end result would be the same. Sharon rested her head on the seat and closed her eyes, confident in her plan.

Chapter Twenty-Three

Michelle sat in the back seat with Damien. He gazed into her eyes for a few seconds at a time, long enough for him to communicate his affection without announcing it to the others. At one point he closed his eyes and silently sighed, and it took every ounce of self-control she had to keep from leaning over and kissing him. She let her mind wander to their time by the river, remembering the feel of his warm lips and body against hers, and she had to stare out the window for a few minutes until the energy dropped.

She allowed herself to imagine waking up next to him in a bed they would buy together and in a house they would call theirs. The kids would come running into their room and jump on the bed to wake them up, and Damien wouldn't yell at them to get out. She couldn't stop her smile and he must have noticed, because his eyes met hers, and he smiled back.

The car was silent for most of the morning. Sharon, Jonah, and Robert dozed occasionally. Finally, when it was nearly noon, Jonah broke the silencc. "Here we go." He sat up straighter in the driver's seat.

Michelle leaned over Damien to see out the windshield. A silver Camry entered the lot and parked halfway between the building and the back of the lot, where Jonah had parked.

Michelle held her breath. She hadn't thought about what would happen once Alex arrived, and now she didn't have time.

The group scrambled to leave the car and approached Alex as he walked onto the sidewalk. He carried a box larger than the one Larry had at his house.

"Funny to see you here," Jonah said when Alex was within earshot.

Alex stopped in a grassy area adjacent to the building and faced the group. Michelle scanned the top of the building: there were security cameras, but only one of them might have been pointed towards them. If they wanted to get away with the jars, they'd have to do so quickly.

Alex shifted his feet. "How'd you know I'd come here? Did Bonnie say something? I told her not to."

"That powder doesn't belong to you." Robert stepped towards Alex.

"I beg to differ." Alex pulled the box to himself. "It was in our courthouse."

"It was there because I put it there. It belongs to me." Robert continued approaching Alex, who stepped backwards a few paces.

"You put it there over a hundred years ago? Nice try." He gestured to the building with a head tilt. "These guys are offering me a good deal. I'm dropping it off now. Excuse me." Alex walked towards the cement path that led to the front of the building.

Robert jogged up to him and punched him in the nose. Alex's head snapped back, and he dropped the box on the grass next to the path. The jars rattled, but Michelle didn't think they broke. Alex stepped back from the box.

Robert shook out his hand. "Consider that retribution for breaking my great-grandson's nose."

Alex cupped his nose with his hand. "Your great-grandson? What the hell are you talking about?"

He didn't know about the powder. Well, not all about it, at least. "Do you know what the powder does, Alex?" Michelle asked.

"No. They just said it was valuable to them and offered me a reward to return it." Alex spoke with a nasal tone as his nose bled over his hand and onto his shirt.

****

Jonah crept towards the men, hoping to grab the box. Alex's attention was on Michelle and Robert, so he might get away with it.

He was close enough to the box to peer into it. The jars weren't broken. They both lay on their sides, bumping against each other.

Jonah held his breath, bent down, and picked up the box.

Alex got Jonah's attention. "If you take that inside with me, I'll split the money with you."

"I don't want money." Jonah moved towards Robert to give him the box. He only made two steps before Sharon stopped him.

"Bring me the box, Jonah." Her voice was low and monotone.

She stood on the sidewalk next to the parking lot. The sunlight glinted off the small gun she pointed at him.

His pulse quickened. Sharon was unstable enough to pull the trigger. For lack of anything better to say, he asked, "Why do you think you need that?"

"I'm taking the powder. I need to keep it."

"Why? Robert should–"

"No, he shouldn't! I need it!" She straightened her arms.

Panic coursed through Jonah's body, and a sharp pain hit his shoulder at the memory of his last encounter with a bullet.

He'd been lucky that day. Dave was a sloppy gunman who'd shot Jonah by accident. This was different. Sharon was cold, focused. And the gun was pointed right at him.

His arms started to shake when he thought of Olivia and the baby.

He couldn't risk being killed and leaving them behind. But this would be his only chance to get all the powder back to Robert. Someone from the company could join them outside at any moment, and the consequences of that happening would be much worse than his own death.

He had to do something.

Taking a short breath to settle his nerves, Jonah stared at Sharon. "Are you really going to shoot me?" He turned his attention back to Robert, hoping he was calling her bluff and not doing something that would get him shot.

"You aren't even supposed to be here."

A loud crack reverberated off the building.

Jonah tipped the box before he dropped it, and the jars tumbled out. The fuller one landed on the edge of the path, breaking into three pieces.

He stood in place, looking at the broken jar and powder strewn on the ground, then at his torso and limbs. He wasn't injured. Who was screaming?

Michelle? She kneeled next to Damien, who lay on his back across the grass and the path. Blood stained his blue shirt a deep purple, and he coughed, spattering blood from his mouth. Michelle covered the chest wound with her hands.

Sharon had fallen to her knees, staring at Damien. She still held the gun.

Two guards ran to them with their own weapons drawn.

Jonah's mind finally processed his surroundings. He ran to Damien and Michelle.

****

Damien tried to figure out why he was looking at the bright sky. His ears were ringing, but the sound of Michelle crying broke through. He turned his head in the direction of her voice. She was pressing her hands on his chest. He wished she would stop because he could hardly breathe. Her tears dripped onto her outstretched arms.

The taste of blood filled his mouth, and he coughed. Blood sprayed upwards, hitting Michelle and landing on his own face. The cough didn't relieve the sensation of choking, and he coughed again.

A male voice he didn't recognize said something after the beep of a walkie-talkie. "We need an ambulance. There's been a shooting, one victim down. We have the shooter in custody."

Someone else approached on his right – Jonah. He took off his shirt and used it to wipe Damien's face and mouth. Damien tried to take a breath, but a mouth and throat full of blood prevented it.

Jonah handed the shirt to Michelle, who took it with blood-coated hands. Jonah moved his hands to cover the place Michelle's had been, on Damien's chest.

Damien turned his head to the side and coughed, expelling more blood onto the grass. He looked up to Michelle. "What happened?"

She didn't respond. Maybe she didn't hear him.

Damien tried to take in a deeper breath, but the weight of whatever Jonah held on his chest prevented it, and his mouth was filling with blood again. "Get off my chest."

"We're trying to cover the wound so you can breathe." Michelle looked at him. Her eyes were filled with distress, and her hands shook as she held Jonah's shirt.

He coughed to the side and tried his question again. "What happened?"

She leaned over him. "You…" She closed her eyes. "You jumped in front of it."

That sounded familiar. He remembered thinking he needed to get the gun away from Sharon. She was going to shoot Jonah. "I tried to tackle–" He gasped when a stab of pain hit his chest, but the blood in his throat prevented it. He turned his head to the side again, but he couldn't make himself cough. He could take only shallow breaths as blood ran from the side of his mouth.

Michelle put the shirt under his check and lowered herself to the ground, facing him. She stroked his face while gazing into his eyes. She didn't make a sound, but her tears dripped onto the grass.

Damien remembered holding Michelle next to the river. But in the memory, she wasn't crying, his chest didn't feel like a bowling ball was on it, and he wasn't scared.

"Am I dying?" His voice barely worked.

Michelle leaned in and kissed his forehead, then cried more audibly.

"I am." He blinked several times. A dark tunnel seemed to close on his vision as little gold flashes appeared.

He brought his hand to Michelle's cheek. "I love you."

She nodded short, rapid nods as she closed her eyes.

"Open your eyes. Please."

She did, releasing more tears. "I wish I could save you," she said in a cracked voice.

His eyes were heavy, but he willed them to stay open. "You already have."

The weight on his chest increased, and he couldn't take another breath.

"I love you, Damien."

Fatigue overtook him, and he closed his eyes.

****

"Come on. Get up." The guard grabbed Sharon by the arms and lifted her to her feet. He put her wrists into handcuffs behind her back.

Sharon wiggled her fingers. Her hands were empty. Where was the gun? She couldn't get the jars back without it.

She scanned the area but didn't see it. Damien lay on the grass. Jonah covered something on Damien's chest, and Damien's mouth was bloody.

She hadn't wanted to shoot Damien. She'd fired at Jonah. Why was Damien wounded on the grass?

He'd rushed her. Threw himself in front of the bullet.

Why would he do that?

The distant sirens grew louder, as did Michelle's cries. Damien didn't seem to be moving. Jonah sat back, looking at Damien and Michelle.

Why was Michelle so upset? She wept like she'd lost a great love.

As an ambulance and two police cars arrived in the parking lot, Michelle sprang to her feet and jogged to Sharon, her face twisted by grief.

Michelle screamed at her. "Why?" She glared into Sharon's eyes, only inches away. "Tell me!"

The officer's voice answered for Sharon. "Ma'am, I'll need you to step away–"

"Tell me! Sharon, I need to know." Her eyes begged Sharon for an answer.

Sharon could only stammer. "I… it wasn't…"

"Do you even know?" Michelle screamed and returned to Damien. Jonah stood and held her before she reached the place Damien had fallen.

Sharon's attention returned to the police officer who held her arm. He guided her into the back of a police cruiser.

She looked past Jonah and Michelle. Robert walked towards the parking lot, carrying the box that held the jars. Another police officer approached him.

The jars. One was broken. The powder had spilled onto the path and into the grass.

And now the police could get it.

Panic coursed through her body like lightning. “Those are mine!” She screamed and struggled against her handcuffs. The metal cut the skin around her wrists, but she didn’t care. She had to get out and get the jars back.

The car pulled out of the lot. Sharon twisted around and watched the scene shrink in the rear window. “Stop! Those are mine!”

Chapter Twenty-Four

Michelle stared at the sterile, tile floor. The sounds of the emergency room – a cable network on TV, a man talking on a phone, a crying child – blended into a distasteful auditory stew.

We did everything in our power, but we couldn't save him.

Her mind couldn't process the doctor's words, though she knew they were true. Damien died before the ambulance arrived. She'd watched the life leave his eyes.

She couldn't cry. There weren't tears left.

Jonah appeared next to her chair, holding a Styrofoam cup full of water. She took it and held it, but she didn't drink from it.

Jonah sat next to her. He sipped his own water.

She thought she might be able to form the question that echoed in her mind. "Do you…" She squinted, unable to figure out how to finish her thought for a moment. "Do you think he did it to save you?"

Jonah looked at her and sighed. "Would that make it easier to accept?"

"Maybe." She studied the reflective sheen of the lights on the surface of her water.

"Then let's say he did."

"But why did she want to shoot you in the first place?" All the words that had been bouncing around inside her head somehow managed to leave her mouth in a coherent manner. She was a little surprised.

"I don't know." He looked at the floor. "She wanted the powder. Maybe I'm just the guy who happened to be holding it when she pulled the gun."

"That's not a very good reason to shoot someone." She sipped her water, but it made her nauseous.

"What's a good reason to shoot someone? She saw me as a threat. I had something she wanted."

"Like a mugging?"

He shrugged.

That didn't sit right. "What did she mean? That you aren't supposed to be here?"

"I think she meant my ancestor. He wasn't part of the original plan. Maybe she saw him, and me, as giant loose ends." He put a hand on Michelle's shoulder. "She obviously wasn't thinking clearly. I'm not sure we'll ever know why she wanted to shoot anybody."

Michelle squeezed her eyes closed, but she opened them again because the image of Damien's life leaving him haunted her memory.

She'd mentally replayed the moment Damien rushed Sharon dozens of times. Sharon was pointing the gun at Jonah, and Damien ran in front of it without hesitation.

Maybe he'd thought he could get the gun away from Sharon before she fired it.

Maybe he'd wanted to save Jonah.

She would never know for sure.

Just a few short hours ago, for the first time in as long as she could remember, she'd dreamed of a brighter future. Before she'd met Damien in Richmond, visions of her future were bleak, full of broken promises and unfulfilled wishes. Damien had changed all that. He'd encouraged her to pursue her career, always asked about her before talking about himself, and she knew he'd loved her simply because of who she was.

Eventually, Robert joined them from outside. "How long would you two like to stay?"

As long as it takes for this not to be real, Michelle thought. But she'd already been sitting there for three hours since the police took their statements, and it was still just as real as before.

She stood, trying to gather the courage to leave the hospital. Damien was here. She loved him. And she had to leave him.

Staring at the door that separated the emergency department from the rest of the hospital, she started crying and dropped the cup, forgetting that she held it. Water splashed on the floor. She looked at the puddle and blinked her tears from her eyes.

She startled when Jonah put his hand on her back.

On impulse, she wrapped her arms around his broad shoulders and cried into his shirt.

He held her. "I'm so sorry."

He must have known about her relationship with Damien. If he hadn't, her reaction since the shooting gave it away. She swallowed and pulled away from him. "I don't know what to do."

Jonah nodded. "Why don't we go somewhere else? We can't do anything here."

She held her breath and walked towards the exit door before she could think about what she was doing.

****

Jonah took the driver's seat of Michelle's rental, thankful that he'd finally talked her into leaving the hospital. He couldn't think there.

Sharon had meant to shoot him. She had enough contempt for him to decide he didn't deserve to live.

He couldn't imagine thinking that about another person.

Had she known he and Olivia were expecting a baby? Was her hatred so thorough that she would deny his child any knowledge of him?

He clenched his jaw, trying to keep his emotions in check.

Maybe if Jonah hadn't challenged her, daring her to shoot him, she wouldn't have pulled the trigger. And Damien wouldn't have rushed in front of it.

If Jonah hadn't challenged her, Damien would still be alive.

His jaw cramped as he tried to keep from breaking down. Michelle needed someone to be strong in this situation. Robert wasn't upset like they were, but he hadn't known Damien as well.

Jonah coughed as a sob escaped. Michelle put her hand on his arm but didn't say anything. He hoped she hadn't reached the same conclusion he did; she might blame him for Damien's death.

After he pulled himself together, he drove aimlessly for an hour and asked, "What do you guys want to do?" He made eye contact with Robert in the rear-view mirror. "Should I take you to the cabin?"

"Yes, we can–"

"Take me to the airport first." Michelle had her elbow on the door and rested her head in her hand, staring out the window.

Jonah glanced at her. "Are you sure?"

"Yeah. I need to go home."

"Okay." He pulled over long enough to set the GPS for the airport before driving back onto the road.

They traveled in silence for most of the trip. "Will you be all right on your own here?" Jonah asked her as he drove onto the airport grounds.

"Yeah."

He pulled into the passenger drop-off area next to the terminal and walked to the back of the car to get her bag. She met him there.

He hugged her. "Call me if you want to talk about it. Anytime."

"Thanks." She walked towards the automatic doors but turned back as they opened. "I'd like to think that some good can come from this."

Unsure of what she meant, Jonah nodded. "Me too."

He watched her walk inside until she was out of his line of sight.

He re-entered the car. Robert had moved to the passenger seat.

"Are you doing okay? You've been pretty quiet," Jonah said.

"There is much to think about. If I hadn't created Deinix, or if we hadn't left it in the safe, Sharon wouldn't have had reason to shoot anyone."

"Do you blame yourself?" Jonah glanced at Robert while driving towards the airport exit.

Robert shook his head. "Sharon made the choice, and I don't believe she intentionally killed Damien. Though her actions show my concern about Deinix was valid."

"What concern?"

Robert turned his body to face Jonah. "It offers great power. I don't know Sharon's exact reason for protecting it, but it was strong enough to warrant killing a man. She was my great-granddaughter armed with a small handgun. Can you imagine what would happen if governments with armies decide they want it?"

Jonah swallowed. It was too much to think about, so he steered the conversation away from the possibility of maniacal governments threatening people. "What did you say to that cop?"

"I told him I was an employee, and I had to get the jars to a secure location. It took some convincing. I couldn't get all the powder that spilled in the grass, however. We can only hope the company will ignore it."

That seemed unlikely. All the company had to do was analyze the powder, and they would know what it was. In the chaos after the shooting, Jonah had lost track of Alex. The police had taken Jonah, Robert, and Michelle to the station for questioning, but Alex was likely questioned at the hospital while receiving treatment for his broken nose. Alex would have had plenty of time to talk to someone at the company, and Jonah wouldn't have put it past him to do so. He could at least show them where the jar broke.

If the company found and collected the powder, they would study it, learn what it did, and develop it. They would be the only company controlling it. Everything Jonah and the other descendants had tried to keep from happening could happen anyway. It was only a matter of time.

"Were you and Damien close friends?" Robert asked.

"I think we were getting there. I wish I knew what he was thinking." Jonah couldn't understand why Damien would risk his life like he did. He remembered the courthouse basement back in January, when he thought he could tackle Dave and stop him from shooting anyone. Maybe Damien's thoughts about Sharon were similar.

Jonah decided that what Damien thought in the moments before Sharon shot him was irrelevant, because he knew one thing for certain: Damien had saved his life.

I'd like to think some good can come from this.

Maybe it could.

"Remember when you asked Sharon the question about one person? Who is one person who deserves the powder?" Jonah asked.

"Yes."

"I know of one."

"And who is that?"

"My brother." He told Robert about Samuel's genetic condition. "Samuel doesn't know what it is to hate or to judge. Everything about his heart is good. The doctors thought he'd be gone by now."

"Would you like to take some powder to him?"

Jonah's pulse quickened; he thought he'd have to persuade Robert into letting him have the powder. "It can't possibly cure him."

"No. It will delay the conditions that would end his life."

Before now, Jonah never thought this was a real option, but in all his talk of not wanting the responsibility of choosing who would get Deinix, Samuel was always in the back of his mind. "Yeah. I'd like to try it."

For the first time that day, Jonah felt hopeful. He'd lost a friend – a friend who saved his life – but gained the prospect of helping his brother.

He took a long breath as the weight of it all settled on him.

****

Sharon woke in a hospital bed. She looked around the room. Why was she here?

She tried to sit up, but her arms were strapped to the bed's side rails.

"Hello?" she called out towards the hallway.

A few moments later, Larry, who had a bandage covering his swollen nose, entered the room and stood near the foot of her bed. "Hey, Shar."

A police officer followed and stood behind him.

"Where am I?" She pulled against her restraints. "Why am I here?" She looked at the cop, then back to Larry.

"They were worried you were a danger to yourself. They sedated you. You've been out all day."

Larry's elusive answers frustrated her. "Dammit, Larry, who are 'they'? What's going on? And why is he here?" She gestured to the cop with a head tilt.

"You remember what happened?" Larry asked.

What was the last thing she remembered? She was in the front seat of a car. Jonah was in the driver's seat.

Jonah. He had the jars – he dropped them. And then Damien was there.

Oh God. "I killed him." She stopped pulling on the restraints.

"Don't say anything else, Shar."

"Did I? Is he dead?"

Larry nodded.

The officer left the room but stood in the doorway, talking to someone. He said she seemed "more lucid."

She fell back into the pillow and stared at the ceiling. What had she been thinking? She couldn't even remember what she wanted when she pulled the gun on Jonah.

Wait. She did remember. He was giving the jars to Robert. She couldn't let him do that. But why?

She remembered something else and tried to sit up again, pulling against the restraints. "One of the jars broke."

Larry furrowed his eyebrows. "Don't know about that."

"We have to find out! They can't have it!"

"Shar…"

"Everyone will know!"

"Stop! Just stop! This has gone on long enough!" He approached the head of her bed. "They've arrested you. They're takin' you into custody, and you'll be charged. You killed a man." He closed his eyes. "There were four witnesses."

She blinked, imagining the rest of his thought that he didn't say aloud. She was going to prison. She would die there.

A nurse entered the room, shined a light into her eyes, and took her pulse and blood pressure. After a conversation with a doctor, the nurse opened the restraints. Sharon's mind barely registered any of this.

Sharon left the hospital in handcuffs.

Chapter Twenty-Five

It was nearly three AM when Michelle arrived in California – too late to pick up the kids. She would get them the next day. Looking forward to seeing them was the only bright spot in her mind, the only thing that made her smile. She'd kept her hand on her necklace for most of the flight. For a few minutes, she'd considered going to her mother's house anyway and waking them up, but that wouldn't be fair to them.

Tonight, she needed to go home. She unlocked her front door and turned on the hall light.

"Mark?"

There was no answer. She knew there wouldn't be. She walked into the kitchen to get a drink, though even this simple act felt different. Since the shooting, everything around her had a shroud over it. The world changed when Damien died, and it was strange that most of the world was oblivious to that fact. People went about their business – texting, laughing with friends, completing mundane tasks – as though someone so special hadn't died hours earlier.

Waiting for a flight had given her time to process what had happened to Damien, at least enough that she could function. Twenty-four hours ago, she'd imagined a life with him, allowed herself to pretend they were a family. She closed her eyes and remembered how he smiled at her. Wrapping her arms around herself, she recalled the feel of his embrace.

Her lips remembered the touch of his, how they moved when he kissed her. Her hands could feel the smooth skin on his chest and the stubble of his jaw, and her body recalled his as he held himself over her on the grass.

Her soul ached at the memory. She turned to place her glass in the sink; what she saw on the counter made her freeze.

A stapled stack of papers rested there. She knew what it was before she looked closely at it.

She put the glass in the sink and picked up the packet. It showed a series of messages – text messages, between her number and Damien's, dating back to early May.

Her tears clouded her vision. She wiped them with an open hand and carried the packet to the living room. Curling up in her favorite recliner, she read every message, reliving her brief time with Damien, laughing when she read his funny messages and mentally filling in the gaps she knew represented messages she'd deleted.

None of the texts individually incriminated her, but in total, they told of hearts longing to be together.

She never guessed Mark would find her texts. She'd assumed privacy laws would protect her. Maybe he'd filed a police report, saying she was doing something illegal, to get them. Or maybe he'd paid someone off.

He'd printed it to show her why he left. He probably thought this packet would break her. Instead, he'd given her a gift.

She turned off the lights and walked upstairs with the packet. Before she tried to sleep, she put it under her pillow.

****

Three days after Jonah left Robert at the cabin, Jonah sat in his car in front of his parents' house in Memphis. He hadn't called to tell them he was coming.

He retrieved a canvas bag from the back seat, walked to the front door, rang the doorbell, and drummed his fingers on his leg while he waited.

His father answered. "Jonah."

"Hi, Dad."

"This is a surprise." His father spoke to him through the glass storm door.

"Can I come in?"

"Oh. Yeah." His dad held the door open for him.

Jonah entered the house and looked into the kitchen. "Where are Mom and Sammy?"

"At the hospital. I was just getting ready to head there myself."

Jonah scrunched his eyebrows. "Why?"

"We didn't want to worry you." His father approached and stood next to him. "Samuel's had three minor strokes over the last week."

"And you didn't think to call me?"

"His prognosis is fair. They're monitoring him now. We would have called if we thought it was serious."

Jonah had to stare at the window to keep from looking at his father. He squeezed his eyes closed.

"Jonah, you knew this was coming. He's already held on longer than everyone thought he would."

"That doesn't make it easier." He strained his jaw, refusing to cry in front of his father. "Let's go see him."

"What's in the bag?"

"It's nothing."

Jonah followed his father to the car. Jonah put the bag on the floor behind the passenger seat. Maybe if he'd arrived two weeks earlier, he might have been able to keep Samuel from having any strokes. He remembered Robert's words: *it will delay any conditions that would end his life.*

Thirty minutes later, Jonah and his father entered a hospital room, where Samuel slept in a bed. Someone had shaved his hair and attached small monitors to his scalp. His mother slept in a reclining chair.

"We have company," his father said.

His mother stirred and opened her eyes. "Jonah? I can't believe you're here."

Jonah took off his cap and bent over to hug his mother in the chair. "I wish you guys had called me."

She squeezed his shoulders.

Jonah stood straight and looked at Samuel, but keeping attention on his brother was difficult. His mother squeezed Jonah's hand.

"What are the doctors saying?" Jonah asked.

"They're monitoring him. The mini-strokes could be a sign of a bigger one to come. He's been unconscious since his last one two days ago."

He faced her. "He's been like this for two days?" He looked back to Samuel and clenched his jaw.

"I'm sorry, honey. We should have called you." His mother released his hand and rose from the chair. "Why don't you sit with him for a little while? The doctors say he can probably hear our voices. Your dad and I will get some coffee."

"All right."

His parents left the room, leaving him alone with a man who looked like the ghost of his brother.

Jonah sat on the edge of the bed and took Samuel's hand. "Hey Sammy. It's Jonah."

Samuel didn't respond. Jonah remembered his previous visits, when Samuel would reach out to touch Jonah upon hearing his voice. He wished his brother would do that now.

"I brought something that might help you. But I think I came too late." His voice cracked at the end of his sentence. "I'm sorry. I hope you aren't scared." He glanced at the table next to the bed and blinked with disbelief.

He released Samuel's hand and picked up the mp3 player, the one he'd given Samuel in November, when he used it to get the key from his brother. Jonah put an ear bud in his left ear, pressed "play", and heard the opening chords of his original song.

He put the other bud in Samuel's ear.

Samuel wouldn't respond, but Jonah liked to think Samuel might remember the moment they shared all those months ago.

Listening to the song, Jonah focused on Samuel. It seemed the jar of powder he'd left in the canvas bag would be no good to him now. Robert had said it wouldn't cure anybody of conditions they already had.

How long would Deinix have prevented Samuel's current situation? Jonah hadn't realized how much he looked forward to sharing his plan with Samuel and his parents – his plan to bring Samuel back to Cincinnati, give him the powder, and take care of him for as long as it lasted. Olivia had even been excited about the idea. Their baby would know his uncle.

Why hadn't his parents called him?

His mother joined him an hour later and sat in the chair. Jonah hadn't moved from the edge of the bed.

"Do they think he'll wake up?" he asked.

"They aren't sure."

"If he does, I want to take him back to Ohio with me."

His mother pressed her lips. "Even if he does wake up, he might not be the same."

"I have something that could help him."

"What's that?"

"It'll sound crazy, but hear me out." Jonah told his mother what he and the others had found in Virginia.

"You think this powder will keep him alive?" She raised her eyebrows.

"I know what you're thinking. But you have to trust me."

"Jonah," she sighed, rose from the chair, and stood next to him, "we all have a time to go. No one can escape it, especially not forever. We knew Samuel's time was coming. He's already beaten the odds. We should be thankful for the time we had with him."

Jonah scowled at her. "You're okay with letting him die? When he might not have to?"

She walked back to the chair and sat down. "I don't expect you to understand."

"You're right! I don't understand what it's like to care for him twenty-four seven. I don't understand what you must have felt when he was born this way. And I don't understand why you didn't call me!" He stared at Samuel, unable to look at his mother. He wanted to punch the wall.

"Would you want to continue living this way?" she asked.

This way? In a coma? "What if he wakes up? Will you let me try then? I'll take him back to Ohio and take care of him. You won't have to worry about him anymore."

"I admit it. Caring for him has been exhausting. We'll never have the kind of family our friends have. But he's my son, and if there was a way to cure him of these strokes, I would do it." She squeezed her eyes closed. "He's suffering, Jonah. I don't want him to suffer."

Jonah was out of words for his mother, so he asked, "Where's Dad?"

"He has a hard time staying here. He's still in the cafeteria."

His father would agree with his mother. They were ready to let Samuel go.

He hoped Samuel would wake up and show them he wasn't ready to go.

****

Sharon walked into a common area of the jail, where the guard said her lawyer waited for her. She looked for a man sitting alone and was surprised by what she saw.

Robert sat at a table with a stranger, who Sharon guessed was her lawyer. She stomped towards them.

She glared at Robert for a moment before sitting and looking at the lawyer, a man who appeared to have just graduated high school. "I'll make this really easy for you. I'm pleading guilty."

"Now, hold on a second." The lawyer held a hand out to her. "Let's talk about a few things first."

"There's nothing to talk about. I killed a man. Four people watched me do it." She looked at Robert. "Why are you here?"

"I've been in contact with Larry."

She leaned towards him. "Was that an answer?" She rose from the table and walked to the guard.

She didn't care why Robert was there. He probably wanted to find out what made her do it. She might have told him, if she had an answer.

She couldn't make herself believe Robert was the reason behind everything that happened. He'd created the powder, he'd used it during the eugenics movement, he'd basically kidnapped the other ancestors, and now he wanted to meddle in her already ruined life. She'd wanted to keep the powder a secret to protect her family. Robert was her family. And she had no interest in protecting or helping him.

Exhausted, she leaned against the wall of her cell, having not slept much in the week since the shooting. She had nightmares, and most of them featured Damien, his face flashing before her as she pulled the trigger. If she believed in ghosts, she would say he was haunting her.

Damien had been a stranger to her. She didn't know if he was married or had children, what he did for a living, or even where he lived. She never cared to ask.

She lay on her hard bed and stared at the stained, tiled ceiling. Her kids knew what she'd done by now. Did they tell her grandkids? Her cousin, the senator, might even know. Liz would have to prepare a statement about her relationship to Sharon, in case the media picked up on it. Liz would have no choice but to disown her.

Defeated, Sharon rolled onto her side and tried to go to sleep.

Chapter Twenty-Six

Three months after returning to California, Michelle moved into a small townhouse with her children. Mark had filed for divorce soon after she arrived home, and to her surprise, the divorce went mostly uncontested. They agreed on how to split assets and arrange custody of the children. He even agreed to help her pay the rent on her townhouse until she finished nursing school while making a point of telling her he was doing it only for the sake of the children.

"Mommy, look!" Grant ran to where she stood by the stove preparing dinner to show her a yellow Play-Doh cookie he'd made. "Eat it!"

She smiled, bent over, and made gobble noises at his hand. He ran back to his room, where she guessed he'd make another cookie for her.

Her children's resilience amazed her. Grant had acted up right after the separation, but he settled after they all became accustomed to their new routines. He often asked why Mommy and Daddy didn't live together anymore, which Michelle found to be the hardest question to answer. Her usual response was *things don't always work out the way we want them to.*

She often imagined how Damien would have interacted with the children. He'd never met them. They didn't know he ever existed. The fantasy of him in their lives was hers alone. Sometimes she wished they had known him, just so she'd have someone to talk to, but she decided wanting her children to carry that burden was selfish. She'd kept Damien a secret from them. And that he must always be.

Michelle had blended well among the sea of grief at the funeral. When anyone asked, she said she was Damien's friend. She'd sat alone in the back row of the church, until someone she hadn't expected to see sat next to her: Elroy. He cleared his throat a few times but didn't say anything. He snuck out the back before the service ended.

Damien had said Elroy was cold to him. Michelle was happy to know Damien's great-great-grandfather cared enough to say goodbye.

Michelle checked the chicken in the pan and turned off the burner. "Go wash up, honey. I need to set the table," she said to Sophie. Sophie picked up the page she'd been coloring and moved it and her crayons to the coffee table in the living room.

"What are you drawing?" Michelle asked.

Sophie held up the paper.

"Can you tell me about it?"

Sophie approached Michelle and stood next to her. She described the drawings while pointing at them. "This is me, this is Grant, and this is you."

Michelle smiled.

"Mommy, who's Damien?"

She inhaled. "Why do you ask?"

"You said his name when you were asleep. I heard you when I got up to go potty."

She had no idea she was saying his name in her sleep. "He was a close friend. Now go wash up."

She watched her daughter skip into the bathroom after putting the drawing on the counter.

Surprisingly, hearing Sophie say Damien's name didn't upset her. Instead, she had an odd sense of calm. "I wish you could have known them," she muttered.

The calm stayed with her through the night while she studied for her next test. During a break, she checked on the kids, who slept soundly in their beds. She nearly cried, but not from despair. She knew that she and the kids would be all right.

It was like Damien was putting his hand on her shoulder, giving her that assurance.

****

Jonah sat in a reclining chair next to the hospital bed, gazing into the deep, blue eyes that saw light for the first time two hours ago. The baby blinked a few times before going to sleep.

Olivia dozed in the bed. They'd been up all night after her labor started in earnest before dinner the previous evening. It took until just before noon for their son to arrive.

A nurse entered the room and asked Jonah to put the baby into the basinet so she could check his temperature. He gazed at the swaddled infant, wondering how something so small could change his whole life. She finished, and he eagerly scooped the baby into his arms again.

"Have you decided on a name?" the nurse asked as she wrote something on a clipboard.

"Yeah. His name is Damien." He didn't take his eyes away from the small face.

"Oh, that's lovely. Is he named after someone?"

Jonah nodded. "The man who saved my life."

The nurse smiled and left the room. It would have been hard to follow up on his last statement, he had to admit.

He'd told Olivia about the name shortly after he arrived home from visiting his family in Memphis. Once she knew the reason for his suggestion, she agreed. Any other possibility felt wrong after that.

Olivia stirred. Jonah walked to her and kissed her forehead.

She removed the blue hat from baby Damien's head and stroked his dark hair. Watching them, Jonah couldn't understand how his heart felt so full.

He handed the baby to her. "How about I go pick up Samuel? He'll want to meet his nephew."

Olivia smiled and nodded. Jonah bent over the bed to kiss her and his son.

He arrived at the respite home twenty minutes later and found his brother sitting on a couch. Samuel's hair had grown back to the length it was before the weeks of his strokes. He'd woken three days after Jonah arrived in Memphis, and Jonah started giving him the powder immediately. The doctors never expected Samuel to walk out of the hospital, but four days later, he did just that.

Robert had said Deinix wouldn't cure Samuel and maybe that was true, but it seemed to keep him from having more strokes. Maybe there was more to it than Robert knew.

"Sammy, it's Jonah." He kneeled next to the couch.

"Jonah!" Samuel squinted at the ceiling and reached out.

Jonah took his hand. "Come on. You have a new nephew to meet."

Samuel laughed. Jonah wasn't sure if Samuel understood what a nephew was, but it didn't matter. He helped Samuel rise from the couch and walk to the car.

All that mattered was his family was together. He looked at the sky and muttered a quiet "thank you."

****

"You're stubborn. Has anyone ever told you that?" Sharon asked.

"Occasionally, yes. Elroy especially." Robert sat across from her at a table at the prison. He held a notebook.

She huffed. "Fine. What do you want to know?"

Robert had visited her every six months since her sentencing three years earlier. She couldn't understand how he thought her being in prison could have softened her.

"I want to know your side. I've interviewed Michelle and Jonah extensively, and I've spoken with Damien's mother and Michelle enough to get his story. Yours is the only one that's missing."

"Why do you want to do this?"

"I'm a writer, and this is a story. It's as simple as that. And it might do you some good to talk about it."

"You'll be outing yourself, you know."

"I'm changing names. Don't worry. I won't out you either."

Sharon shook her leg under the table and leaned into her arms. "Four years ago last November, I received a phone call from an historian in Richmond. It was the first Monday after my retirement."

She told Robert what she could remember about Alex's call, finding the key, and everything that followed, hoping he'd be so disgusted by her side of the story that he wouldn't want to include it. Who would want to write about their murderous great-granddaughter?

By the time she finished and he left, she felt different. It was difficult to name the emotion; maybe hashing out everything she'd kept inside had a cleansing effect. She felt lighter.

Jonah and Michelle had gone on with their lives. Robert had told her about them when she asked. Michelle was a nurse and was raising her kids. Jonah had a three-year-old son and a new daughter, and he was taking care of his brother. They'd moved past the tragedy she caused in New York. Sharon didn't have that option.

And then there was Damien, the fourth descendant, whose life she'd cut short. He was an environmental engineer. What things might he have accomplished? She remembered being upset about an oil spill around the same time Alex had called her. Damien might have been able to solve that problem.

She wondered if other murderers thought about their victims this way.

The guard led Sharon into her cell and locked the door behind her.

It all happened because she'd wanted to protect her family, which was ironic, because if she hadn't fired the gun, Jonah wouldn't have dropped the jars. The powder wouldn't have fallen into the grass for the company to find. They hadn't seemed to do anything with it yet, but she figured they would, given enough time.

She sat on her bed, leaned against the wall, and opened the book she was about half-through reading. It was one of Robert's books, a suspense novel published under one of his many pseudonyms.

Considering all the information she'd given Robert, she could read her own story this way.

She wondered if she would want to read it.

Epilogue

Our top story tonight: a pharmaceutical company in New York has released a statement saying they've developed a 'fountain of youth pill', which slows the process of aging dramatically. Flag Pharmaceuticals says results from animal studies are promising, and they hope to begin human trials soon.

Robert shook his head and turned off the TV, wondering if the company would claim infertility as a side effect of the drug he'd created. It would be a great irony.

He wandered outside and found Gao walking towards the cabin from the river.

"They're releasing statements about Deinix," Robert said.

Gao shook his head. "I'm not sure I want to see what happens." He set his fishing rod against the wall near the door and entered the cabin. "It's good Elroy isn't around to find out."

Robert watched Gao clean his catch of the day, silently agreeing with his statement about Elroy. Their friend had passed away the previous summer at the age of one hundred thirty-two, five years after the jar broke in New York. It had taken Robert and Gao several weeks to figure out how to live at the cabin without him.

"Should we do anything about it?" Gao asked.

"I've asked myself that question many times since the jar broke."

"Do you have an answer?"

Robert shifted his feet. "I might. Let's think this through. If we had not hidden the jar in Richmond, and our families never knew about it or about us, what would we be doing?"

"Living here, the same as we are now."

"Right. But things have changed."

Gao twisted around to look at him.

"It would make sense for our actions to change as well," Robert said.

"What do you mean?" Gao wrapped the filets in plastic, put them into the refrigerator, and walked into the living room, where he sat on the couch. Robert stood near the desk.

"Deinix is out because I sent that letter to the company after we hid the jar. The company has always had the control, I just didn't know about it until our descendants opened the safe."

"Okay. So?"

"So, how do we take back the control?" Robert walked to the couch and sat next to Gao, turning his body to face him. "I fear the company will greatly misuse Deinix. They will come to control everything, even the government, because they can buy officials with it. You know what they say about absolute power." Robert glanced at the floor and shook his head before he looked back to Gao. "We can't go after them directly. They would kill us or have us arrested. So…" He grinned. "We need to plant the seeds of a resistance."

Gao's eyes narrowed. "How?"

Robert shifted towards him. "We'll go to smaller towns and live there long enough to know who to trust. I'll teach that person how to make Deinix. We'll explain everything we know about it, and it will be available to anyone who wants it. The people in these communities will likely be the only ones in the country to know the complete truth about it."

"But how will this be a resistance?" Gao asked.

"When we finish in one town, we'll move on to another, and then another, in different parts of the country. Over time, these communities will outlive everyone else and know the truth. My hope is there will be enough people when needed to effectively stand against the company."

"But won't there be a risk of those we teach misusing Deinix as well?"

Robert nodded. “There will always be that risk. But doing nothing is not an option. We can only hope they will choose to be on the right side of history, when the time comes.”

“What is the right side of history?”

Robert grinned. “I wish I knew.”

THE END

Readers like you make a big difference to a writer like me! Please stop by Amazon and leave a review – a 5-star rating is always appreciated!

Acknowledgements

Thank goodness for people who are smarter than I am, or this book would have been much more difficult to write.

Thanks to Noel Shelton for walking me through the basics of police procedure and for not laughing when you realized how clueless I was.

Thanks to Rebecca Mast for sharing your knowledge of first aid and for continuing to be one of my greatest cheerleaders.

Thanks to fellow author Dan Alatorre, first for encouraging me to keep going with this project when it got frustrating and then for walking me through the indie-publishing process. And for making me laugh along the way.

Thanks to my friends at Critique Circle, who slogged through the early drafts of each chapter, offering your expertise and perspective even when things got mushy. The book is better because of you.

Finally, thanks to my family and friends who served as beta readers, cheerleaders, and promoters of my writing throughout this process.

About the Author

Allison Maruska started her writing adventure in 2012 as a humor blogger. She wrote her first novel, a Young Adult mystery called Project Renovatio, in 2013, which was accepted for publication by 4RV publishing. While it went through the process of traditional publishing, Allison continued working on other projects, including The Fourth Descendant and posting on her blog. She is also co-authoring a series of eBook marketing books with Dan Alatorre.

Allison is a certified interventionist at an elementary school in her area. She's a wife, mom, coffee and wine consumer, and owl enthusiast.

Connect with Allison on the interwebs!

Blog: http://www.allisonmaruska.com

Facebook: http://www.facebook.com/allisonmaruskaauthor

Twitter: https://twitter.com/allisonmaruska

Amazon Author Page: http://amazon.com/author/allisonmaruska

Made in the USA
Middletown, DE
06 July 2016